# Stay for the Holidays

## Mildred Gail Digby

*Quest Books*
*by Regal Crest*

ISBN 978-1-61929-452-3


First Edition 2020

9 8 7 6 5 4 3 2 1


Cover design by AcornGraphics


Published by:

Regal Crest Enterprises


Find us on the World Wide Web at
http://www.regalcrest.biz


Published in the United States of America

# Acknowledgments

First off, I'd like to say a huge thanks to Cathy, Patty, and Staci at Regal Crest for all their help and invaluable support in preparing this manuscript. Also a big thanks goes out to my fellow RCE authors K. Aten and JS Frankel for help with naming characters, grammar of the English variety, and most of all, for being all-around awesome people. Finally, I must mention my eternal gratitude to Aja Marie Ussrey, for her timely and wise advice that allowed me to write this novel without including the word "buttcrack".

## Dedication

For my partner, Masa. You are the star of my life in the way you guide me, bring me light, and also are really fucking hot.

# Chapter One

FLAT ON HER back, knees bent and legs spread wide, Jade's entire consciousness was focused on the sweet, dripping wet slit above her. Two fingers came down and slowly rubbed the jutting clit, teasing her with the luscious treasure that was just out of reach. In time to the slow passes, the young woman over her rocked her hips, thrusting into the V of her fingers. Jade's hips bucked in response, pushing against nothing but air.

"Oh Jesus," Jade croaked. "Connie, sweetheart—fuck I need you."

An angelic face with a mischievous smirk looked down at her, framed by short blonde hair. The hand that wasn't buried between her legs gripped the headboard.

"You want this?" Connie asked. She drew her fingers over Jade's swollen nether lips, spreading Jade's juices over them. The scent caught in Jade's nose, an addictive mix of musk and honey. Connie's voice, usually a bright soprano, came out in a low purr that she only got when she was turned on.

"Uh huh," Jade said. She couldn't look away from the gorgeous sight of Connie straddling her head. Her sex twitched in response, her inner muscles tensed with the craving for touch, for anything to ease the hot tension in her groin.

"Hmm," Connie hummed the word in a husky alto. "You need to ask nicely."

"Please, baby girl. Please let me taste you," Jade gasped. She would do anything Connie asked of her. Nearly six feet of tattooed butch muscle, Jade melted into jelly in front of the elfin young woman who loved her like nobody ever had before—or ever would.

"That's better."

Connie spread her knees. Jade's cry of relief was drowned out by the wet press of pouty lips to her mouth. With a growl, Jade gripped Connie's hips and pulled her into a devouring kiss. Jade lapped the juices before they could spill wastefully down her face. She thrust deep into Connie's willing entrance before she circled the swollen clit with her tongue. The headboard rocked with the movements of Connie meeting her with pumps of her hips. Jade's breath came out in harsh grunts, her fingers dug into the softness of Connie's ass. With every thrust, the muscles bunched and relaxed. The soft cries of pleasure Connie made urged Jade on like nothing else. She existed only to treasure and worship her.

A persistent buzzing cut into Jade's consciousness, breaking her rhythm. Jade pulled away with a lascivious grin.

"Did you smuggle in a toy, sweetie?"

A pause.

"No," Connie said. "I guess you didn't either."

"Englebird Humpercunt," Jade barked. There were only two people in the world who called her, and one of them was sitting on her face. Jade was just going to ignore it, but Connie dismounted and curled up on the pile of pillows like a small, sexy kitten.

"I can wait," Connie said. She tweaked a nipple in a teasing way. "For a few minutes."

Disgruntled, Jade reached out one hand and rummaged around in the pile of discarded clothing on the bed. Once she found her smartphone, she sat up and raked back her long brown hair impatiently. She swiped across the phone screen, making sure it was audio only.

"Talk to me Young. And it better be fucking important."

"Caught you at a bad time?" Detective Irvine Young's gravelly voice grated on Jade's nerves.

"Something like that," Jade said. She put the phone on speaker and plopped it down on the comforter while she gathered up her hair and jammed it messily into a clip.

"I got something for you, kid."

Jade half-grinned at the old nickname. Even though the insistent throb of unspent desire tormented Jade, she couldn't stay pissed off at Young.

"What is it, big guy?"

"You got plans for lunch tomorrow?"

Jade raised her eyebrows and met Connie's surprised look with her own.

"Not yet," she said. "Why?"

"A new case came across my desk, and I think it's right up

your alley, if you get what I mean."

"I hear you," Jade said. "What's the story?"

"How about I tell you over lunch? It's kinda sensitive information." Young paused. "Is Connie around?"

"Yeah, she's here," Jade said. She reached out and took Connie's hand in hers and gave a gentle squeeze.

Ever since the case that first brought them together, Young had a definite soft spot for Connie. Jade couldn't blame him. Connie's sweet strength captured her heart and soul and Jade was never getting either of them back.

"Great. Have her come with, if it's no trouble."

Connie piped up, "That's fine. Want to meet up at Dixie's Diner? That place right across from my office."

"Sounds good," Young said. "So does one-ish work for you two?"

"Perfect," Connie said. She pressed up against Jade's side as she spoke. Jade held herself still and didn't feel the need to complain about the close quarters at all. After a short round of good-byes, Jade ended the call.

"I wonder what that's all about," Jade mused aloud.

"We'll find out tomorrow," Connie replied. She tilted one shoulder forward, causing her soft, full breasts to swing with the motion. Jade's mouth fell open. Her clit jolted to attention. Connie speared her with a dark look, one that held the promise of many good things to come. Connie lowered her thick lashes over her stunning, green eyes before she said, "Tonight belongs to us."

Jade let out a happy *ooh* as Connie launched herself into Jade's arms and they tumbled into the crumpled comforter.


THE CRISP OUTSIDE air followed Jade into the office of Goode Fire Extinguishers Ltd. She shrugged under her lambskin jacket and strode through the door.

After the incident which left one member of the company dead, another under arrest, the boss fired and Murel the receptionist bailing like a flea off a drowning rat, the company underwent significant restructuring. Gone were individual desks, replaced by a number of oval tables with jacks and outlets for laptops and tablets. Connie's former position in customer service was outsourced, and the office was given over to the R&D

Department, which was convenient since Connie was the newest member. Except for a small cluster of four brown-vested administrative workers at a table in one corner, everyone else wore coveralls.

The remaining staff was small, the atmosphere technical and egalitarian. Jade always felt welcome and at home whenever she visited, which was often as she didn't have much else going on. She liked hanging out with Connie and the other members of R&D. At first, Jade worried about her presence being too intrusive so she discussed it with Connie, who didn't mind Jade being there at all. She pointed out it made networking over their other job as paranormal investigators easier if anything came up.

The blasting strains of some boy band's ode to Christmas greeted Jade when she breezed into the main office. She stood in front of the glass display case and gazed around the room. The blinds were festooned with tinsel and sparkling glass balls, hundreds of blue snowflakes covered every wall. Someone had set up a huge fake tree in one corner where it hovered like a benevolent alien entity. The needles were pink and white and it was draped with red and white lights, plastic candy canes, and a whole shitload of ornaments. Even the sample fire extinguishers on display hadn't escaped the holiday treatment. Someone had put jaunty wreaths over each one.

Jade bellied up to the reception desk. On the other side of the desk Nora, another member of the R&D department, put together a line of miniature snow-covered houses and shops. The empty boxes were creased and bald at the corners. Crumpled tissue paper was stuffed into them, a testament to their solicitous treatment.

"What the hell happened in here?" Jade asked. "It looks like Santa Claus exploded or something."

"Just getting into the holiday spirit," Nora said. She ducked under the desk and the miniature town blazed into light.

"That's cool, but I'm not gonna help you clean all that up next month."

"You might as well," Nora said. She tugged the worn coverall into place over her solid form. "You know, we're gonna have to start paying you, the amount of time you spend here."

"No way, if it means I have to wear a coverall and actually do work," Jade said. Nora belted out a laugh.

"If it's Connie you're looking for, I just saw her go into the storage room. Give her a minute and I bet she'll be coming over."

"Great." Jade crossed her arms and lounged back against the desk.

As predicted, Connie emerged from the storage room only a moment later. Her face broke into a bright smile and she galloped across the room. Jade couldn't help but echo the expression. God, Connie was fucking sweet. On the surface, Connie was dainty and innocent-looking but when it came to the bedroom — Jesus Christ, the things she could do to Jade. Just one of the many things she loved about Connie.

Since Jade first met her three months ago, Connie had changed. Her hair was longer and wavy then. Now, cropped in the new pixie style Jade thought was cute as hell, her waves turned into a halo of golden curls. The changes weren't only physical. Free from her previous soul-destroying job, Connie was happy and blossoming into the person she was meant to be. Like Jade, she still had a few issues to work through, and Jade was honored to be with her on that journey.

For a moment, Jade thought Connie was going to jump into her arms, but instead she stopped short. She was in the regulation blue coverall and managed to look both scientific and fucking hot in it at the same time. Jade considered the fact she was a little bit biased in her opinion.

"Ready to go to lunch?" Jade asked.

"Sure," Connie said. She shrugged into her coat en route to the duty board. She flipped her nameplate before she joined Jade at her post. Back at Jade's side, Connie threaded her fingers through Jade's in a way that had her gulping down the rush of heat that swept from her heart to her knees, with a significant bump in the middle.

THE FREEZING DASH across the street from the office building to the diner took Jade's breath away. She stomped snow from her boots at the entrance and paused as once more her senses were overwhelmed. The diner had also been hit with holiday spirit. "Jingle Bell Rock" was on the jukebox, the counter was decorated with bunches of holly, and the glass pie stands had big red bows on the handles.

Instead of sitting across from Connie, as she usually did, Jade slid into the bench next to her. Connie sat by the wall and she stowed the small mountain of their coats beside her. Jade shoved the menu into the holder next to the napkins. Neither of them ever bothered reading it. Sturdy and welcoming as always, Dixie came over with her order pad.

"What can I get you gals today?" she asked. "The lunch special's roast turkey, and we got a fresh apple pie on the counter, just waiting for me to cut it."

"Miss Dixie, you sure know how to tempt a person." Jade wiped her mouth on one cuff. "I'll have the special. For now."

"Me too," Connie said.

Dixie bustled off. Warm and comfortable, Jade stretched her legs out under the table. She sipped at a cup of coffee mostly in order to resist the urge to put her hand on Connie's thigh and give her a squeeze. The door clacked open. Young entered along with a whirl of cold air.

Muttering a brief greeting, Young got settled at the table. His sparse hair stood up after he pulled off his woolen cap. He dabbed at the melting snow on his bushy moustache. Their hellos were interrupted by Dixie appearing with two heaping plates. She gave Young a big smile when she saw him.

"That the special?" he asked.

"Yup," Jade said around a mouthful of turkey and potato. She scrubbed a crumpled paper napkin across her face. "Recommend it."

"Nice to see you again, Irv. What'll you have today?" Dixie leaned one generous hip against the table. She whipped out her order pad.

"I'll go with the special," Young said.

"Coming right up."

Young watched Jade for a moment before he said, "Gotta admire you, Mayflower. The way you put away that turkey like it's gonna run away from you."

"That's nothing. You should see how she eats pie," Connie said. She leaned her cheek on one hand and said, "It's a thing of beauty."

"Mgrf," Jade agreed as she shoveled the last bit of her lunch into her mouth. She put her cutlery down, grabbed her water, and chugged it.

Connie was almost finished and Young was just starting on his food.

"Got room for pie?" Jade nudged Connie.

"Definitely," Connie said.

Dixie brought over the coffee pot for refills.

"We'll have two pieces of your good pie, Miss Dixie," Jade said.

"You got it."

Dixie swept over to the counter. Jade twisted around in her seat so she could watch the sacred ritual of the first cut. She didn't take her eyes off the scene until the golden crusted piece of perfection sat in front of her. Jade closed her eyes and savored the moment. Then her spoon fell into her hand and she dropped down over the pie just as easily and naturally as a bird of prey on a fleeing rabbit.

Once she was finished, Jade sat back against the seat and covered her satisfied burp with the back of one hand. Connie scraped up the final bits of apple and held her fork to her lips. She caught Jade's eye and deliberately ran her tongue over the morsel before she drew it slowly into her mouth. She finished by sucking on her bottom lip.

With a strained, "Oh fuck," Jade bent over as a rush of pure lust raged through her and landed right between her legs. She glanced across the table. Young was rooting around in his briefcase and didn't seem to be paying attention. Jade took that opportunity to slide next to Connie and whisper in her ear.

"Naughty girl. Save that tongue for me."

Connie just replied with a quirk of her kissable lips. Suddenly overheated, Jade fanned herself with a napkin. A bead of sweat trickled down between her breasts and vanished into the band of her sports bra.

"So tell us about this case you mentioned," Jade said. She ditched her napkin and folded her hands on the table. Young pulled a folder out of his briefcase and placed it on the table. Dixie helpfully came over and cleared away their empty plates.

"You ever heard of this place called Emerald Resort? It's on the south shore, out in South Aisling."

"Nope," Jade said. She looked over at Connie, who shook her head.

Young shuffled around in his folder and pulled out a photo.

It showed a sprawling mansion with gabled windows and a large wraparound porch. Masses of trees filled the photo on either side of the house. "It used to belong to an old-blood local family, the Prewetts. They went way back in that town. The last one to live there, Edwina Prewett, never married. She had no relatives anyone could find, just a bunch of cats. It was empty for about ten years, then it got sold last year. The new owners fixed it up and made it into a kind of getaway type place. Re-opening is next week."

"Looks nice enough now," Jade said with a shrug. "What's that got to do with us?"

"Seems like they had a bit of trouble. Last Thursday they had an incident. The department's treating it as a one-time case of vandalism but I think there's more to it than that. It's not gonna stop and probably will escalate. Anyway, see for yourself. I'm gonna warn you, it ain't pretty." Young tossed several photos onto the table.

Jade leaned forward and shuffled the photos around.

"Salted scrotum jerky," Jade breathed.

The photos had all been taken in the same room, which appeared to be a slightly fussy sitting room furnished with a number of sofas and potted plants. But it was the wall behind them that stood out.

The entire wall was scarred, crisscrossed with words that were scraped deeply into it. Chunks of plaster and ripped shards of wallpaper decorated the floor. Whoever had done it was strong and determined—and angry.

```
choke the dyke dead
rape her straight
enjoy hell cuntlicker
```

Jade slammed the photos back into the folder and shoved it at Young.

"This is no fucking ghost," Jade snapped. "*Nothing* starts out this strong. Unless somebody's covering up previous incidents, which is also shady as fuck, this was done by a person."

Young held up a hand. Jade bit the inside of her cheek. He said, "There's a reason why this case needs you on it."

"Don't think you can pass me this kind of stuff, no matter

how gay I am," Jade said. "I'm not going to investigate some ass-hole who's just going to insult me and there's no way in hell I'm putting Connie in that situation either. Did you suddenly forget the kind of stuff we do? I don't deal with the living. You people have a hate crimes division. Let them take care of this bullshit. I'm out." Jade stood to leave, but Young's words stopped her.

"Mayflower, wait. Don't make a decision until you take a look at the details," Young said. "Just hear me out, okay?"

Jade scowled and raked both hands through her hair. "I'm giving you one more minute of my time and that's all," she said.

"Nobody was in the house besides the owners. The place was locked down tight with the security system on and nobody else on the premises. No evidence of break-in or tampering either. No *earthly* person could have done this. Even the folks involved are thinking that the perp isn't, you know, corporeal."

"For fuck's sake." Jade leaned one hip against the table. "One of the owners did it. Case closed. Normal people don't use ghosts as a go-to excuse unless they're trying to hide something."

"I have good reason to believe they didn't carry out the van-dalism." Young put down another photo. "These are the owners. Melinda and Doreen Hadley. For the record, they're not sisters."

Jade stared at the photo. The two women looked to be in their fifties. One was round and the other husky. They looked kind and friendly. Ironically, they were sitting on the sofa that appeared in the crime-scene photos, except the wall behind them was unblem-ished. A black lab lay at their feet and a small, shaggy dog of some kind perched between them.

Connie reached over and gently took Jade's hand in hers.

"Maybe we should help them," Connie said.

That small act alone took the righteous anger completely away from Jade. She returned Connie's squeeze and focused on Young again.

"Tell us more," Jade said. She dropped back onto the wide bench seat.

"I saw the police reports, not really much in them, but I got a gut feeling about this, kid," Young said. "That house has got his-tory. Lots of opportunity to pick up a 'tenant'. Something hap-pened there and it left a mark that's either just showing up now or it's been there for a while and finally got strong enough to cause serious damage. The key is finding out what it is, which I can't do from here."

Jade hummed to herself for a moment as her mind worked. She said, "If it's a historical building, they might have some stuff about it in their tourist information center."

Connie looked up from her phone. She sparkled with energy and interest. "The local library has a photographic archives. That might be a good place to look as well."

"So, what do you say?" Jade leaned her elbows on the table. In spite of herself, a smile tugged at her lips. "Should we take it or not?"

"Let's take it," Connie said. She wriggled in her seat as if she wanted to get up and start dashing around. "We should go and check out the area in person as soon as possible, before anything worse happens."

"You'll have a good chance to look around next week," Young said. He placed a glossy fold-out brochure on the table. "I pulled some strings and got you two booked as last-minute guests for their grand opening. On the house."

Jade picked up the pamphlet and stared at it. The title declared: LGBT COUPLES' RETREAT in looping, rainbow letters. She speared Young with a long stare then let out a guffaw. "Aw shit big guy, you had me going. This is our Christmas present, right? You old softie."

"Actually, it's not," he said.

"Oh," Jade said.

Connie said, "It's a great opportunity. If there's a homophobic *something* there, the retreat will probably really make it angry. Spur it into acting out and revealing itself." She clenched one fist and cracked her knuckles. "Then we can take it out."

"That's the spirit," Young said. "With the two of you on the case, it won't stand the ghost of a chance."

Jade fixed him with a withering glare.

Young coughed into his fist. "Uh, sorry. Anyway, I've arranged for the two of you to go down there a day early so you can take a look around and get a feel for the place without a bunch of other people in your way. See if there's anything hanging out that shouldn't be."

"Good idea," Jade said. She picked up the pamphlet and stuffed it into her canvas messenger bag. She swiped the check and waved Young off. "I got this. Anything else we need to know?"

"Just the owners want to keep it quiet. For the record, they know who the two of you are, but nobody else will, and they want to keep it that way," Young said as he picked up a toothpick. "It's their grand opening to-do and they don't want a bunch of bad publicity."

"Got it. We'll be discreet."

After Young left, Jade walked Connie back across the street. The wind had died down somewhat and chunky flakes rained down on them.

"When do you think you'll finish tonight, sweetheart?"

"Probably about five," Connie said. She got that sweet, mischievous look on her face that never failed to send Jade's hormones into the stratosphere. "Are you going to invite me over to your place? On a weeknight?"

"Hell yes," Jade said. "We can start prepping for the new case. Ahem, among other things, if you're okay with that."

"I'm super okay with that," Connie purred. She gazed up at Jade. "My skillet's still at yours, so I can make you a nice big breakfast tomorrow. You know, because I'm going to do my best to work up your appetite tonight."

"Oh yeah, I'd love that," Jade said. "How about I zip home, whip up some dinner and come back to pick you up?"

"It's okay, I can take the bus," Connie said.

"It's freezing out," Jade said. "Plus, I want to check the new snow-tires on the truck and I don't trust the bus drivers when it's snowing like this. Could have black ice too."

"All right, I appreciate the offer, my white knight," Connie said with a smile. The dimple Jade considered the most adorable thing in the world appeared on one rosy cheek.

"Fuck me Connie, you're so cute," Jade murmured.

# Chapter Two

"OOH, LOOK THEY'VE got pole dancing lessons and a massage workshop," Connie said when Jade entered the bedroom. The hardwood floor was silken under her bare feet.

"Massage, maybe, but pole dancing?" Jade raised her eyebrows. "Oh hell no. You couldn't pay me enough."

Connie laughed. "Me neither. I can see Benny doing it, though."

Jade couldn't help but grin at the mental image. Benny ran the bookstore on the first floor and, in addition to being the son of Jade's former cellmate, was the gayest and sassiest thing around. The fact that Jade had seen more of him than she needed to when she'd accidentally walked in on him and his boyfriend Jordan, in post-coital bliss on the bookstore's floor, didn't help.

She grabbed a clip from the dresser and twisted her long hair up behind her head. Once she was free from distraction, Jade sat down behind Connie. She wrapped her arms around Connie and breathed in the scent of shampoo on her still damp, blonde hair.

They were both in sleepwear, Jade in a tank top and drawstring cotton pants and Connie in a flannel nightshirt Jade's Aunt Addie gave her as a not-Christmas present. Because Connie was saving up for a car and both Benny and Jordan had student loans to pay off, they declared a ten dollar spending limit per person. Addie was an expert at finding loopholes, the latest being she'd bought the nightshirt online for herself, but accidentally got it in Connie's small size and didn't want the hassle of returning it. Jade detected bullshit but didn't call her aunt on it. The nightshirt was soft as cashmere against Jade's bare arms and Connie looked completely adorable in it.

Jade peered over Connie's shoulder to study the pamphlet on the quilt in front of them.

Connie pointed. "I don't really know what they mean by 'periodic, random, and intimate mystery questions', but what do you think of couples' pottery?"

"We might not have time to do all that, sweetie," Jade said.

She shifted so Connie was tucked more securely between her legs and in her arms.

"I know," Connie said. "But it is a five-day retreat. Even if we spend a few days getting rid of the ghost, we're still there for the week."

"If it really *is* a ghost," Jade said. She bent her head and placed a soft kiss on the tempting bare skin of Connie's neck. Under Jade's lips, Connie tilted her chin up with a murmur of appreciation. The action summoned up a wave of heat inside Jade. She couldn't stop herself as she trailed kisses down the side of Connie's neck. Her lips brushed Connie's skin as she said, "I'm not really in the mood to talk any more. How about you, sweetheart?"

"No," Connie said in a breathy voice. "I think you know what I'm in the mood for."

Jade's heart pounded. A hot, tight feeling gripped her right between her legs. Jade swallowed the rush of arousal down and said, "Maybe, maybe not. Show me."

Wordlessly, Connie took Jade's hands and drew them up to cup her breasts. Jade sucked in a hard breath as her palms filled with the most exquisite softness. Connie let go of her and unbuttoned the front of her nightshirt.

The nightshirt fell open. Jade groaned deep in her throat as her fingertips met the first brush of bare flesh.

"Fuck, you're so sweet," Jade said in a heated whisper. "You hot, sexy research and developer."

Connie let out a short laugh at that, but it turned into a moan as Jade found a taut, hard nipple and rolled it under her fingers. Connie threw her head back with the sweetest sound of longing. The movement disturbed the pamphlet and it fluttered to the floor where it lay forgotten. Jade held Connie for a moment before she stroked her hands down over the plane of Connie's midriff. Jade's breathing got rougher with every inch.

"Stop right there," Connie said. Her voice was low and husky with arousal.

She got up on her knees and turned in Jade's loose hold. Jade got one second's worth of her predatory expression before Connie pushed her back against the pillows. Connie's lips met hers in a deep, hungry kiss. Jade moaned into Connie's mouth as Connie's tongue sought hers. Jade sprawled back against the pillows with

Connie's body held between her thighs. The kiss didn't end. They sucked in breaths where they could. Jade thought she would explode. She ran her fingers through Connie's hair and cradled her head.

Without breaking the kiss, Jade bent her knees and pressed the bottoms of her feet into the quilt. She canted her hips in a silent plea. Jade bit off a moan as Connie rocked into her spread thighs.

"Fuck, Connie that's really good," Jade managed to grit out. She couldn't stop herself from meeting Connie's deft thrusts. Her body was primed. The cotton of her pants slipped over her sex, already slick and wet. The indirect contact was maddening. Jade was hungry for more. She wanted Connie's hands on her. "Connie, baby, I need you so fucking bad."

Connie stilled. She raised herself on her hands and looked down at Jade. She licked her bottom lip while she gave Jade a slow once-over. Her nightshirt was fully unbuttoned and Jade got an eyeful of the most amazing view when Connie rose to her knees. She shrugged the nightshirt off completely and it pooled around her legs, which upgraded the view from amazing to breathtaking. Jade swallowed hard. She shifted her butt against the quilt, desperate for even the slightest relief from the pressure building up between her legs.

"Now you," Connie said.

Jade didn't need to be told twice. She ripped her tank top off and chucked it away somewhere. She reached down and grabbed the drawstring of her pants, but was stopped by a slender hand on hers.

"Let me," Connie said. She bent down and Jade couldn't help but breathe out a reverent word as two of the most perfect breasts swung down in front of her face. Connie's skin was milky-pale and at rest, her areolas were almost invisible. Now, however, they were pebbled and pink, her nipples clenched like little cherry pits. Connie glanced up with a secret smile on her lips that foretold of only good things in Jade's future.

Connie moved to one side to free Jade's legs in order to pull the cotton pants down. Jade kicked them off with an impatient movement as soon as they got to her knees. Fully nude, Jade stretched back. She raised her arms over her head and rested them on the pillows. Jade had to admit she liked her own body, especially when she was bare before Connie. Jade's arms were long and muscular, the extensively tattooed right one as well as the scarred left. The newest tattoo, a small but perfect star on the underside of her arm swam into her vision for an instant before Jade returned her attention to the woman above her.

Jade reveled in the way Connie looked at her. A buzzing warmth grew in the depths of her belly. She always felt more naked under Connie's gaze than any other time and she loved it. Connie never shied away from Jade's scars, she paid just as much attention to Jade's imperfections as she did everywhere else.

Connie nestled between Jade's spread legs. She dropped her head to claim Jade's neck with her open mouth, kissing and tonguing both the unblemished skin and scarred areas just as hungrily. Her hands came up and lightly brushed over Jade's aching nipples. The instant Connie touched her, Jade's back arched and she let out a groan.

"Sweet Jesus," Jade said. Her clip dug into the back of her head but she barely registered the small discomfort. Her chest heaved, her breasts rose and fell with each breath.

Connie raised her head. She gave Jade a naughty smirk before she bent and her lips came down over one nipple. Her fingers tweaked the other. Jade gnawed at her lower lip to keep a lid on her moans. She was on fire. She was gone, lost already to Connie's affection. Connie pressed a wet kiss to the valley between Jade's breasts and continued lower. Between Jade's legs, Connie wriggled as she inched her way down. The press of skin-on-skin ignited Jade's desire. Connie's weight on her was the best feeling she ever had. Jade panted into the air. She kept her hands over her head even though she ached to grab Connie by the hips and grind into her.

When it came to the bedroom, Connie was in charge and Jade was more than happy with that. Each breath came out in a harsh moan as Connie's slow journey continued. A tongue circled her navel. Connie didn't stop there the way she always did. She dipped her head and painted a line down Jade's belly. Soft lips brushed a kiss over the patch of coarse hair at the apex of her legs. Startled, Jade gave an involuntary twitch.

At the sudden movement, Connie paused and looked up. She was flushed and breathing hard. Her pupils were fully blown, her lips swollen and wet.

Jade reached down with one hand and stroked through Connie's hair. The tiny smile that blossomed on Connie's face sent a shock of fire through Jade. While she secretly dreamed of seeing that tousled blonde head buried deep between her thighs, Connie hadn't gone there yet. That night it seemed Connie was in the mood to try something new.

"Keep going," Jade breathed.

"Really?" Connie asked in a hushed voice. She dropped her gaze and Jade felt it like a tangible thing. She couldn't help but grind her butt against the bed as a gush of wetness trickled from her.

"Fuck yeah," Jade said. She lay back onto the pillows and spread her legs wider. "You can stop anytime you don't feel right, but God I want you to do me with your mouth."

That was the end of the discussion. Connie gave Jade one last, burning look before she bent down. Jade's breath hitched as deft fingers parted her. She threw her arms over her head once more and grabbed handfuls of pillows. Connie slowly ran her fingers first down, then up Jade's length. Connie's breath ghosted over Jade's trimmed curls and super-sensitive flesh. Gentle, hesitant fingers spread Jade's wetness from her opening, over her inner lips, up her crease and finally onto her primed clit. A jolt shook through Jade at the first contact.

"Wow," Connie said softly to herself.

Jade couldn't help but agree as Connie settled down between her legs. Connie held Jade open with her fingers. Jade trembled with anticipation of what was coming. A firm tongue swiped into her slit, first up, then slowly down. It took all of Jade's willpower to keep still as Connie slowly teased and explored her. Jade panted into the air. The urge to move won and Jade rocked her hips, pushing herself to meet Connie's wet caress. Her body was tense and shivering, she was on the edge but couldn't quite make the drop. As much as Jade loved each pass of Connie's tongue, each soft kiss, it wasn't enough.

Jade unclenched one fist, dropped her hand, and drew her fingers through Connie's blonde tumble of curls.

"That's really good, but I want you up here, baby girl," Jade said in a low growl.

Connie straightened and licked her lips in a way that made a fist of arousal clench in Jade's belly. She crawled up Jade's body until they were nose-to-nose.

"You are so fucking beautiful," Jade purred. She didn't even think before she put her hands on either side of Connie's face and pulled her into a kiss. Jade had never tasted herself on anyone's mouth before that moment. It was a lot more exciting and intimate than she imagined. Jade slipped one thigh between Connie's legs. Connie met her with a pleased hum low in her throat.

"You're sopping wet," Jade murmured against Connie's mouth. She ran her hands up and down Connie's back. She shivered under Jade's touch.

"Yeah," Connie replied eloquently. She let out a whimper as Jade stroked her fingers down over her belly. Connie buried her face against Jade's shoulder. Jade could feel her jaw muscles clench.

"Be as loud as you want, sweetheart," Jade said.

"But your aunt—" Connie once again bit off a cry.

Jade dropped a kiss onto Connie's shoulder and whispered, "The walls are thick. Plus, Addie's been around the block more than a few times. What the fuck does she think we do when we spend the night together? Play Cribbage?"

Connie's quick laugh turned into a gasp as Jade's fingers found her. Connie's wetness covered her as Jade gently circled her clit, stiff within the sleek folds.

"Like that?" Jade asked.

Connie hummed and ground herself against Jade's fingers. Jade knew exactly what she wanted and slowly but firmly pushed two fingers into her. At the sight of her fingers sinking deep into Connie, Jade's inner muscles clenched. A wave of urgency gripped her. She couldn't wait for her turn.

"Do you think you could do me too?" Jade asked. "Like, at the same time."

"Oh yes," Connie said. She shifted and blinked eyes bright with need.

Jade took Connie's hand and brushed a light kiss over her knuckles before she drew Connie to her. Jade grunted in pleasure as Connie entered her. She couldn't believe the feeling that stole over her. Shocks of pleasure streamed from her sex where Connie was pushed deep within her, just as Connie's trembling walls held her in a hot, tight sheath.

Jade shifted and started to thrust, gently at first then harder as Connie moved along with her.

"Fuck this is so good," Jade said. "Oh yeah, like that, fuck me, Connie."

In time to Connie pumping into her, Jade's breath came out on sharp pants. Jade opened her legs and rocked her hips as she took Connie deep. Connie's walls clutched at Jade as she buried herself in her lover's wet opening. Their movements got sharper and harder. Jade realized anew the benefits to being on the bottom when Connie's breasts rocked in front of her face, bouncing with each pump. The smack of hot skin and the wet sounds of sex filled the room. Jade's thighs tensed. Her belly cramped. Above her, Connie shivered. Her hips jerked back and forth.

"So close," Connie said. "Jade, I'm so close."

"Don't fight it. That's it, sweetie," Jade said.

Connie arched her back in pleasure. That time, she didn't swallow the cries of ecstasy. Her movements got ragged and desperate. Jade was right behind her. Meaningless words fell from Jade's mouth as her body rocketed toward climax. Their position had Connie's palm flat against her clit and Connie's weight on her. Each thrust sent a volley of pleasure straight from her clit to her gut. Jade wasn't going to last much longer. She closed her eyes as the first sparks rippled through her.

"Coming," Jade grunted out. "Shit, Connie, I'm fucking there. Jesus!"

The last word was ripped into a cry. Her body shuddered as Jade let go. On top of her, Connie held still for an instant before a gush of wetness came down over Jade's hand. Silken muscles clenched hard on her fingers.

"Yes baby, come for me," Jade said between sharp breaths. She eased in and out of Connie as the waves of release broke. The shuddering jolts peaked. Connie threw her head back as she rode Jade hard. The sight was breathtaking. Jade stroked circles around Connie's engorged clit, not touching directly, but pressing into the delicate skin around the sheathed bud. The final shocks turned into a gentle rocking rhythm, then stillness as Connie fell into Jade's arms and nuzzled against her.

"You okay?" Jade asked. She smoothed sweat-damp hair from Connie's forehead. Against her chest, Connie's breaths were deep and slow.

"Mm hm," Connie said. "For now."

She stretched and draped herself over Jade once more. With a murmur of happiness, she pressed her spent sex to Jade's thigh and lightly ground against her. In spite of her own euphoric post-climax state, Jade's breathing kicked up a notch. Jade hoisted herself up on one elbow and looked down at the young woman who lay in her bed, who held Jade's entire universe in her eyes.

"That was fucking amazing," Jade said. She pulled off her clip and shook back the long cape of hair that spilled down over her shoulders. She chuckled as Connie reached out to brush the brown lengths back. In the process, her fingertips grazed Jade's still-hypersensitive nipples in a way that was no accident. A jolt of arousal sparked from the slight touch. Jade hissed in a breath before she caught Connie's wandering hand and kissed her fingers.

Jade said, "Keep doing that and I'll keep you up so late you're gonna have to call in sick tomorrow."

Connie raised an eyebrow and replied, "Actually, I already told Bill I'm telecommuting tomorrow. On flex-time."

Really?" Jade said in a conversational tone. Her thighs buzzed with renewed arousal. She sat up and grabbed her clip. With a practiced twist, Jade's hair was secured. "Since you put it that way, there's really only one thing left to do."

With a predatory growl, Jade threw herself forward and into Connie's arms where a happy squeak welcomed her.


"THESE ARE THE best eggs I've ever eaten in my entire life," Jade said around the forkful of scrambled eggs she shoved into her mouth.

Across from her, with her own mound of golden, buttery eggs, Connie laughed. "You just have an appetite from last night's workout."

"Sure do. You were insatiable, my lady," Jade said. Connie clapped a hand over her mouth to cover her smile. Jade grabbed a piece of toast from the basket in the middle of the table and spread a thick layer of marmalade over it. She shifted in her chair as her body remembered the activities of the previous night. After several more orgasms, they shared a shower and finally collapsed into the big, fluffy bed where they passed out in each other's embrace.

Jade looked across the table to where Connie, whole and healthy and, most of all, happy, was enjoying her breakfast with gusto. Was it only three months ago she was in limbo, her body in a coma and her spirit begging Jade for help? Jade wouldn't ever forget the sight of Connie's battered body in that hospital bed. Luckily, the joy she experienced at Connie's side pushed it further into her memory with every passing day.

Heavy footsteps on the stairwell preceded an older lady who burst into the kitchen.

"There you are, Janie," Addie said. Her head swiveled to take in the scene of domestic bliss. "You didn't tell me Connie was coming over, I would have made a pot roast. Good morning dear," Addie said. She gave Connie a squishy, one-armed hug before she plunked herself down in a chair.

Frustrated anger pounded in her chest but Jade refrained from correcting her aunt yet again about her name. Instead, she drew in a breath, held it for a moment, then slowly let it out. Her counselor would be proud. Calm again, Jade said, "You can't just come barging in like that. What if we were naked or fucking on the table or something?"

Connie sputtered with laughter and a piece of egg flew out of her mouth. Apologetically, she scooped it up with the paper towel she was using as a napkin.

Unfazed, Addie said, "If anything was going on, I would've just let myself out again and gone about my business." She adjusted her homemade shawl and stood once more. "Anyway, I was just on my way to get a cup of Benny's good coffee before I head out to the market. I was going to offer to get you something, but I see you've got plenty here. I'm almost tempted to pull up a chair and join in."

"You're welcome to," Connie said and smiled, showing off the dimple that was just begging for Jade's kiss. "There are lots more eggs and my skillet's finally perfectly seasoned, thanks to your great advice, Addie."

"Oh pshaw, just common sense, which doesn't seem too common nowadays. Although you seem to have it in spades, my girl."

Jade sat back in her chair and cradled her coffee cup in her hands. She watched her aunt and her girlfriend chatting like old friends. Connie glowed as she spoke and the last traces of Jade's irritation faded under the barrage of such happiness. The day they found the old iron skillet at a flea market resounded in her memory. Since then, Connie became something of a breakfast connoisseur and Jade was happy to share in the results.

After Addie breezed out and clomped noisily downstairs, Jade stacked their empty plates and took them to the sink. While she lathered up the sponge, Jade said, "Addie sure loves you. You know, if I don't marry you, I think she will."

A squeak behind her prompted Jade to whirl. Connie sat at the table, face pink.

"I didn't mean like right away," Jade stammered. She wiped a soapy hand across her forehead and bit back the urge to curse.

"That's okay, I love Addie too. Not more than I love you, of course," Connie said.

Jade's own face went a bit pink at those words. Connie didn't say them too often, and Jade never got tired of hearing them. After she drained the last draught of coffee, Connie brought over her mug and handed it to Jade, who dunked it into the sink. Connie tucked an errant curl behind her ear and looked perfectly adorable as she leaned back against the counter. She started to say something but stopped.

"What is it, sweetie?" Jade asked. She shuffled the silverware into the dish rack and dried her hands on a towel.

"I was just wondering," Connie said. "Why Addie calls you Janie and not Jade."

"Yeah, that," Jade said. She hung up the towel and shoved her hands into the pockets of her jeans. She was silent for a moment, before she said, "Addie's my mother's older sister. My mother gave me that name and it's all we really have left of her. I guess she doesn't want to give up that connection. But to me, Janebeth Trescott is someone I never want to be again. Someone I can't be again."

Connie was silent for a moment before she darted forward and hugged Jade tightly around the waist. She buried her face against Jade's shirt. Jade couldn't help but wrap her arms around Connie and hold her close.

"Thank you for telling me," Connie said. Her breath was hot against Jade's shoulder.

Jade pressed a kiss to her temple and said, "I don't tell stuff like this to just anyone."

"I know."

On the table, Connie's phone chirped. The screen lit up with a series of text messages.

"You gonna get that, sweetie?"

"I guess so," Connie said. She stepped back and looked up into Jade's face with a quirk to her lips. "But I'm hoping for a 'to be continued' on that hug."

"Anytime," Jade said.

Connie leaned one hip against the table. She picked up her phone. A smile broke over her face. She got busy tapping away. Jade's heart filled with warmth at Connie's expression. Only a few months ago Jade would have died to see that smile. Hell, she nearly did. Jade glanced at her once more before she turned and tidied up the few remaining things from breakfast.

"What are you smirking about over there?"

"Benny and Jordan are taking me shopping tomorrow," Connie said with a sparkle in her eyes. "For a fancy dress."

"Why do you need that?"

"You didn't read the pamphlet at all, did you?" Connie huffed out an annoyed sigh, but her dimple gave her away. "On the last night of the retreat, they're holding a formal Christmas Eve dance. And you're wearing your tux."

"That old thing? Ugh, if you insist," Jade said.

"I do, you look amazing in it."

"So you're looking for a new dress?"

"Yup," Connie said. She wrinkled her nose. "Something a bit warmer than the one I wore to the beach. And that doesn't smell like seaweed. Yours cleaned up a lot better than mine did."

"Cool. I'll get a scarf or something to match."

"I'll get your scarf. You have to wait until the dance to see my new dress."

"Aww," Jade said.

"No aww," Connie told her. "I want it to be a surprise."

"I can't wait," Jade said. She glanced at the clock. Already half-past nine. "Shit, you have to get to work. Why don't you use the office?"

Together, they meandered down the hallway.

As they walked, Connie reached out. She brushed her fingers over Jade's. She said, "You have work to do as well and I don't want to kick you out. I'll just set up in the kitchen or living room."

"No way," Jade reached over Connie's head to open the door to the office. "I want to go downstairs and hang out with Ben for a while."

Connie arched an eyebrow.

"Uh, and of course prep for the new case."

"Of course," Connie said. She crossed the small room and got settled behind the desk. She tucked a pencil behind one ear, then propped her elbows up on the desktop behind the laptop, at once both professional and unbelievably cute. Jade leaned in the doorway to take in the scene. Connie started typing, but stopped after a moment and looked up with a question in her eyes.

"Sorry, babe, just enjoying the view," Jade said. She easily caught the pencil Connie pitched at her. "Shoot me a text when you're taking a break. I'll come up with coffee and muffins."

"Sounds good, thanks." Connie beamed. "Oh, and can you return my pencil?"

With a smirk, Jade tossed the pencil back. Connie bent her head over her task and Jade eased the door closed. On her way out, Jade swiped the pamphlet from the bedroom floor. She took a brief detour through the laundry room and dumped the contents of the hamper into her small front-loading washing machine. While the machine sloshed away, Jade went down to Benny's bookstore which took up the first floor of the building.

Talking and laughter filtered through the frosted glass door at the end of the stairwell and Jade poked her head out. On the other side of the glass, emblazoned in proud gold letters, were the words: *Mason and Mayflower Investigations.*

As usual for that time of the day, the café corner was full. Benny stood behind the counter with a purple bandanna on his head that matched his purple apron. He didn't miss a beat as he simultaneously poured one of his fancy coffee drinks, popped something into the toaster oven, and held his own in the banter-laden conversation buzzing around him.

"There you are sleepyhead," Benny sang out as Jade tried to sneak past him to the newly refurbished reading corner. "Late night, hmm?"

Jade only replied with a knowing smirk.

"How about a coffee for the road?"

"Nah, I got my fix upstairs," Jade said. "I'll get a couple later to go."

"Sure thing," Benny said. He crossed his arms, tilted his head and said, "Well?"

"Well what?"

"Are you going to spill why exactly Connie needs a fancy-shmancy dress all of a sudden?"

In response, Jade slapped the pamphlet down on the counter.

Benny let out an ear-piercing shriek and snatched it up. He raised his head from the glossy pages with a look of complete awe. "Jaaaade! You *go* girl! How on earth did you manage to wrangle a reservation there? I heard that place has been fully booked for *ages*. And their inaugural too!"

Too many people were paying attention to them. Annoyed, Jade grabbed the pamphlet and shoved it under her arm. She lowered her voice and growled, "It's not recreation. We've been asked to look into a situation, that's all."

"Uh huh," Benny said. He didn't look convinced. "At any rate, I'll make sure the dress Connie gets is gonna knock you off your feet. Don't worry at all about your little cupcake, she's in good hands with me and Jordan. He's got an ex who works for Spangle and he can hook us up with designer stuff for cheap."

Even though Jade had no idea what Spangle was, she said, "Thanks Ben. You're the best."

"You know it. I take it you're driving down?"

"Yup," Jade said. "It's not too far."

"Good. At least I don't have to worry about your old car crapping out and leaving you stranded somewhere since you got your truck."

"Hey, I liked that car," Jade groused. "But yeah, my truck is pretty sweet."

Benny tinkled a laugh.

"Oh, and before I forget," Jade dug into her pocket and came up with two crumpled ten dollar bills. "We're coming back on the twenty-fifth, but it could be late. Here's your and Jordan's Christmas presents."

"Excuse me?" Benny fixed her with an incredulous look as if she was offering him used tissues.

"What's wrong with cash? That way you guys can get whatever you want. I don't know what the fuck you all like."

"You could have at least gift-wrapped them."

Jade clenched her jaw. For twenty years, Jade survived by

regarding any kind of gift with extreme suspicion. Things didn't work that way on the outside. She'd fucked up again. Her gut twisted. She was just about to withdraw the offer when Benny's expression softened. He gently patted Jade on the hand and trotted over to the cash register. He returned with the donation box.

"How about making a donation to LGBT youth camps in our honor?"

Relief washed over Jade. She stuffed the bills into the box.

"I hope you splurged and got something nice for Connie," Benny said.

The thought of what waited in a small velvet box upstairs warmed Jade's cheeks. A tight, electric feeling awoke in her chest. She shook her head dismissively and said, "Not for Christmas. I stuck to the price limit for that."

Benny raised an eyebrow but didn't reply. Jade left the counter and he waggled his fingers at her before he twirled over to the espresso machine.

She dodged a group of students and found a beanbag chair in a quiet corner. Jade spread the somewhat crumpled pamphlet over her knee and studied it. She focused on the brief description of the renovated property and history of the area. Apparently, the building itself was over two hundred years old and consisted of the main house, a boathouse, and a renovated barn that claimed to be an event space. Jade guessed the fancy dress party thing would be held there.

Even though she grumbled about it, Jade was glad for the excuse to wear her tux. She liked the look of the tailored lines on her long limbs. Most of all, she liked the way Connie looked at her when she got all dolled up in the formalwear. A burst of laughter from the café corner caused Jade to glance around in alarm. Her shoulders came up in self-defense mode.

Even after over a year of living as a free person, Jade still didn't like public places with lots of movement and noise. She couldn't shake the instinct that told her to look out for people using the noise as cover for an attack. Unconsciously, she moved so her back was firmly against the wall with no chance of anyone sneaking up on her.

Her hands shook. With a frustrated growl, Jade clasped her hands on one knee and stared out the window to distract herself. Cars hissed by in sprays of slush. After the previous night's snowfall, the fresh snow was dazzling in the sunlight. People bustled by on the sidewalk between snow banks that already streamed ice water over the pavement. Most of them carried some kind of shopping bag. Inside, the bookstore was warm and the scent of cinnamon and nutmeg wafted through the air.

That Christmas would be only the second one in twenty years Jade wouldn't spend freezing her ass off, locked in a building with people who would just as soon fuck her up as fuck her. Neither were high on Jade's list of priorities. Early on in her incarceration she learned to project a stay-away-from-me aura as well as the fighting skills to enforce it.

Now Jade was free, but she couldn't quite lose the shackles. Not yet. Large chunks were missing from her life. What was her normal for almost half of her forty-three years suddenly wasn't anymore.

Some days Jade woke up and for a dizzying split second she thought she was still in that cell and she'd dreamed the past year. With a shake of her head, Jade brought herself back to the present.

She gnawed at the cuff of her shirt and stared at the uninformative pamphlet. While a lot of places in the area boasted about their supposed haunted state, Jade could understand why the owners of the resort wouldn't flaunt the fact they had a ghost, particularly a homophobic one. If the place actually was haunted. Jade wasn't quite convinced she and Connie weren't walking into a trap.

# Chapter Three

THE SNOW CRUNCHED under the truck's tires as Jade pulled into the long driveway. The huge building loomed up in front of them, looking much bigger and more foreboding than in the brochure. Only one window in a far corner of the building shone with yellow light. The rest were black. On either side of the driveway, snow-capped hedges blotted out both the wan streetlights and the floodlights that turned the vast lawn into a glittering white carpet.

The truck nosed up to the guest parking spaces. Even with the radio blaring cheery holiday tunes and hot air blasting from the dash, Jade felt a chill trickle down her spine. It could have been the eerie silence of the place, mixed with a good helping of nerves. Jade didn't like going into a new place, particularly one where she wasn't sure of the rules.

She cut the engine and turned to Connie. "What do you think? Spooky enough for you?"

Connie looked up from her phone where she was updating Benny on their progress. She tilted her head and pursed her lips.

"I'm sure it looks more welcoming in the daytime."

"Hope so," Jade said. She stared at the blank windows of the resort as if challenging them. Her instinct pinged. "Let's leave our stuff in the truck for now. I don't want to have to deal with dragging a bunch of shit around while we check the place out."

"Good idea," Connie said.

Jade opened the door. She'd unzipped her jacket in the hot cab of the truck and didn't bother to do it up again. She stepped into the night and freezing air punched her in the chest. Ahead of her, Connie bounded up onto the porch. She stopped in front of the door. Like the rest of the building, it was huge and old-looking. The door sported a gigantic bauble-laden wreath that glittered in the faraway floodlights.

Connie raised her hand, hesitated, and turned to look back over her shoulder.

"Do you think we should knock? I mean, it's still someone's

house and the retreat doesn't officially begin until tomorrow."
Connie's lips quirked up. "Do you think they have a butler?"

Jade's laugh sounded forced and faded in the bleak night air.
"I hope not. I never know if I should tip those guys or not."

On a whim, Jade tried the doorknob. It was unlocked. Jade
eased the door open and stepped into a vast entrance hall. She
skimmed her hands along the wall but failed to find a light
switch. The click of the door closing behind them seemed very
loud in the silent, dark house. At least it was warm. Jade shivered
off the lingering chill. She peered into the darkness. A heavy,
waiting feeling stole over her, like something was lurking just out
of sight.

"Shit-crusted bastard," Jade muttered. She backed up against
the door. The doorknob dug into her hip, which snapped Jade's
mind back to the present. She got out her penlight and clicked it
on. The pale circle of light revealed a row of sturdy hooks stud-
ding the blue floral wallpaper. Each hook had a rubber mat under
it with a pair of slippers propped against the wall. Jade's penlight
weakly illuminated a lobby-like area with sheet covered, hulking
shapes that could have been sofas like the one she saw in the photos.

"Hello?" Jade called out. She couldn't help but keep a protec-
tive arm out in front of Connie.

A thundering ruckus started up from somewhere deep inside
the resort. Jade tensed, on high alert. It sounded like a train had
grown legs and was coming straight at them. Over the thuds, a
jingling sound lent the ominous welcome committee a cheerful
overtone.

Suddenly the room flared into light. Jade only had a split second before a big, black mass impacted with her legs and sent her
reeling back a step. Her penlight flew from her hand. A smaller,
fuzzy mass scampered around both her and Connie, yapping and
occasionally twirling around. Two tails wagged nonstop.

"Frog, Lady! Sit, girls."

Jade's heart was still pounding in her throat when a pair of
women burst into the lobby, who she recognized as the owners of
the resort. The first one to reach them was nearly as tall as Jade,
stocky and suntanned. She had a graying crew-cut and frowned
as she scolded the dogs in a stern voice, but the laugh-lines on her
face were a testament to a cheerful disposition. The woman

behind her was small and round and looked as if she'd be soft like a dinner roll if you squeezed her. Her blonde hair was tied back in a ponytail and her mouth was thin. She hung back as her partner reached them and grabbed both dogs by their collars.

"Sorry about the girls," she puffed. "You're okay with dogs?"

"Yeah, fine," Jade said in the heartiest voice she could manage. The only dogs she was familiar with were the ones who walked with the guards and were trained to bring people down. The black lab snuffled eagerly into the air. Her sleek head swiveled as she turned her attention from Jade to Connie, who crouched down and regarded the dog calmly. A pink tongue flicked her on the cheek and Connie pitched over with a squeak. She got up somewhat sheepishly. Jade pressed a hand to her lips to cover her chuckle.

The woman let go of the dogs and stood. She held a hand out and both of them obediently sat on their haunches. Tails thudded against the hardwood floor. Once the dogs were still, she said, "I'm Mel Hadley. That lovely lady over there is my wife, Doreen. And you've met our girls. The big black one is Frog and the little white one is Lady. They're too friendly for their own good. Worst guard dogs in the world."

"Nice to meet you." Jade took the offered hand and shook it. Mel's grip was sure and her hand calloused. When Doreen didn't offer, Jade shoved her hands into her pockets and said, "I'm Jade Mayflower and this is my partner Connie Mason. Detective Young contacted us about looking into your case."

"The ghost hunters," Doreen said with a derisive curl to her upper lip.

"I'm a licensed private investigator," Jade said through a tightly clenched smile. Her hand twitched to where her P.I. license rested in its black leather holder. "Our clients just happen to be slightly different than normal."

"We run Mason and Mayflower Investigations," Connie said. She dug out one of their newly printed business cards and handed it over with a proud flourish.

Doreen took the card and read it. Her face fell. "Oh. So partners in this case means business partners. Detective Young led us to believe—"

"No, we're totally together," Jade said. She winced at her overeager tone. It sounded blatantly fake. She draped an arm around Connie and pulled her close. Connie nestled against her without a moment of hesitation. The guarded look on Doreen's face eased a bit.

"That's good to know, Ms. Mayflower," Doreen said.

"Jade's fine. I hate that formal shit."

"All right then, Jade it is." Doreen looked at the business card one more time, then back up at Jade. "I hope Detective Young told you how important it is word doesn't get out that you're here looking for ghosts." She said the last word with sarcasm, which Jade didn't find particularly encouraging.

Jade squared her shoulders in defense. "Yeah, he did."

"Good," Doreen said. "Because we've sunk our entire savings into this place and if some farfetched rumors start driving away our guests, it's not going to be pretty. No cameras or funny gadgets, no weird stuff. I also expect the two of you to participate as regular attendees of the retreat and as a *couple*. This retreat is for people who are having intimacy issues and for some of them, it's their last chance. I don't want you messing that up. Got it?"

Jade regarded Doreen through narrowed eyes. She simply nodded. She didn't trust her voice not to spit out a lungful of expletives.

"Dor," Mel said. "That's not how they work. Detective Young made that clear."

"It bears repeating," Doreen said. She looked from Jade to Connie. Her eyes were calculating, as if she was trying to measure something. "We've prepared a room for you two. I assume you're fine with sharing a bed?"

Jade was too confused to answer, but Connie piped up, "Of course we are." She slipped her arm through Jade's and smiled up at her. "Isn't that right, honey...uh, butt?"

Jade couldn't help the snort of laughter that exploded from her. Connie followed her, dissolving into giggles behind the hand she clapped to her mouth. Doreen crossed her arms over her chest and gave Mel a pointed look.

In the silence that followed their outburst, the strained atmosphere got even tenser. Jade forced the nervous grin off her face. Maybe Connie's rare foray into sappy nicknames could have been better timed.

Mel broke the tension by asking in a bright voice, "How about joining us for dinner? We've got our private rooms in the back, if you're okay with home cooking. The staff don't start until tomorrow."

"That sounds great," Jade said. She relaxed a fraction. "I've got some questions about the property and the case I'd like to discuss with the two of you."

"We don't know a whole lot, but we'll try to be as helpful as possible," Mel said.

Doreen was silent.

DINNER TURNED OUT to be Shepherd's Pie. The dogs chased each other around the table and snuffled happily at anything and everything. Lady seemed especially taken with Connie and sniffed her ankles for a while, then plunked her fuzzy little body on Connie's slippers. After the initial excitement wore off, Frog retired to a braided mat in the corner with her chew toy.

The dining room wasn't large, but it was cozy and welcoming. The walls were plain in contrast to the rest of the resort, which bordered on overdone and stuffy. They sat around a table decorated with a number of candles that added to the warm atmosphere and almost made up for Doreen's sour expression.

"Normally, we'll keep the dogs in here," Mel said. She scooped generous mounds of Shepherd's Pie onto everyone's plates. "I hope you don't mind them. I can shut them in the kitchen if you find them a bother."

"Not at all. I think they're adorable," Connie said. She glanced under the table with a smile. "And we're the ones invading their turf. I like having them here."

"Me too," Jade said with an indulgent glance at Connie.

"Glad to hear that," Mel said. She picked up her fork and said, "We don't stand on ceremony here. Dig in, folks."

Jade was ready to spring in with the questions, but she figured the first thing she brought up shouldn't be the possibility their resort was haunted either by a hate-spewing ghost or a huge fucking bigot in sheep's clothing. She shoveled in half of her pie and tried to find a way to ease into the conversation, maybe catch her hosts off-guard so they'd give her more info than they planned.

Connie saved the day.

As Mel poured glasses of sparkling juice for everyone, Connie asked, "Is Lady a Bichon Frise? She's so friendly and playful."

Mel beamed and even Doreen looked a bit less guarded.

Doreen said, "That's right. We rescued her from a puppy mill. She'd never been outside, never even learned how to play, but look at her now. Frog's a rescue too. She was found tied up at a campsite, badly abused and almost starved to death, poor thing. It took us a long time to get her to trust people again."

Connie's eyes glistened in the soft light. She shook her head. "How can anyone be so cruel to innocent animals?"

At the pained tone in Connie's voice, Jade's chest gave a lurch. She reached out and took Connie's hand.

"Hey, it's okay, sweetie," Jade said in a soft voice.

"Sorry," Connie said. She took a sip of her juice and turned her attention back to the conversation. "Frog is an unusual name for a dog, especially such a big one. I bet there's a story behind it."

"There is," Mel said. "When we first got her, she couldn't bark, only made this kind of croaking sound and just like that, Britt started calling her—" Mel stopped talking abruptly and looked around the table. "Listen to me blathering on, I'm sure you've got some questions about the resort. How about some more carrots? They're grown locally, fresh from the farmer's market."

Jade pounced. "Who's Britt?"

Mel glanced across the table at her wife and gave a shake of her head.

Without acknowledging the look Mel threw at her, Doreen raised her chin and said, "Britt is Brittney. Our daughter."

With a resigned air, Mel said, "I'd say she's about your age, Connie. She'll be twenty-five next March."

"That's pretty close to me," Connie said. "I'll turn twenty-five in June."

Doreen clapped her hands together. "Goodness, so young! I think it's great you've found each other, you know, you seem so different. No offense." Doreen cocked her head and asked, "How long have you been together, if you don't mind my asking?"

"Your daughter, Brittney. Is she here?" Jade asked. She wanted to get the topic off herself and Connie.

"No, she isn't," Mel said sharply. "She lives and works in Portsmouth, where she is at the moment."

The temperature in the room felt like it plummeted several degrees.

Mel suddenly changed to a cheerful smile. She said, "How about the two of you? Any plans for kids?" Her jolly tone was just a little bit too bright.

Connie answered with a non-committal shrug.

Jade matched Mel's manufactured joviality. She said, "We're not trying, but we're not preventing either. Heh heh, if you know what I mean, right sweetie?" She followed up the remark with a chuckle and a joking prod with her elbow to Connie's side. Connie didn't move.

"I think Connie would make a great mom," Mel said. "Imagine a house full of little blonde babies!"

The words ignited a flash of anger. More harshly than she intended, Jade said, "Why do you just assume Connie's gonna be the one to get knocked up? What if I wanted to take one for the team?"

Connie's gasp cut through the sudden silence.

"It doesn't have to be an either or situation," Mel said. "There's no reason why you both can't participate equally. Who knows, you may even find a nice gay male couple and trade."

"Uh, yeah, that's an idea," Jade stammered.

"Jade, you're what, forty?" Doreen asked.

"Around there," Jade said in a guarded tone.

"You don't want to leave it too late," Doreen said. "If you're serious about starting a family, you two had better get things rolling ASAP. It takes a while to find a donor. Be prepared for surprises, though. The older you are, the more things can go wrong. You're looking at massive changes to your entire lower region, even in the best-case scenario. Worst case, you're ripped to shreds and nothing ever feels or works right again."

Unconsciously, Jade crossed her legs.

"Don't scare them, honey," Mel said. She reached out to put a hand over her wife's, but Doreen moved away before they touched. Mel continued as if nothing was amiss, "If you don't want to be a birth mother, there are always other routes. How do you feel about using a surrogate?"

Jade shifted in her seat. She wanted to be the one asking questions instead of answering and definitely not about such a personal subject. Her hand clenched on her fork.

"We've discussed adoption," Jade said. Beside her, she felt Connie tense. Maybe the topic was too personal for her as well. To be honest, they hadn't really discussed it. Jade had mentioned she wasn't too keen on babies and favored adoption, but that was all. At the time, only Connie's disembodied spirit had been in attendance, which complicated matters even more. She might not even remember the exchange. Jade hoped she didn't come off as too unenthusiastic about the whole kids situation for Connie's sake.

"I hope you're ready for some scrutiny," Doreen said. "It's a hell of a hassle to get approved, especially if you want an infant. If you've got any skeletons in your closet, pretty much forget about it."

Jade tried not to hunch her shoulders defensively. Exonerated or not, two decades in a federal penitentiary was a pretty big skeleton.

Doreen waved a hand and said, "Best to make one yourself. Who knows, you might get lucky and your body bounces back to the way it was in a year or two. Or you could end up in a diaper for the rest of your life. But having a family is worth it, right?"

Connie flinched. Instead of answering, Jade took another mouthful of pie and practically swallowed it whole. She felt like shit. The investigation wasn't going anywhere except down Discomfort Street. Jade wracked her brain for anything non-confrontational to say when, once again, Connie came to the rescue.

"I can't believe how gorgeous this place is. The pictures in the brochure don't do it justice," Connie said. "It must have been a huge job, turning a one-family home into a beautiful resort like this. Did you do the renovations yourself?"

"Yeah, most of them," Mel said. She puffed up with pride. "We did all the cosmetic stuff like wallpapering and painting, and also some repairs. I got pretty handy with a buzz-saw, 'cept for one time I nearly took my thumb off. You should've seen it, blood everywhere." With a flourish, she rolled up one sleeve and proudly displayed a curved, white scar at the base of her hand.

"Ooh, I bet that hurt," Jade said. She picked up her glass without thinking and didn't miss the sudden glances both Mel and Doreen gave her at the burn scars that started on the back of her hand and vanished under her cuff. Jade put her glass back down with a thump.

Mel said, "We left the electrical and plumbing to the experts, though. Each room has its own en suite, just showers though. If you want a bath, you can reserve the one on the third floor. It's got a whirlpool big enough for two."

"Nice," Jade drawled. She fixed Connie with a look. "I think we should definitely take advantage of that feature while we're here."

Connie blushed but nodded. Her dimple caught the candle-light and gave her the air of a mischievous angel. Jade caught her breath. She was so sweetly sexy, Jade wished the interminable dinner was over and she had Connie alone in their room. Hopefully the mattress wasn't squeaky or else their hosts would be in for a musical night. Jade hid her lascivious grin behind a big gulp of juice.

"Thanks for squeezing us in," Connie said. "I hope we didn't inconvenience you or force anyone else out. I heard your retreats are already booked up for all of next year."

"It's no problem," Doreen said in an offhand way. "That room's not supposed to be for guests, anyway. Britt stays there when she's here."

Jade didn't miss the alarmed look Doreen's words brought to Mel's face. She filed it away in her mind. Before Mel could speak to deflect the topic, Jade jumped in.

"So Britt stays here a lot?"

"From time to time," Doreen said. "She helped out with—"

"Anybody got room for dessert?" Mel got to her feet and started stacking dishes in an overly loud way. She waved off Connie's offer of help and scooped up a bouquet of silverware in one large hand. "We've got carrot cake, fresh from the best bakery in town this afternoon. Their cream cheese frosting is decadent."

"Sounds good," Jade said to Mel's back. The dogs, perhaps sensing the excitement in the sudden flurry of activity, jumped up as well. Like two furry shadows, they pelted into the kitchen after their owner. Scampering paws and jingles filled the air.

"Decaf okay?" Mel hollered from the kitchen.

"Sure," Jade replied. She glanced over at Connie, who looked thoughtful. The look was followed by the soft press of Connie's stockinged foot to Jade's. Either she was giving Jade a secret message or she was playing footsies. Jade suspected the former, although she appreciated the hint of the latter. Jade shucked one slipper and tapped Connie back without meeting her eyes.

"Doreen, honey, could you give me a hand in here?" Mel poked her head into the dining room. "I want to make sure the dogs have some food too."

Doreen's thin lips thinned even more, but she excused herself and got up.

The rest of the meal was taken up by Mel cheerfully dominating the conversation with tales of their renovation adventures. Jade played dumb and followed along. She actually had a pretty good time, all things considered.

# Chapter Four

"THEY'RE HIDING SOMETHING," Jade said. She set down their bags and leaned back against the door. The cold night air streamed from her, sharp and clean in the slightly cinnamon scented room. The room was lit by a single stained-glass lamp. The bed was a solid double, with a carved mahogany headboard that looked antique. The heavy curtains over the window and dark, patterned wallpaper added to the feeling of being in a time-warp a hundred years into the past.

"Come here and let me warm you up," Connie said from her perch on the bed. She held out both arms and Jade fell into them. She slung herself over Connie's body and buried her face against her chest with a happy sigh. Soft hands stroked over Jade's hair and back, electric heat streamed from every place they touched. Connie's voice hummed through Jade as she said, "And for the record, I agree."

"We need to get them apart," Jade said. Connie released her and Jade rolled over onto her back. She pillowed her head on her arms and gazed up at Connie. "They play off each other, run interference. I think Mel's more open to the idea of us being here, but Doreen definitely knows something."

"Good plan," Connie said. "We can divide and conquer."

She stretched out down next to Jade. Connie languidly trailed a finger over Jade's lower lip, down her throat and finally in a line down the middle of Jade's body, lingering between her breasts. Ripples of arousal started up at the light touch. Jade stifled a groan. She wanted to close her eyes and lose herself in Connie's arms.

Jade tried to concentrate on the details of the case, but the lamplight casting Connie's green eyes into sultry darkness, along with the softness of her breast just brushing up to Jade's own made thinking straight quite difficult. Jade couldn't stop herself as she freed one hand from behind her head and cupped Connie's cheek.

"I want to kiss you so bad," Jade breathed.

"Why don't you?" Connie's eyes sparkled in the low light. Her lips quirked up. Jade leaned forward. Her heart gave a great kick, she wanted Connie's mouth so much. Connie's eyes fluttered closed and she tilted her head in clear invitation. Jade was almost there when a faraway, nagging sound brought her back. Jade froze with her eyes unconsciously trained on the door.

"Jade, what—?"

"Shh," Jade placed a finger on Connie's lips. The soft resilience was almost unbearably tempting. "I hear something."

Connie stilled. Both of them held their breaths. The muffled but unmistakable sound of raised voices filtered through the air.

Jade sat up. She winced at the squeak of the box spring. After their enforced silence, it seemed much too loud.

"I'm going to see what that's all about," Jade said. She rolled off the bed. Her feet searched for her slippers for an instant before she shuffled into them.

"Should I stay here?" Connie asked.

"Yeah," Jade said. She quickly brushed an errant strand of hair from Connie's forehead. "If I get busted, I don't want them to lose trust in both of us."

"Okay," Connie said. She rose to her knees on the bed and looped her arms around Jade's neck. She pressed a quick kiss to her cheek and whispered, "I'll be here, keeping the bed warm for you. Hurry back or I'll start without you."

"Ooh," Jade said. Her knees buckled. She had to grab onto one of the bedposts to keep upright. "Really?"

"Of course not," Connie said with a mischievous tilt of her head. She made shooing motions with her hands. "Go. And good luck."

As quietly as she could, Jade slipped into the dim hallway. Even if Doreen hadn't spilled the information, it was obvious their room was, at best, a spare. It didn't even have a number on the door. All of the guestrooms were on the second floor, but theirs was tucked away at the end of the hall. A large linen closet stood between them and their next door neighbors. Across the hall was a narrow service stairwell, which led quite close to the owners' rooms and served as a funnel for the sounds of the faraway argument.

The only illumination was provided by green glowing squares placed at intervals at ankle-level on the walls. The voices grew in volume and clarity with every step Jade took down the old stairwell. She braced her hands on the walls on either side of her on her careful descent. The stairs were soft and ancient, untouched by renovations other than the guiding stickers. Jade rolled her weight as much as she could to avoid creaks. One stair near the bottom gave off a sharp pop when Jade eased her foot down onto it. She sucked in a breath, but the voices didn't pause.

Jade breathed again. At the bottom of the stairwell, she leaned against the door until it opened a crack. She held her breath and concentrated on listening. It was clear Mel and Doreen were having some kind of heated discussion. The first words Jade could make out were Doreen's.

" — secretive ever since this whole business started."

"But that didn't give you the right to look at her phone." Mel's voice was lower than Doreen's, but similarly tight with anger.

"It was locked anyway. I know you think that's why she's barely talked to either of us since that morning, but I *know* it's something else."

"Dor, honey, I just think we shouldn't jump to conclusions, that's all."

Doreen interrupted. Her voice was shrill. "Oh no. You've obviously made your decision and my opinion doesn't matter. You always were too soft with Britt. You always took her side, spoiled her. It's your fault this happened."

"Mine? Dor, I know — "

"No, you *don't*." Doreen interrupted again, speaking over Mel. In her hideout, Jade winced at the harsh tone of the words Doreen machine-gunned at her wife. "You didn't wreck your body for her. You didn't have to give up your dignity, you didn't have go on frikking pills and go to therapy, did you? She damn well owes me for all that. So if you think being *nice*, acting like she can do no wrong, trying to cover up the truth with supernatural nonsense that *nobody* believes is going to make up for that, you are so wrong."

Mel said something that Jade couldn't catch. It must have been some kind of apology because Doreen suddenly laughed, a harsh, bitter sound.

"Sorry? You're sorry? No, you don't get to be sorry. I'm the one who's sorry." A pause. Doreen spoke in a softer voice. "Mel, I love you but I don't want to interact with you right now. I need to find my center before the guests arrive tomorrow. Good night."

Footsteps and the slam of a door brought the discussion to an end. Jade waited for a few extremely long minutes more until she heard a second set of footsteps, heavier and more purposeful than the previous ones.

A door opened and closed with a rattling, metallic sound. Jade brought the floor plan of the building into her mind's eye. A sunroom advertised as a smoking area had the best possibility of being Mel's destination.

Jade came to a decision. She crept down the hallway until she came to the sunroom. It was a lot nicer than she thought, more like a glassed-in study with armchairs and an actual fireplace at one end. The lights were off but a nice glow came from a roaring blaze in the fireplace. The room was bathed in orange and yellow. Jade eased the door open.

Mel was in one of the armchairs. She twisted to look over her shoulder as Jade came in. Mel held a slim cigar and a spiral of fragrant smoke plumed from one end. In the other she had a glass with some kind of amber liquor in it.

"Hey, fancy meeting you here," Jade said. Her voice sounded, too high, perky, and fake. She discreetly coughed into one hand as she let the door bang shut behind herself. She swaggered into the room with the air she had every right to be there and dropped into the armchair next to Mel's. "Very nice setup you have here," Jade said in her usual throaty growl.

Mel leaned forward to tap her cigar into an ashtray on the small table between them. "Yeah, Doreen let me have this room as my own personal project. I like to think it turned out pretty well." She held up her cigar. "Do you smoke? I can offer you a fine hand-rolled Cuban from my collection."

"Nah," Jade said. "I don't smoke, but I like the smell."

"Glad it doesn't offend," Mel said. She nodded to the bottle standing between them. "Could I interest you in a brandy? This is one of my favorites."

"Sure," Jade said even though she'd never tasted brandy in her entire life and was sure she'd find it foul. She accepted the glass and clinked it with Mel's before she raised it to her lips. The scent was like a punch to the nose. Jade kept her mouth closed until she lowered the glass to rest on the table again. The trace of liquor she licked from her lips filled her mouth with an acrid burn not unlike disinfectant. Jade hid her grimace behind a hum of approval. Silence fell, but it wasn't uncomfortable. A log in the fire popped.

"So you believe in ghosts?" Mel asked. She got a sheepish look on her face. "Sorry, dumb question."

"No, it's a good question," Jade said. She traced the rim of her glass with a finger. "I believe in what I've seen. I believe a person's life energy can exist separately from their body. I also believe an act of sudden violence or deep emotion can leave an echo, like a mark on a place where it replays that moment over and over. It seems Doreen's a bit skeptical."

"She thinks…" Mel trailed off. She took a drag of her cigar.

"Mel, you have to be honest with me," Jade said. "What does she think? Come on, you know I'm going to hear it from her sooner or later. This is your chance to give me your side first."

Mel's posture drooped. She sighed and nodded. "Fair enough," she said. "Okay, here it is. Doreen thinks that Britt's responsible. You know, for the vandalism."

"Why does she think so?"

Mel shrugged. Her eyes were fixed on the snowy expanse outside. Here and there the glittering surface was dimpled with dog-shaped imprints. She took a quick sip of brandy before she said, "It's probably a coincidence but every time something's happened, Britt's been here."

"Every time?" Jade fixed Mel with a hard look. Still, the other woman didn't turn away from the window. "I was told it happened once. Damnit, Mel." Jade slammed her hand down on the table. This time, Mel turned to her. "Don't bullshit me. I may be some woo-woo weirdo to you guys, but I'm doing my best to help you out here. At least give me the tools to do that."

Mel straightened. "You're right. You deserve to know. We had several other incidents before the last one. It all started about three months ago. Before that we didn't have any trouble at all," she said. Her voice was dull and defeated. "They were smaller, just smashed things in the hallway and a few words on the walls. We fixed everything before anyone saw. The last one, though, we didn't catch it in time. The electrician we hired came in early. He saw it before we did and called the police. There was nothing we could do." She massaged her temples. "But Britt was just as surprised and outraged as the rest of us. The last one especially upset her. She's not that good an actor. I know she didn't do it."

"Doreen thinks she did," Jade said. "Did anyone ask her about it?"

"No. I asked Doreen not to bring it up with Britt. It would only escalate into another fight," Mel said. "I can't see Britt propagating that kind of thing — all those awful words."

"Is Britt straight?"

"Yeah. She's had a couple boyfriends, nothing serious yet. But she's always been super accepting of her mom and me. She's been to Pride with us and all that. She's a solid ally."

Jade faked another sip to think over her next question. She didn't want Mel to know she'd eavesdropped, but she needed more information. Jade wished she was as good at all that talking bullshit as Connie.

"How's Doreen's relationship with Britt?"

Mel pressed her lips together. She took a drag of her cigar and let the rich smoke out slowly.

"Not great," Mel said. She sighed into her brandy. "Doreen blames Britt for her...problems. It didn't help that after Britt was born, Doreen didn't bond with her very well. She wasn't capable of taking care of a newborn, so I did pretty much everything. I don't blame her for that."

"What happened?" Jade asked. She tilted her glass. The firelight sent a golden glow around the line where liquor met glass. "Like, PPD?"

"That, among other things." Mel's face clouded. "Everything was fine up until the birth. It was traumatic, very invasive. This was before we could get married. The hospital had been really accommodating and understanding until that point. The doctor in charge of her delivery was some new guy. He suddenly decided he wouldn't let me in with her, so I was stuck in that damn waiting room, pacing like a caged tiger."

"Shit," Jade said in sympathy. "And this doctor guy fucked up?"

"I don't know. Nobody would speak to me directly, and Doreen never received much explanation either." Mel's voice faltered. "They did things to her without her consent, put her dignity and health second to the baby. I didn't know until it was over and I saw what they'd done to her while I was stuck outside. She was in such an awful state. A lot of it was my fault. I didn't protect her."

Jade's fingers clenched around her glass. The liquid inside rippled from her shaking grip. She couldn't imagine the agony she'd feel if anyone violated Connie like that. A fist of rage squeezed Jade's chest for a moment.

"It left her with a lot of damage, mental and physical," Mel said. She swirled the liquor in her glass as she spoke. The amber depths glowed in the light of the fire. "It didn't just affect how she got along with Britt. It changed our intimacy, it changed everything. We've spent the last twenty-four years coming to terms with what happened and re-learning how to love each other. That's why we decided to start our retreat. To help others with what we've learned."

"Okay," Jade said. She felt like a big dumb rock. "I want to talk to Britt. In person, if possible."

"I thought you might," Mel said.

"Is she coming home for the holidays?" Jade winced. "I guess we kind of kicked her out of her room."

"No, she was planning to spend Christmas with friends from the start. And that last incident, well she just took off like the place was on fire. I don't think it's good for her to be here," Mel said. She shifted in her chair with a look of discomfort. "She's been avoiding me since that, so I really hope she'll talk to you."

Jade mulled that over. She could be running from a supernatural threat, or from her own guilt.

"I'll text you her address, and I'll let her know about the two of you. She's not answering her phone, but she is at least reading her texts."

"Great," Jade said.

Mel knit her fingers together. "Since we're doing this full disclosure thing, there's something else I should probably let you in on."

"Shoot."

"This whole house has a bit of a strange vibe sometimes, but I think there's *something* in that room, Britt's room."

Jade sat up. She abandoned her brandy in favor of leaning both hands on the table to face Mel squarely. "Why? Have you seen anything? Felt anything?"

Mel shook her head. "Nope, but I'm probably the least sensitive person to all that. I have noticed stuff, though. For example, sometimes the dogs go crazy in front of that room. Neither of them will enter it, but sometimes they sit in the doorway, barking at something nobody can see. Maybe something's there or maybe that's just them being silly fuzz-butts. It was the previous owner's spare room and it was just rank with the stink of cats. Maybe that's it."

"Could be anything," Jade said. "Sometimes animals are more sensitive to certain things than humans. Anything else?"

Mel said, "There are a couple other things, like light bulbs burning out faster there than anywhere else, and how sometimes the curtains look like they're moving even when the window's closed." Mel shrugged. "But those can be explained any number of ways."

"Yeah, especially in a house this size and age," Jade said. "Plus the fact that ghosts don't exist."

"Jury's still out on that one," Mel said. She shot Jade a wry grin, took a quick drag, then let out a puff of smoke. "The main thing that worries me is, in the deed to the house, there was a note from the owner to leave that room empty and never let anyone stay there. Nothing about why, and to be honest, none of us wanted to dig deeper than that." She tapped her cigar absently against the rim of the ashtray. "We figured as long as we weren't renting the room out, it would be okay. Evidently not. I, uh, hope you don't mind we put the two of you there."

"It's cool," Jade said. "In fact, I think it's probably a good idea."

Her mind full of new information that was not quite fitting together, Jade slouched back into her chair and gazed into the fire while she tried to make sense of it all. She needed to talk it over with Connie.

The room was warm and the armchair soft. A wave of sleepiness hit her. A huge yawn split her face open. Hurriedly, Jade covered her mouth with one hand.

"Sorry, but I'm beat. I should probably head upstairs."

"All right." Mel glanced at her watch. It was large and solid. "I'm about to head in myself. Big day tomorrow."

Jade stood. She wondered if she could pull off downing her brandy in one shot, but rejected the idea. While she felt bad for wasting something probably really expensive, it was also really gross. More than likely she'd puke it right back up. She settled for holding out a hand for Mel to shake.

"Thanks for the brandy and the honesty."

"No problem, I appreciate you keeping an open mind about this case."

Jade retrieved her hand, stepped back, and gave an abbreviated salute.

As soon as Jade slipped back into their room, Connie greeted her with a running hug. Jade gathered her up and bent to kiss her. Just before their lips met, Connie stopped and wrinkled her nose.

"Were you drinking?" she asked with a surprised expression. "And is that cigar smoke?"

"I hung out in the smoking room with Mel and she gave me a brandy," Jade said. She scrubbed the back of one hand over her mouth. "I didn't really drink any but I guess it still stinks. Give me a second and I'll take care of it, okay sweetie?"

"Okay," Connie said. She draped herself over the bed in a seductive pose. "But hurry because I want you in my bed. This is the last night we won't have neighbors after all."

"Yes ma'am!" Jade hustled into the bathroom where she scrubbed her mouth out with a whole shitload of toothpaste and sprayed herself liberally with room freshener. She debated going back out in the buff to save time, but she loved it when Connie undressed her, so she changed into the new pajamas she got specifically for the retreat. They were deep blue silk with white piping on the cuffs and collar. Jade studied herself in the mirror with an air of satisfaction. With her hair pulled back neatly in a low ponytail, she was nearly six feet of pure class. Jade felt like she needed one of those velvet robes to complete the outfit.

Connie's eyes lit up when Jade re-entered. She didn't speak, just rose to her knees and beckoned Jade with one finger. Only too eager to comply, Jade launched herself from the bathroom doorway, clear across the room to land on the bed. Connie stroked one hand down the front of Jade's pajama top.

"I like this, it looks gorgeous on you," Connie said. The predatory note in her voice sent a thrill straight to Jade's clit. "And it's going to look even better on the floor."

"Mmph," Jade replied as Connie caught her full on the mouth in a sudden kiss. She fell back onto the bed. Already Connie's nimble fingers were on her buttons. Connie's tongue pushed into her mouth and Jade greedily accepted her. Jade stroked both hands down Connie's back until she reached the luscious swell of her backside. She groaned deep in her throat when Connie got to her last button. Jade reluctantly removed her hands from the firm little treasure they were holding to strip her pajama top off. The air on her bare breasts was cold only for an instant before Connie's hands were on her.

"Fuck yeah, I'm yours baby girl," Jade panted into the air as soon as her mouth was free. Connie's lips came down over her nipple. Her tongue teased Jade fully erect. Jade's breath sobbed in her throat. She bit her lip as desire threatened to overwhelm her. At first, Jade thought the bed was shaking from their bodies rocking together, but when Connie's switch to her other breast brought a sick lurch like something heavy rammed into the bedframe, Jade couldn't ignore it.

"What the fuck?" she breathed.

Connie raised her head. Her tongue swiped over her wet lower lip.

"What is it, Jade?" Connie asked.

A screeching noise filled the room. Jade twisted to look over her shoulder.

The mirror opposite them held a dark shadow. The glass shook as if the thing inside was pounding fists on it. A silver splintering sound echoed through the room as the glass split into a spiderweb of cracks. The dark thing slid down the ruined mirror and spilled onto the wallpaper, leaving a trail of deep scratches in its wake. The shadow hit the floor and raced across the carpet, coming right at them.

"Nutsack ass-wanker!" Jade threw Connie out of the way. She didn't have time to move before the thing hit her. Reality flicked off. Jade's mind filled with guttural whispers. Hissed insults roared louder until her ears rang. Something huge hit her. Jade fell backwards into nothing. She threw out her arms to try and stop herself, but she only felt cold air. Heavy blows rained down over her again and again. The words wouldn't stop. They were raw with hate. Jade cradled her head in her arms to try and protect herself. A blinding pain ripped through her gut. Jade cried out. She had never felt pain like that, not even when she was burned. A gush of something warm and wet spilled down over her body. She was ripped in two. Her lungs wouldn't work.

She was dying.

"Jade, come back to me. Listen to my voice, come back."

The words were a rope of salvation. Jade snapped back into herself. She was on the floor, cradled in Connie's arms. Her breath heaved in ragged gasps.

"Breathe with me," Connie said. Her voice was soft and calm. "In for three...hold, there you go. Now out. Slowly. Okay, again."

The repeated words hummed through Jade like a mantra. Connie coached her through the steps. Gradually, her heartbeat came down from the stratosphere. Grounded once more, Jade sat up and dragged her hair back from her face with both hands.

"Are you all right?" Connie asked.

"Yeah," Jade said even though she didn't really think so. She looked down and ran a hand over the unblemished skin of her midsection. "Thank God," Jade breathed. A quick glance revealed the room was also back to its original, undamaged state. Jade hugged her arms to her chest, at once too aware of her nakedness.

Connie quickly stood and grabbed Jade's pajama top and draped it over Jade's shoulders.

"You're shivering," Connie said. "What did you see?"

"More like heard," Jade said. She shrugged into her top and tried to get her numb fingers to do up the buttons. Connie gently took over. She buttoned Jade up with a clinical touch.

"What did you hear?"

Jade paused for a moment, solidifying the memory before she said, "It was saying those words, the same insults that were scratched on the walls. Then something started hitting me and I think I was stabbed or something."

"Wow," Connie said. She wrapped her arms around Jade, who moved to meet her for a kiss, needing the contact and reassurance more than anything. Jade froze as the lamp flickered and a low, threatening growl echoed through the room.

"What is it?" Connie asked.

"Looks like something's not a big fan of girl-on-girl," Jade said.

Connie drew back with slow reluctance. "Maybe we should cool it for tonight."

"Yeah, we probably should," Jade said. She reached down and adjusted her pajama bottoms where they stuck to her. Mentally, she wasn't in the mood anymore, but her body was still raring to go. Her clit throbbed. Her lower belly was heavy and tense. She had a bad case of blue uterus. "Fuckity McFuckfurters," Jade gritted.

Connie clapped a hand to her mouth. A few giggles spilled out. In spite of her unfortunate state, Jade's face relaxed into a grin.

"At least we know this place is actually haunted," Jade said. Her eyes were trained on the mirror, whole and innocently reflecting the room without any clues something else lurked behind its glass facade.

"That's one thing at least," Connie said. She joined Jade in the bed and snuggled under the heavy blankets. Jade held Connie in her arms and experimentally stroked a hand through her silken gold curls. Nothing came from it. Apparently snuggling passed under the clit-blocking ghoul's radar.

Jade relaxed into Connie's warmth. She whispered into her hair, "The other news is, I had a very interesting talk with Mel."

Connie turned in Jade's embrace. Her sweet expression of interest tugged at the lingering heat in Jade's gut.

"Tell me," she said.

Jade reported the conversation while Connie lay heavy and soft in her arms. Connie didn't speak other than a few thoughtful hums.

When Jade finished, Connie said, "What happened with Britt is the key to what's happening now. The truth is spilling from the past to the present."

Jade paused to let Connie's words sink in.

"You're exactly right," Jade said. "And I love it when you talk like a movie trailer."

Connie's bright laugh filled the air. She rose up onto her elbows and turned off the bedside lamp. "Goodnight Jade," she whispered. "My white knight."

# Chapter Five

THE ROADS WERE clear and the morning sun shone on the dazzling snow. Jade rolled her window down and filled her lungs with the fresh, albeit freezing air. Hot gusts from the dash competed with the rush from the opened windows.

"Not too cold?" Jade asked.

"Nope." Connie replied. She leaned one cheek on her hand and grinned back at Jade. "It's nice to get out of the city. The air here's different."

"Yeah, it is."

Traynor's Port was full of classic stone buildings and small eclectic shops. In contrast, South Aisling felt organic. The houses looked like they were made out of gingerbread and grew from the land like mushrooms instead of being built. Everything was wooden and painted in a variety of counter-intuitive colors. They passed a turquoise church hall that advertized something called a box social on a whimsical signboard out front before the truck rolled into the most heavily-trafficked area of the town. The main street boasted several cafés and souvenir shops, most of which were closed. A few antique shops hung on, festooned with wreaths and tinsel, vying for the attention of the few people wandering around outside.

Jade parked in a free lot. She stashed her keys, then jumped out to the ground. Her cowboy boots hit the packed gravel with a satisfying thud. She shoved her hands into her pockets and looked around. Already Jade felt alive, ready to go poking around and bothering people. Connie scampered around from her side of the truck. She leaned shyly against the driver's side door instead of on Jade's arm the way she usually did. Jade knew why and didn't blame her. Time moved slower the farther you got from the big urban centers. Traynor's Port wasn't the most progressive place in the world, but it was easily a few decades ahead of the sleepy town around them.

"We made good time," Jade said. She checked her watch. "Okay, I'm going to head over to the tourist information center, try to dig up the dirt on the old Prewett place. If you strike gold at the library, let me know, okay? And if you don't, you know where I am. Come over and join me."

"Sure thing, partner," Connie said. Her cheeks were pink from the cold. Under her cheerful knit cap, short golden tufts of hair framed her face. She whipped out her phone and scrolled through multiple maps and diagrams while Jade gazed at her. Connie was vibrant, capable and damned cute. She looked up at just the right moment. Their eyes met. Connie's lips quirked up. "Jade, you are so busted."

"Sorry, I couldn't help myself," Jade said. She bit back a curse as the frustrated heat from the night before rose up within herself once more. Shit. Not now. Jade was really glad she wasn't a guy because her bomber jacket wasn't long enough to cover any unfortunate symptoms of her arousal.

Even though the parking lot was fairly sheltered from outside gazes, Jade glanced around before she cupped Connie's cheek in one hand. She brushed her thumb over Connie's lower lip.

When Connie spoke, the words felt like a kiss. "When should we meet up?"

"They're serving lunch at one and we have orientation at three," Jade said. "Doreen will kick our butts if we're late. How about we plan on moving out at around noon?"

"Okay," Connie said. She closed her eyes and pressed against Jade's palm for an instant before she pulled back. With a cheerful wave, she turned and trotted off, phone in one hand.

The tourist information center was a short jog from the parking lot, sandwiched between a fussy-looking shop full of knick-knacks and an old-timey barbershop. Jade let herself in and stomped the snow from her boots at the entrance. The room was dominated by a large wooden desk covered in pamphlets. The walls were plastered with yellowed photos of various events and groups of people. Instead of the ubiquitous Christmas tunes Jade was getting used to being bombarded with at every turn, a small black radio on the desk was tuned to their local news channel. A staticky telephone interview about something to do with river conservation filtered into the air.

A middle-aged man with slicked back, thinning brown hair looked up as the door swung closed behind Jade. He was a head shorter than Jade, decked out in a bright green sweater liberally decorated with reindeer and snowmen. A plaque on the desk proclaimed self-importantly: Percy Havarth at Your Service. A framed Tourist Management diploma hung on the wall behind him.

The man, who Jade assumed was the eminent Percy Havarth, didn't disguise the fact he disapproved of Jade as his eyes travelled from her face, down over her bomber jacket and long denim-clad legs to her white cowboy boots, and back up again. Jade clenched her fists in her pockets. She bared her teeth in a smile while picturing how easy it would be to kick his ass.

"How may I help you there, miss?" His voice was twangy and nasal with the local accent, a byproduct of the little town's age and isolation.

Jade tried to keep her stance neutral and unthreatening even though she inwardly bristled at being called *miss*. She was forty-three years old and that ranked at least a *ma'am*, although she hated both and would just as soon be called by name or nothing at all. But this wasn't her turf. She couldn't start a pissing contest. Not yet.

"I'm interested in old buildings," she said. "Particularly the old Prewett place. Do you have any information on it?"

Jade bit the inside of her cheek at the derisive look on his face.

"I'm assuming you're interested in the property before it got turned into that *resort*," he said.

"Yeah," Jade said. "Do you know if anything happened there? Like, anything bad?"

"Other than those *people* moving in and turning it into their little festival of debauchery?"

"Other than that," Jade said. Her gut clenched.

"Oh, I know a few things," he said with an air of superiority Jade wanted to smack off his face. Percy rocked back on his heels. "Yes, a few things that I probably shouldn't say. You know, in case it's bad for business."

Even though it galled her, Jade grasped onto that thread and gave a yank. She forced a smirk and said, "That's what I'm hoping."

"In that case, there is one incident that comes to mind," Percy said. He turned away from her and marched over to a small, outdated computer terminal set out for public use. He leaned over it and tapped away with two fingers. "Here's the article."

"Thanks," Jade said. She waited for him to move away from the single chair in front of the terminal. He didn't, simply hovered with a look of expectation.

"Well, aren't you going to sit down and read the article?"

"Not unless you step back, sir," Jade said. She squared her shoulders and swallowed the vitriolic curses that welled up in her throat.

Percy looked surprised, then defensive. "I'm not doing anything wrong. What, do you have a problem with me?"

"Nope," Jade said. "Just don't like people getting behind me."

Even though he looked like he didn't believe her, Percy eased away from the terminal. With a courtly gesture that could have been sarcastic, he bowed and presented the chair with both hands. Jade slung herself down into it and peered at the article on the screen. The date was twelve years ago.

Local Man Charged with Manslaughter in Boathouse Killing

Jade skimmed the article.

"Dangling donkey-cocks," she breathed.

Her skin prickled and she whipped around to see Percy standing behind her. One hand rested on the back of her chair. If he moved it up, his palm would be against her back.

"Do you mind?" Jade snapped before she could stop herself.

Percy didn't move. He pointed to the screen with his chin. "I went to school with Link Porter's father, I knew that whole family. Ruined that young fella's life, it did."

"I'd say the girl he stabbed to death in the Prewetts' boathouse got her life ruined more," Jade retorted. She twitched her chair away. Her heart ached as she read the victim's details. Teresa Kendall was only twenty-four. The same age as Connie. One of the attached photos showed a young woman smiling at the camera. She was vibrant, fine-featured, and cute. Also like Connie.

Jade drummed her fingers on the table. There wasn't enough information. She felt like something significant was missing.

"Anything else I can help you with?" Percy's voice startled Jade.

"Actually, yeah," Jade said. "She was just passing through, the article said. They didn't even know each other. Why do you think he did it?" Jade asked.

"No idea," Percy said with a shrug. "When Link was on trial, he didn't say much. What I think, if you ask me, is she must'a sassed back or disrespected him. His father didn't put up with women thinking they were better than him, and he brought up Link the same way after his mother took off."

"Wonder why," Jade said under her breath.

Percy continued as if he hadn't heard, "He was sentenced to a couple years. Got out early, but he was never the same. Prison changes a man."

Jade wanted to add it changes women too, but she kept silent. Percy obviously knew more about the case than was written in the article, which was only the bare bones. "Do you know where Link Porter is now?"

"Yep," Percy said. "Shady Pines Cemetery. Hung himself in that same boathouse. His father was beside himself, thinking he'd run away. They finally found him after a week when somebody's dog got the scent. Ever since then, nobody's wanted to go near the place. Can't say I blame them. I guess it's only right those unnatural folks took it over." The last part was said in a contemptuous tone.

Jade was too deep in thought to take offense. "Anything else come to mind?" she asked.

"Not really," Percy said. "My family's been here for six generations. Porters just as long. What happened to poor Link was really a tragedy."

"I'll say," Jade muttered. "Hey, mind if I get a copy of this?"

"It'll be twenty cents," Percy said. He leaned over Jade. With a flash of panic, she leapt from the chair and stood with her back pressed to the wall. He looked at her with a puzzled expression before he tapped a few keys and straightened up. From behind the desk, a whirring sound started up. Jade distracted herself by yanking out her phone. She had a text message from Connie.

No luck at the archives. Heading your way.

Instinctively, Jade relaxed. She smiled at the screen, which Connie decorated liberally with heart stamps. She had just fired off her response when Percy came over with a printout in his hands. Jade dug out some coins and swapped them for the paper.

"Thanks, Perce, uh Percy," she said. "Mr. Havarth. I appreciate this."

"No problem," he said. Now that the topic had shifted somewhat, Percy's expression became warmer and a lot more solicitous. "Are you just passing through, or are you staying here for the holidays? We have several good B&Bs I could introduce to you. Make sure you mention I sent you. It's not much, but the center gets a very small commission for every recommendation we send along."

A cheerful jingle ushered Connie into the room. An evil compulsion seized Jade. She scooped Connie up in a hug. Connie gave a happy squeak. Even though they had an audience, she wrapped her arms around Jade's shoulders and nestled against her.

"Thanks for coming, sweetie," Jade murmured into Connie's honey gold hair. She looked up at Percy. "Actually, we're staying at the unnatural resort of debauchery."

"I didn't mean — well — I mean," Percy stammered. His face was beet red. His mouth flapped around uselessly.

"Don't worry about it. Seriously, Percy, don't be an ass to your new neighbors, okay?" Jade said. "They're good people and they're doing their best to make a place here in the community. I hope there's room for everybody in South Aisling, not only the boring old farts."

Jade didn't wait for Percy's answer before she took Connie's hand. Together they went into the brilliant white light of the day. The air was fresh and colder than in Traynor's Port. Snow crunched under their feet. A few cars passed them, but their fingers remained twined about each other.

When they were back in the truck, Jade let the engine idle for a moment to get the cab warmed up.

"I'll show you mine if you show me yours," Jade said. She waved the printout in the air.

"I've already seen everything you have," Connie replied in a low, teasing voice.

Jade coughed. "Yeah, okay, but not this."

Connie's eyes tracked the paper with interest. "Did you get something?"

"Yup," Jade said. She passed over the article. Jade threw the truck into reverse and backed onto the main road. "I don't know if it's a coincidence the vic's the same age as Britt."

"Maybe it is, maybe it isn't," Connie said. "There's not really much to go on here."

"Yeah," Jade said with a grimace. "It's the only thing we've got so far. Let's see how it goes."

Connie nodded before she turned her attention to the article. She pursed her lips in a cute, sexy way that had Jade struggling to keep her eyes on the road. Connie's lips were pink and delicately full and Jade loved having them on her body. She ached to reach out and stroke one hand over Connie's leg, trail up to where her thighs met and dip into that hot, tight place between them.

Jade's body was seized by a deep hunger. To try and distract herself, Jade shifted in her seat. She kept both hands on the wheel, away from temptation. Connie didn't make that any easier when she shrugged out of her coat and tossed it into the narrow cargo space behind the seats. Under her bulky coat, she wore a body-hugging green knit top that flattered her curves. Jade loved Connie in any color, but green was by far her favorite. Jade's face flushed. Her breathing picked up.

Sweat popped out on her brow. Jade struggled out of her own jacket at the next stop sign. Connie helped by grabbing her cuff and pulling.

"Thanks, babe. What did you find out at the archives?" Jade asked. Her voice was only a little strained.

"Not too much," Connie said. "I found a bunch of pictures of the old house before it was renovated, plus a couple of the original owner. You can see them when we get back to the resort. I've got them in my phone."

"Good girl."

The shops and houses thinned out. A few minutes later, all signs of civilization disappeared completely. Both sides of the road were filled with trees. The forest was old-growth, one of the few places that hadn't been razed by loggers. The overhead was so thick in places, the ground was mostly bare of snow, rusty red with fallen pine needles.

As they drove, Connie seemed tense. She fiddled with the stereo without any real purpose before she twisted her fingers together. A few minutes of heavy silence passed, broken only by the quiet strands of the country song on the radio.

"Jade?" The word was soft, hesitant.

"What is it, sweetheart?"

"Um, could you pull over? And like, drive down and park in that clearing over there?"

"Sure thing," Jade didn't even think to question the gentle request. She rolled the wheels over the soft shoulder and as far into the surrounding forest as she could get the bulky truck to go. She killed the engine. "What is it, Connie?"

In response, Connie unsnapped her seatbelt. She scooted over until she was pressed up against Jade's arm. One hand trailed up Jade's thigh until it reached the apex of her legs, echoing what Jade had fantasized about doing to Connie. Jade unconsciously spread her legs a bit and leaned into the pressure of Connie's fingers on her with a low hum of pleasure. The arousal she'd been fighting since the night before instantly flamed into life.

"Ooh," Jade let out an involuntary sound as Connie rubbed up and down over her. Even through the denim, Jade felt Connie's warmth. Her clit sprang to full alert, wetness seeped into her underwear.

"Is this okay?" Connie asked in a soft, husky voice that set Jade on fire.

"Yeah, this is nice," Jade murmured. She bit off a frustrated growl when Connie's fingers stopped their brief massage.

"It could be nicer," Connie said. She drew back and looked Jade straight in the eyes. Jade caught her breath at the desire in Connie's expression. "I can't stop thinking about when I went down on you the other night. It was such a powerful connection. I've never felt anything like that before, even though I couldn't finish you that way. But I really want to do it again. Like, now. If, um, if you're okay with that."

"Oh hell yeah," Jade said. Her face broke into a huge grin.

"Good," Connie said. In a voice that brooked no opposition, she said, "The truck's facing away from the road so if the windows fog up, nobody will notice. Don't turn on a thing, not the heater, not the hazards, okay?"

Jade nodded dumbly. She was rock-hard and soaking wet between her legs.

"Take off your jeans and prop your knee up on the steering wheel. I want you spread wide and ready for me."

"You've been thinking about this, planning this out, haven't you?" Jade whispered.

"Every minute since last night," Connie said.

Connie grabbed the fleece blanket Jade had stashed under the seat and wrapped it around her shoulders. She pulled two wet wipes from the pack between the seats and scrubbed at her fingers, which set Jade's body off even more. Her clit throbbed with the need to be touched. Jade couldn't believe what they were about to do. Her heart pounded. She made a move to start taking off her jeans, but Connie's hand on hers stopped her.

"Let me get that," Connie said. She gripped Jade's belt buckle and pulled it open with a desicive yank.

Obligingly, Jade raised her hips and Connie tugged her jeans and boxer briefs down in one swift motion. Jade kicked herself free of them. She obligingly spread her legs. The cool air of the cab hit her harder where she was wet. Her harsh breaths were loud in the confines of the truck. Wordlessly, Connie urged Jade's knee up. She spread the blanket over Jade's legs and burrowed under it. Connie was slim and petite, she fit in the small space perfectly.

Soft kisses rained down over Jade's belly, trailing down to where her throbbing sex was waiting. At once, two fingers pushed into her. Jade let out a breath in surprise. Connie was just going to go for it. No warming up or anything. If Jade had to be honest, she'd been in various stages of warmed-up since the previous night. It wasn't going to take much to drive her over the edge.

"Shit, I'm so fucking hot for you, do it Connie," Jade said. She reached down under the blanket to lightly draw her fingers through Connie's hair, instinctively smoothing the short strands away from her face. Jade threw her head back and let out a long moan as Connie's tongue invaded her. Jade couldn't help herself. She let go of Connie and arched back to grab the headrest with both hands.

Jade kept up a soft refrain of *oh fuck* as Connie relentlessly batted her clit, swiping away to tease her indirectly when Jade got too close to the edge. Tension clamped down in Jade's groin. She wasn't going to last much longer.

"Fuck, don't stop, I'm coming," Jade gritted. The steering wheel bit into her knee, but Jade didn't care. White light broke over her as she came. Jade's hips lifted clear of the seat. A gush of wetness spurted from her at the force of her climax. The only thing she was aware of was the sweet, persistent mouth latched down over her, the rhythmic pumping in and out.

Connie didn't let up and Jade had barely recovered when a second climax ripped through her right on the heels of the first. Jade had never done that before. Her fingers ached from their death-grip on the headrest. Her hips bucked, her breath sobbed into the hot air of the cab.

Slung across two seats and the gear-box, Connie's body rocked along with hers. Her slender hips wriggled, her sweet little ass pumped up and down as if she was thrusting into Jade with more than just her fingers. The sight drove Jade into the stratosphere. Not for the first time, she wondered what it would be like to have Connie with a strap-on between her legs, drilling into Jade with every piston-like thrust of her hips.

The image brought a raw, desperate edge to Jade's arousal. She could only make guttural grunts as waves of release broke over her again and again. With stamina that left Jade breathless, Connie chased her climax until Jade couldn't come any more.

"Okay baby, I'm done. You fucking finished me," Jade panted at last. She sagged back against the resilient cushions of the driver's seat, chest heaving, sticky, sex-streaked thighs quivering. Jade patted Connie's tousled hair gently and said, "Sit up, sweetheart."

Connie did as Jade asked. She thoughtfully left the blanket over Jade's lap. Connie sucked her lower lip into her mouth. Her eyes were half-closed, her breath came in quick bursts.

"Was that okay?" she asked.

"Okay? Connie, sweetie, it was fucking amazing," Jade said breathlessly. "Give me a minute and I'll take care of you."

With that, Connie lifted an eyebrow. "Really?"

"Really," Jade said. She grabbed onto the holy shit handle above her head and hitched herself higher in the seat. Her arms felt weak. Her entire body was limp and glowing. Jade had never come like that, and she wanted to repay the favor. She glanced over at the passenger's seat and got an idea. Jade very rarely let her alpha side out around Connie, but that day she couldn't hold back.

"Baby girl, listen to me," Jade lowered her voice to a feral growl. "I'm gonna go around to your side. I want you stripped and waiting for me, wrapped in that blanket. Okay?"

"Wow, that's sexy," Connie said. Her eyes were bright with need and anticipation. "And definitely okay."

High on the feeling of power, Jade shimmied into her jeans again. The crotch of her briefs was soaked through. Jade hoped her jeans weren't the same. Connie looked so sweet and sex-tousled Jade ached to drag her into a kiss. She resisted in favor of what she wanted to do next. Connie gave Jade a puzzled look when she tugged her belt off and left it on the seat. Jade just answered with a knowing smirk. Mindful of the lingering impression of the steering wheel on her hands, she grabbed a couple wet-wipes just as Connie had.

Once Jade was somewhat decent, she opened the driver's side door and staggered into the snow. The second her boots hit solid turf, her knees buckled. She slammed her elbow onto the hood to keep from face-planting.

Jade rounded the truck. She shouldered her way inside and settled into the passenger's seat. True to her word, Connie was waiting in an eager, fleecy ball.

"Come here, sweetie," Jade said. She held out her arms in invitation. "I want you on me."

A little shyly, Connie crawled over to Jade. She rose to her knees before she straddled Jade's lap. The blanket opened just enough to give Jade a glimpse of what lay underneath. Her breath kicked up and her sorely abused clit jolted. Jade shut out her body's plea for action. It was her turn to be there for Connie.

"God you're so beautiful. I am going to absolutely love fucking you," Jade murmured. She looked into Connie's face. For a moment, she dropped her alpha persona. "Are you okay with this? One word from you and this all stops. You're the one in charge here."

"Yeah, I'm okay," Connie said. She let go of the blanket enough so it slipped down over her shoulders, caught on the soft swells of her breasts. Her voice was breathy but urgent. "You can do whatever you want. Just hurry up."

Jade cupped the back of Connie's head in one hand, while the other stole under the blanket and gripped her bare hip. Jade pulled Connie into a hard kiss, the quick intake of breath against her mouth only drove Jade further. The hand holding Connie's hip slipped around to cup her backside. Jade urged Connie to rock back and forth, rubbing her spread sex over Jade's lap. Jade moved to kiss her neck. She kneaded Connie's ass, then slipped down to lightly tease her from behind. She ran a finger over slick lips, then lightly circled her opening but didn't enter her. Connie's gasps became whimpers.

"Good?" Jade asked.

"Uhn, more. I need more." Connie arched her back with a wanton moan. Jade could feel her heat and wetness even through the demin of her jeans.

Jade stroked her hand down from Connie's nape, over her shoulder. She skimmed over one breast before she drew her fingers down over Connie's belly.

"Yes, yes," Connie murmured. She looked up and met Jade's look with an absolutely wicked one of her own before she dropped the blanket.

All of the breath in Jade's lungs whooshed out of her. Proud and tall, Connie threw back her shoulders in an unashamed display of her nakedness. She rose slightly on her knees. Her breasts heaved with each breath, the gentle swell of her hips gave way to a tightly curled thatch of light brown curls between her thighs. Her legs were spread, pouting lips parted to reveal her clit, firm and proud in the fleshy sheath.

"Oh fuck me," Jade whispered in complete awe. Connie's hands grabbed onto Jade's shoulders. She lowered herself once more to Jade's lap. She pumped herself hard against Jade once, twice. Jade couldn't help but groan at the firm pressure on her crotch. Connie leaned forward and pressed her breasts to Jade's.

"No, you're going to fuck me," Connie purred in Jade's ear. "Now."

Jade didn't get a chance to reply verbally. Connie took Jade's chin in her hand and guided Jade into a long, deep kiss. Connie's tongue demanded Jade's, her body trembled with tension. Jade couldn't keep her waiting any more. She stroked down between their bodies. Her fingers met Connie's heated wetness and pressed further in, two fingers hovered at the edge. Without pause, Connie dropped down, taking Jade fully into herself. The connection was instant, blinding.

Connie had never been that demanding, Jade loved it. She loved the fact Connie gave her everything, her trust, her most intimate moments, her entire being. The thought was both daunting and incredibly hot.

Their sudden union was met by a low, hungry growl deep in Jade's throat. Connie echoed her. Jade gripped Connie's hip with her free hand as Connie rode her hard. Their breathing matched in pace, their lips never broke the ravenous kiss. Jade brought her hand from Connie's hip around front to tease her clit. She kept her fingers in one place and let Connie move against her. The hard bud raced over her skin, rubbing up and down in frantic pumps along with the movement of Connie's hips. A sudden tremor gripped Connie's frame. The tight inner walls grabbed at Jade's fingers. Connie let out a cry and bore down hard.

"That's it, yeah, do it, baby," Jade panted into Connie's mouth. Jade couldn't help squeezing her own legs together. The tension between them was like nothing she felt before. She wasn't even being touched directly, but she was hurtling toward another climax, right along with Connie.

The faint sheen of sweat on Connie's skin caught the sunlight as she threw her head back. Outside, the forest sprawled out all around them. Jade felt like they were the only two people under that searing white sun.

Connie pulled up one knee and took Jade deep. She didn't seem to care, or even be aware of the spectacular show she gave Jade as she lost herself to the pleasure of their lovemaking. The sight of her riding Jade's fingers, rising up until she almost pulled free, then sinking back down, taking Jade to the hilt was the most erotic thing Jade had ever seen. Jade gritted her teeth as a shudder ripped through her.

At once, Connie grabbed Jade's hand between her legs and held her deep and tight. Her hips thrust one last time before she cried out. Connie's tight channel clamped down over Jade. Her body shivered and bucked. Her inner muscles held Jade in a death-grip. Jade couldn't stop herself. The tension clenched in her groin broke and she came hard. Their breaths were in perfect union, Connie's soft rhythmic cries perfectly echoed Jade's own lower ones, as if they were one.

Automatically, Jade stroked her free hand up to hold Connie steady until the last jolt faded from her. Only then did Connie let her go and Jade gently withdrew. The loss of connection hit her in the gut. Limp and shivering, Connie collapsed onto Jade's chest. Jade carefully drew the blanket around Connie's shoulders and held her. With a happy sigh, Connie snuggled closer to Jade. She closed her eyes and hummed softly. Connie's chest rose and fell against Jade's with every deep breath.

Jade didn't even think about it when she brought her fingers to her lips. She licked them, then sucked Connie's essence from her skin. The scent was musky and sweet, the taste uniquely Connie. Jade savored every bit. With the way things were at the resort, she didn't know when she'd get a chance to taste her again.

They were both in need of a shower and a change of clothes, and the resort's lunchtime was getting perilously close, but Jade was in absolutely no hurry. With a loving touch, Jade carefully brushed back the sweat-damp hair from Connie's brow. She moved so Connie was sitting more comfortably on Jade's lap instead of spread over her. Jade didn't speak. Connie usually needed a short time to regroup especially after a particularly intense orgasm, and that last one had been a doozie—for both of them.

The small sounds from outside slowly filtered back into Jade's consciousness. The faraway clacking of the wind through the trees, the almost inaudible gurgling of a nearby creek. Jade licked dry lips. Careful not to disturb Connie, she patted around with one hand and found the water bottle she had in the cup-holder.

Jade twisted the cap off and offered it to Connie.

"Thanks," Connie said. Her voice sounded harsh. She took a few gulps of water before she handed Jade the bottle and sat up. One arm held the blanket over her breasts. She was tousled and gorgeous, practically glowing. Slowly and deliberately, Connie stretched both arms over her head. The blanket slithered from her body and pooled around her hips. The sip of water nearly went up Jade's nose at the sight.

"Jesus Christ," Jade choked. She wiped a sleeve over her mouth as dribbles of water fell onto her shirt. "Fuck, don't get me started again Connie, we'll never get out of here."

"Sorry," Connie said, but her dimple hinted she wasn't.

"We're gonna be late for lunch," Jade said with a reluctant glance at her watch.

"That's okay, I already ate," Connie said.

Jade couldn't help the peal of laughter that filled the cab.

With a carefully innocent expression, Connie leaned over and gathered up her clothes. Lithe and graceful even in the cramped cab, she slipped into the space behind the driver's seat where she started to get dressed. Jade quietly hissed out a 'God dammit' to herself. On the driver's seat, there was a noticeable damp patch. Jade hurriedly folded the blanket and put it over the spot. A grin cracked her slight discomfort. The truck had officially been baptized.

Jade looked down at her disheveled clothing with a grimace. "I should grab a shower before orientation."

"Me too," Connie said. With her back to Jade, Connie pulled her top on over her bare skin. She glanced back over one shoulder and said, "How about we skip lunch and go through a drive-thru somewhere? That way we have until three."

"Good idea," Jade said. She took out her clip and rubbed a hand through her long hair. "Just give me a few minutes, okay? I don't think I can move for a while yet. Connie, you did me really fucking good. My legs feel like jelly."

"Why don't I drive back?" Connie asked. "I want to keep in practice for when I get my own car."

"Sounds good to me," Jade said.

Connie slipped between the seats and slid into the driver's seat. Instead of reaching for the ignition, she put something soft into Jade's hand. Surprised, Jade opened her fingers and found a soaked pair of pink and white striped panties. Connie leaned over and pressed a quick kiss to Jade's cheek.

"That's a souvenir from today," Connie said. "Just so you know exactly what you do to me."

Jade fixed Connie with a slow, knowing smile. "Don't think I'm giving these back anytime soon." She deliberately stuffed them down the front of her jeans and pretended not to see Connie clapping her hand over her giggles. Connie was still smiling when she eased the truck back onto the road.

# Chapter Six

HERALDED BY THE flapping of her slippers, Jade raced down the stairs, skidded on the hardwood flooring, and slammed into the dining room just as the clock struck three. The assembled people turned as one to look at her. At the front of the room, Doreen fixed Jade with a disapproving look. Beside her, Mel gave her a half-shrug. She gestured for Jade to enter with the hand that wasn't holding a pile of handouts.

Self-consciously, Jade rubbed at her damp hair, which lay sleekly over her new flannel shirt and down her back. She tried to slow her breathing as she threaded her way between the tables to the one where Connie was already sitting with another couple, a pair of men about Jade's age. One was swarthy and well-built, the other smaller and refined-looking in a button-down shirt and jacket. The handwritten nameplates in front of them identified the men as Basil Martinez and Garrett Phelps.

"Hey, is this seat taken?" Jade joked weakly. She plopped down in the chair next to Connie, who scooted closer to her. "Sorry I'm late, sweetie."

"You're just in time," Connie said. She slipped her hand under the table and gave Jade's a squeeze. Jade squeezed back. The men across from them exchanged a knowing look, but Jade didn't care. They didn't have to hide. Jade swelled with pride. She could even sit Connie on her lap and give her kisses through the lecture if she wanted.

A small spatter of applause brought Jade's attention to the front of the room. Mel walked around, handing out stapled sheaves of paper while Doreen stood at a podium. She had a microphone clipped to one lapel of her smart dress.

"Can you all hear me?"

A bunch of people called back in the affirmative.

"Great," Doreen said. "Welcome to the first LGBT Couples' Retreat here at Emerald Resort. I want to thank you all for coming and making a commitment to intimacy, honesty, and self-discovery. First things first. If you'll look at the handout, you can see a short summary of our facility."

As Doreen spoke and everyone rustled their papers, Jade surveyed the room in awe. The lecture faded into the background. Outside of the Pride Parade, she had never seen so many same-sex couples. Twelve other couples were seated at tables similar to theirs, one of the tables held three couples, but the rest had two. She guessed her and Connie's last-minute inclusion necessitated a shuffle in table-partners. A gentle nudge brought Jade back to the present.

She gave Connie an apologetic look. As she surveyed the room, more surreptitiously this time, Jade was very aware that Connie was the youngest in the room by easily two decades. All of the other attendees besides the ones at their table looked to be around fifty or older. While Garrett and Basil were on the young end of the spectrum, they had the air of a couple who had been together long enough to know exactly how to annoy each other. Jade shifted in her chair. She remembered the purpose of the resort and felt like a complete fake.

Doreen said, "For our first activity, I'd like you to introduce yourself to your table-mates. You will be seated together for all meals, so it might be nice to get to know each other. Introduce yourselves, say a bit about your partner and how you met, feel free to talk about your goals for this retreat. Remember to be courteous and positive." She stopped and shot Jade a warning look. An instant later, Doreen was back to business. "All right, you have fifteen minutes. Go!"

"I guess I'll start," Garrett said. He smoothed down the front of his shirt. Jade forced her attention back to the table with a manufactured smile. She hated shit like that. She walked out on her counselor when she tried to make Jade do the group therapy thing with all that blah blah about yourself bullshit. Beside her, Connie was her usual cheerful self. Jade wished she was that comfortable around new people. By missing lunch and nearly being late to the orientation, Jade was already on thin ice with Doreen so she couldn't very well fake a headache or something and escape.

"As you can see, I'm Garett Phelps, my pronouns are he and him." After his introduction, Garrett waved his hands as he spoke about his business, something about art galleries and whatever. Jade tried to look interested as she frantically tried to think of what to say when her turn came to speak. The truth was definitely too farfetched for the unitiated. She hadn't expected all that meet and greet stuff. Jade wished she'd thought of getting their story straight with Connie before. The falafel Jade stuffed down her throat while Connie was in the shower lay in her gut like a rock.

Garrett turned to Jade and asked, "So how long have the two of you been together?"

Jade's mind went blank at the sudden question. She stammered out, "Three—"

"Years," Connie supplied. She clasped her hands on the table and tilted her head.

"Yeah. Three years," Jade echoed.

"Interesting," Garrett said. Beside him, Basil sighed. Garrett didn't seem to notice. "And Jade, may I ask how ever did you meet such a sweet young thing like Miss Mason here?"

Jade didn't like the tone Garrett used. There was something mocking and fake in it. She clenched her hands under the table and wished for the whole stupid orientation bullshit to be over. Jade swallowed the flash of anger. She said, "Through work. We, um, collaborated on a project."

It was the truth, barely. Jade didn't mention the project in question was the investigation into Connie's attempted murder, proposed by Connie's spirit while her body lay in a coma as a Jane Doe.

"Really?" Garrett said. He leaned his chin on one hand. "I wasn't aware you worked in a junior high school. And I always thought dating your students was frowned upon."

A crash resounded through the room as Jade's chair hit the floor. She lunged across the table and grabbed Garrett by the collar. Her lip curled in a feral snarl. "Don't fucking start with me," Jade growled. "You have no idea who you're dealing with."

Garrett's face blanched and he helplessly slapped at Jade's hands. Jade's world narrowed to the man in front of herself. Her fists shook with rage. A light touch on Jade's shoulder broke the spell. Jade came back to reality. Everyone in the entire room was staring at her. Connie was also on her feet. Her hand rested on Jade's shoulder, not restraining her, just reminding Jade she was there.

"It's okay Jade," Connie said softly.

After a heartbeat, Jade let go of Garrett. Automatically, she held up both hands as she backed away.

"Everything okay here?" Mel trotted over.

"Yeah, great," Jade said.

"It seems *someone* can't take a joke," Garrett said. He straightened his collar with an air of superiority.

"Let's keep things positive, people," Mel said. "Are we copacetic?"

Jade nodded. She bent down and righted her chair before she slung herself down in it. Mel clapped Jade on the shoulder before she walked purposefully over to another table with a cheerful greeting. Around them, talk buzzed back into life. Jade's knee bounced under the table.

"How about you not be an asshole?" Basil shot to his partner in a tight whisper. "For once."

Jade and Connie exchanged a glance.

"Oh, so I'm being the asshole now," Garrett retorted. "Fine, whatever, always take their side. I told you this whole retreat thing was a stupid idea."

"Anyway," Connie said brightly, "Basil, you said you've got a concert coming up next month. Where exactly is it going to be?"

The conversation resumed. Jade managed to get a few normal sentences out while quietly wishing to be anywhere but there. She didn't care about what anyone thought of her except Connie. Blowing up in front of her was not what Jade wanted to do. Connie had enough crap in her life without having to deal with Jade's.

The interminable introduction time ended with an announcement from Doreen.

"We have a number of workshops set up this week," she said. Beside her, Mel placed some photocopied papers down side by side on the long table at the front of the room. "Space is limited, so it's first come, first served. Remember to leave some free time to go sighseeing around our little town of South Aisling. We have maps and coupons at the reception desk if you're interested."

Like a well-dressed rocket, Garrett was out of his chair and the first to the front. Around him, the other guests milled about. Excited voices filtered through the air. Connie wriggled in her seat.

"Let's go sign up for some workshops."

Jade looked at the tightly-packed group at the front table. She drew a hand over her forehead. "Connie, why don't you go ahead? Choose anything you want."

"Anything? Do you trust me?"

"Implicitly," Jade said.

"We're going into the city tomorrow, right?"

"That's the plan."

"I'll leave tomorrow open, but I'll choose something fun for today," Connie said before she scampered off.

Jade stretched out her legs and pondered their next move. She not only wanted to talk to Britt, she wanted to hit up Young for some more information on the murder case. Jade was familiar with echoes that remained long after the traumatic event had passed, but why now? Mel said the incidents started recently. Something triggered them. Jade leaned her elbows on the table, so deep in thought she didn't notice Doreen sitting down next to her.

"What?" Jade jerked back reflexively.

"Don't worry, I'm not going to tell you off for nearly throttling Garrett."

"Is he always like that?" Jade asked.

"He means well, and I thought you and Connie might connect with him and Basil. Still, if you want to change table mates, I'll see what I can do."

"Nah, it's cool," Jade said. She cracked a grin. "I don't want to have to break in another set of people."

Doreen looked at Jade with unsettling comprehension in her eyes. She took a small purple envelope from her pocket and passed it over. "Here's the first mystery question. I left everyone else's this morning but I didn't want to go into your room now that you've got all your luggage in there." Doreen glanced around the room before she leaned closer and said, "I wasn't going to bother you two with them, but Mel thought it might be a good idea in case anyone else mentions them. Plus, who knows, you might figure some things out. You know, about your relationship with Connie. Make sure the two of you are alone when you open it."

"Sure thing," Jade said. She felt as if she'd missed something. Unconcerned, Jade shoved the envelope into her shirt pocket. Doreen got up just as Connie returned. She was pink-cheeked and bouncing around with energy as she slipped into the chair next to Jade.

"Do you want to know what we're doing this afternoon?" Connie asked. She looked entirely too excited for Jade's peace of mind. "It's going to be really fun."

Jade let out a theatrical groan and clapped a hand to her head. "Tell me it's not pole dancing."

"No, not pole dancing," Connie said. She clasped her hands in front of herself with the air of a mischievous sprite. "Decorative vegetable cutting."

Jade spluttered in indignation. "I cut veggies fine."

"Just kidding," Connie said. "How do you feel about massage?"

"Nice," Jade said. She stretched out her arms over her head. "I'm feeling a bit stiff after, uh, after the long drive yesterday. Yeah."

Connie lifted one brow and gave a low hum.

Finished with their schedules, the other guests filed out of the room. Jade hung back. She stuffed her hands in her pockets. Her conscience buzzed. Jade had to say something.

"Sorry for jumping at Garrett." Jade yanked her hands out of her pockets and looked down at them. She clenched them into fists. The scar tissue on the back of her left hand pulled tight with the movement. "I didn't mean to go off like that. It's just, he disrespected you and I couldn't let that slide."

"It's okay," Connie said. Her cheeks stained a delicate pink that took Jade's breath away. "I would do the same for you."

Garrett's loud voice caught Jade's attention. He stood in the doorway, wedged between Mel and Doreen. "I saw your darling Bichon," Garrett said. He held out something that looked like a business card. "If she ever has puppies, we would love to bring one of the litter into our family. Of course with generous compensation for your time and resources. What do you say, hmm?"

Doreen crossed her arms and said, "Lady is a rescue. It would be unethical to breed her."

"What a waste," Garrett said. He pocketed his card and breezed from the room. Basil followed with his head down.

CONNIE SAT DOWN on the bed. She patted the empty spot

beside her in an invitation for Jade. Happily, Jade sprawled out. She rolled over onto her back and looked up at Connie. She wanted to reach up and trail her thumb over Connie's pouty lower lip, but decided that might lead to activities that incurred the wrath of their ghostly chaperone. Instead, Jade pulled out the envelope from Doreen.

"Mystery question number one," Jade announced.

"I'm curious. Open it, Jade." Connie lay on her stomach with her chin propped up on her hands.

With a flourish, Jade pulled out the card inside the envelope. Her eyes bugged out and she hurriedly stuffed it back in.

"What is it?" Connie asked. She launched herself at Jade, who caught Connie in her arms with a surprised *oof*. For a second, Jade lay there with Connie's soft resilience pressing down over her. Connie bent her head and whispered against Jade's neck, "It's okay, ask me the question."

"All right, you win," Jade said. Connie sat up and clasped her hands in her lap. She waited with a sweet, expectant expression. Jade cleared her throat and read aloud, "Tell me what you think is hot about me."

"That's easy," Connie said.

"Exactly. There's nothing hot about me," Jade muttered. She chucked the crumpled up card at the trash can. It hit the rim and fell to the floor.

"Asshole jacker," Jade muttered. She rose, grabbed the card, and pelted it into the can.

"What do you mean nothing?" Connie said. She studied Jade with an intense look that brought a flush to Jade's cheeks. "There are so many things I find hot about you. For example, the way you just blushed."

Jade rolled her eyes. She threw herself back down onto the bed. She pillowed her head on her arms. Connie seemed sincere. Jade kicked off her slippers and stretched out once more. "Okay. And?" she asked.

"And when you pump iron, and how you look when you get really focused on something, like doing a crossword puzzle or cooking something new for me," Connie said.

"That's just normal stuff," Jade muttered.

"No it isn't. Jade, you are the sexiest person I've ever seen." Connie got a blush of her own. "Not that I've seen a whole lot, but it's true. I love your body, how you're so strong and so gentle at the same time. I love when you touch me, and when you let me get close to you. I love everything about you. And I find everything about you absolutely hot."

Deep in Jade's chest, a warm feeling started up. She'd caught Connie checking her out quite a few times, but to hear the words lit a fire inside Jade. She couldn't form the words to reply, though. Not yet. She wasn't used to hearing good stuff about herself. Insults, threats, things like that became Jade's normal. She trained herself to let them pass through her, never to believe them. Jade didn't get compliments. Even her counselor never laid it on that thick, and Jade paid her by the hour. Jade wanted to believe Connie. She ached for it.

"You don't have to say it back," Connie blurted out. "I mean, I'm not fishing for anything."

"I know," Jade said. Her gaze softened. She wanted to reach out and gather Connie up against her. She wanted to smooth the worried look from her face, tease her sweet, kissable lips. God, Jade wanted to touch her. She sat up with a lurch. "What time does the massage workshop start again?"

Connie stretched to grab her phone from the bedside table, giving Jade a nice view of her bare belly as her shirt rode up. Jade was seized with the urge to run her fingers up and down the softly yielding flesh, slide her hands into Connie's shirt and lift it clear off. She wanted to buff her lips over Connie's breasts, suck her nipples into hard peaks. Jade stifled a frustrated groan. She wished they were back in the truck in the middle of the woods. How come when she wasn't allowed to do something, suddenly that was all she could think of?

"Whoops, five minutes," Connie said. She stood and shoved her phone into her pocket. "We should get moving. It's upstairs in the Wellness Room. Here, put on your name tag."

Reluctantly, Jade got up. She clipped on her name tag, which was the repurposed name card from orientation, then followed Connie from the room. Instead of the creaky, narrow stairwell Jade used the night before, Connie led her up the vast main staircase. It rose from the lobby and was finished in the same dark inlaid wood floor as the hallways.

Jade's slippers flapped as she climbed up behind Connie, who moved with ease and grace. Between fighting with her slippers and navigating the stairs, Jade managed to get a few glances at Connie' trim jean-clad rear end, which jiggled just enough to be really cute. Jade knew each firm cheek fit perfectly into her hands. Her palms tingled with the memory. Annoyed at herself, Jade resisted the urge to smack herself across the forehead for being such a single minded perv.

The Wellness Room was across from the private bath. It was accessed from the hallway by large double doors that were thrown open so Jade could see the full wall of windows that looked out onto the front yard. The floor was shining hardwood, the room airy and open. Jade stopped short in the doorway. Lounging on a blue foam yoga mat, in a designer jogging suit, was Garrett. Another couple, two grey-haired women with nametags that identified them as Helen and Lisa, were also in attendance. Jade squared her shoulders and swaggered into the room.

"Oh wonderful," Garrett remarked airily. "I was wondering if we'd get another helping of angry dyke today."

"Lucky you. I've got a double order coming right up especially for you," Jade said. She didn't miss Basil rolling his eyes and shaking his head, but she also didn't care. The way Helen looked at Connie as she walked past them to get a mat from the holder in the corner pissed Jade off more. Helen looked at Connie with a mixture of pity and motherly concern. Jade knew it was probably from her show in the orientation. Mentally, Jade dared Helen to give her an opening to do it again.

The instructor breezed in. She was young and smiley in a horsey kind of way, with straw-colored hair and freckled skin. She was wearing a T-shirt with a glittery peace sign printed on it and one of those long cotton skirts that Connie favored when she was relaxing around the house on weekends. Jade eyed her and decided she seemed all right.

"Hi all, I'm Trillium," she said. She plunked herself down on a mat at the front of the room and pulled her bare feet into her lap in an easy lotus position. Jade winced. Trillium continued blithely, "I've been doing massage therapy for seven years and I think you're all in for a treat today. The key is communicate. Use your words, let your partner know when something feels good. If you want something, say it. No judgement, okay? Anyway, let's get started. Hands up, who's more comfortable on the bottom?"

Without even thinking of it, Jade stuck her hand up. A snicker erupted beside her. Jade turned to glare at Garrett, who had a hand over his mouth.

"Oh, *that's* unexpected," he tittered. "A bottom, are we?"

Jade swallowed the epithet she wanted to throw at him. She didn't particularly care what people thought about that whole top-bottom bullshit, it was a private matter between her and Connie. Jade just shrugged. She casually unbuttoned her shirt and pulled it off, displaying the full sleeve of tattoos on her right arm and the extensive burn scars on her left. Garrett let out a little gasp.

In only a tight tank top, Jade gave a careless stretch, incidentally flexing her pumped biceps and toned back muscles on the way down. Even though it stretched her scars, Jade drew the moment out as long as she could. Behind her, Jade heard Connie hum in an appreciative way. Jade gloated silently, yeah okay, she could put on the sexy butch look when she chose. Lisa stared hard at Jade with her mouth slightly open until Helen poked her with an annoyed grunt. Jade didn't care. They could ogle as much as they wanted, she belonged to Connie.

Trillium swished over to them and said in a perky voice that had to be at least half-faked, "We're going to start with a simple shoulder massage. Bottoms, face-down on the mat. Tops, shake out your arms, flex your hands, you're going to use them soon."

"Trilly, sweetheart," Garrett called from where he was sprawled out on his mat, "Please tell me you know what top and bottom means. You know, in the *gay* sense of the words."

"Of course," she said with a slighty confused expression on her face. "It's self-explanatory. The top gives the massage and the bottom gets it. I didn't think there's anything inherently gay about the terms, though. I use them all the time when I do workshops."

"Okay, let's go with that," Garrett said.

Jade bit her lip to keep from snorting in laughter. She lay down on the mat and rested her cheek on her folded arms. Beside her, Connie earnestly followed the instructor's example of some finger stretches and wrist circles. Jade tried not to think about the magic Connie's fingers were capable of. She shifted slightly as her jeans suddenly felt a bit warm around the crotch.

"All right, tops, get into posisiton," Trillium called out.

Jade felt a light touch on her shoulder. She twisted to look up at Connie who regarded her with a calm, sweet gaze.

"Are you okay with me behind you?" Connie asked softly. "We don't have to do this if you don't want."

"I'll be okay," Jade said. She appreciated Connie's concern for her limits. Jade put her head down and let out a breath.

"That's not going to work," Trillium said. "Connie, you need to get on your partner. We're doing this for maximum skin-ship and trust."

"No, this is okay," Connie said.

Jade considered the option for a moment. More than having someone behind her, being held down was a major trigger for her. But it was Connie, the person Jade trusted most in the world. She didn't want her stupid hang-ups to control them.

"You heard the woman," Jade said. She turned to give Connie a grin. "Get on me and do your best."

"If you're sure."

"Yup."

Jade couldn't help but tense as Connie straddled her and settled down on her back. Connie started at her shoulders. Waves of warmth drove away her tension. Connie's hands felt like magic on her. Jade couldn't stop the low moan of pleasure as Connie worked her stiff muscles.

"Good?" Connie asked.

"Fucking great," Jade said. She closed her eyes as Connie stroked down her back and kneaded around her shoulder blades. Jade wished they were alone so they could at least be naked. The thought of Connie spread over her, slick and bare, rubbing up and down slowly over the small of Jade's back as she rocked back and forth with the massage nearly had Jade moaning aloud again. She clenched her ass cheeks together, desperate to keep from bucking her hips into the mat. Above her, Connie gave a tiny chuckle that meant she understood only too well what Jade was thinking.

Rustling and flapping sounds, followed by an annoyed sigh came from the mat beside her and pulled Jade back to reality.

"Ouch!" Garrett said. "Basil, you're so ham-fisted, you're not doing it right at all. You're killing my neck with your meaty paws. No finesse at all."

"What do you want me to do?" Basil sounded tired.

"Not what you're doing, that's for sure. God!"

"Good job, Connie." Trillium's voice filtered into Jade's ears. "You're a pro at this."

"I don't know about pro, but it's fun," Connie said in her cute, shyly pleased way. Jade muffled her smile in her arms.

"Why don't you try—"

An itching tingle ignited Jade's survival instincts. Jade twisted and snapped her hand around Trillium's wrist, stopping inches from her shoulder. The room went silent. Jade gritted her teeth. She released her death-grip on the instructor's wrist and tried to make her face into a harmless smile.

"Sorry, I uh don't really like that," Jade stammered.

Garrett let out a hoot and said, "No touchies, Trilly. You do *not* want a taste of Jade's angry dyke moves, now. She'll snap your head off and piss down your neck."

Trillium's smile looked brittle. She backed away.

"You know what, I'm just going to leave you alone to do your own thing," Trillium said.

"Thanks," Connie said. She scooted backward until she was perched on Jade's backside. She rested her hands flat on Jade's lower back, just above her waist. Slowly, softly, Connie pressed down, then stroked up again. Jade's discomfort melted. Connie really did have magic in her fingers. Jade was almost asleep when footsteps near her broke into her reverie.

Mel squatted down beside them with a grin on her face.

"Enjoying yourself?" she asked.

"You bet," Jade said. She hoisted herself up onto her elbows and rolled her shoulders. "Nearly forgot where I was."

"I wish *I* could," Garrett said in a snide voice.

"How about I help you with that," Jade said. "I heard an angry dyke boot to the head works wonders for memory issues."

"Uh huh girlfriend, I'd like to see you try," Garrett said.

"Play nice, kids," Mel said in a tone light enough she could be construed as joking but a steely glint in her eyes told Jade otherwise.

"Yes ma'am," Jade said. She flopped down and relaxed onto the mat. She was actually having a good time sparring with Garrett. Benny never gave her that level of sass, and if she threatened him, he'd probably cry, not to mention his mother would kick Jade's ass the next time they went to visit her at Dorvelle

Women's Pen.

Mel stuck her hand into the file-folder she was carrying and pulled out a number of small purple envelopes, which Jade recognized as the next mystery question. This time, Connie was the one to receive it.

"You know the drill, folks," Mel said. "Discuss when you're alone, got it?"

The assembled people murmured their agreement.

"Great." Mel went to the front of the room. A somewhat subdued Trillium was sitting on her mat, drinking from her water bottle. Mel said, "Dinner's at six-thirty, so free time until then. Check out our reading room if you want. We've got board games, puzzles, and card games you are all free to use. Have a good afternoon and see you all in the dining hall later on."

Connie got up and Jade quickly put the mat away. She shrugged back into her shirt and bounced on the balls of her feet. She really did feel like a million bucks. She wanted to jump around and shadowbox. Instead, Jade returned to Connie's side. She greeted Jade with a cute little smile. Jade shoved her hands into her pockets to keep from reaching out and running her thumb over Connie's rosebud lips. Gay-friendly atmosphere or not, Jade didn't want to deal with any more of Garrett's snark.

"What do you want to do next?" Jade asked. For a moment, she considered suggesting they get in the truck and go for a "drive," but she was actually pretty beat and didn't think her clit could take another pounding like that. Not until maybe tomorrow.

"How about hanging out in our room until dinner?"

"Sounds like a plan," Jade said. She muffled a yawn with the back of her hand as she wandered into the hallway.

Helen's voice rang from the Wellness Room, "Connie, you dropped something."

Connie stopped in the doorway with a look of confusion. She patted her pockets and gave Jade an apologetic look. "Sorry, you go ahead," she said. "I'll just be a sec."

"Okay," Jade said.

On the way back to their room, she swung by the reading room and left with a couple books by an author she'd enjoyed reading in the past and thought Connie would too. She kicked off her slippers as soon as the door to their room closed behind her, and sprawled out on the bed. Jade got comfy and opened one of the novels. She was halfway through the first chapter when her instincts prickled. Connie was taking a long time. Jade chewed her bottom lip. She wondered if she should go and investigate, in case Connie was in trouble or something.

Jade sat up and put her book on the bedside table. She hovered in indecision. Maybe Connie was just chatting or something. If Jade charged in like a rampaging elephant for no good reason, she'd only add to her asshole reputation. Most people didn't walk the line between the living and the dead, and had no idea of what lurked just under the surface of reality.

A circle of warmth against Jade's hip startled her. She slapped at the bedspread but met nothing. The warmth moved slightly, and a sound almost like a purr resonated through Jade. She held her hand over the area, trying to gauge what the hell was on her. The warmth vanished with the slam of the door. Slippers flapping, Connie stomped across the room. Her eyes looked stormy and her lips were pressed together.

"What happened, baby girl?" Jade asked.

Connie flung herself onto the bed and laid her head in Jade's lap. She let out a long, angry breath through her nose. "I didn't drop anything," she said. "It was just Helen. She kept asking me all these questions like do I have a safe place, can I move freely, and stuff like that. I couldn't believe it at first. Then she tried to give me her phone number but I wouldn't take it. As if I need it!"

Anger flared into life within Jade. She clenched her jaw to keep the growl in check. She gently brushed Connie's golden curls away from her face while she seethed.

"I would never hurt you," Jade said. Her voice was harsh and low.

"I know that," Connie rolled over and gazed up at Jade. She twined her fingers around Jade's, She pressed a quick kiss to Jade's palm before she brought Jade's hand to rest on her chest. "I don't care what anybody thinks of me being with you. I'm happy with you and that's it. Oh, hey, did you get some books?"

Connie sat up, at once her cheerful mood was back. Jade blinked with wonder at how she could do that. Just one more thing Jade loved about Connie, she was terrible at holding a grudge.

"Yeah, I thought you might like them," Jade said. "They're

kinda old, but pretty good. The one on top's this kind of cross-dressing western historical thing, which is pretty fun, and the other one's about hockey. They're both great, the author, Emma Jerome's, really good at adding twists and writes a hot love scene."

"Oh, I'll go with the western one," Connie said. She curled up against the pillows with her book and started to read. Her face in concentration was the cutest thing Jade had ever seen. Normally, she would have joined Connie in reading, and probably snuggling, but her pulse was still pounding from the assumption Helen made about her. Jade got to her feet. She couldn't sit still. Pacing the room wasn't going to help and punching the wall would only upset Connie. Jade glanced out of the window to the vast backyard. A black missle-like thing was bounding happily through the snow, kicking white spray up everywhere. Jade felt a crooked grin on her face at the pure exuberance of the dog.

"I think I'll go outside for a bit," Jade said. "Looks like Frog's having a fun time out there."

"Okay," Connie said without looking up from the page. She waved one hand absently as Jade left.


OUTSIDE THE RESORT, the snow was deep pink from the setting sun, the shadows a velvety blue. The winter days were short, but Jade no longer feared the night. For the last twenty years, she dreaded it. Her nights had been stifled silence, vigilance, and soulless fluorescent lights. Her only directive; protection of herself as well as the chosen few who made their way into the family of her heart. Jade had been on guard for so long, it became part of her consciousness. Now that she was free from the constant threats of violence, she had to figure out how to live like a human again. Her breath steamed into the chill air as she rounded the house.

Off the shoveled path, the snow came up to her knees. She waded over to where Frog galloped around in great bounds. The dog whuffed and snuffled into the air, obviously having a great time. Jade paused with her hands in her jacket pockets. Frog's snow-speckled ears perked up. She sniffed the air before she whirled and barreled over to Jade. This time, Jade sidestepped before the dog collided with her. Frog pranced in a circle around

Jade, welcoming her like an old friend.

"Hey there girl," Jade said. She patted the dog's head, smoothing off some of the snow. In response, Frog shook herself and unleashed a volley of snow all over Jade.

"Aw, assfruit hole humpers," Jade muttered and brushed herself off. She slapped the snow off her leather gloves before it melted.

Mission accomplished, Frog bounded off. She returned with a stick in her mouth. She dropped it into the snow in front of Jade and looked up at her with anticipation in her liquid brown eyes.

"You wanna play?" Jade asked. She felt a bit silly talking to an animal, but then again, she regularly talked to ghosts, which were a bit more on the out-there scale than dogs.

"Whuf!" Frog replied. She lowered her snout and stuck up her backside, her tail wagged madly in the crisp air.

"Maybe we should ask your mama first."

Jade looked around. She didn't see either of Frog's owners around. She wasn't sure what the procedure was for randomly playing with someone's pet. On a whim, Jade trundled through the snow until she faced the sunroom. Sure enough, Mel was inside, nursing a cigar and reading the newspaper. Jade shouted out a *hey* and waved. Mel put down her newspaper and opened the French door to the yard.

"What can I help you with?" Mel asked.

Frog and her stick galloped in circles around Jade, kicking up even more snow.

"Is it okay if I play with Frog?"

"Be my guest," Mel said. "She'll come in by herself when she's ready, so don't worry about leaving her alone when you get tired."

"Great," Jade said.

Mel made a go ahead gesture with one hand as she slid the door shut. Jade bent down and picked up the stick, which caused Frog's tail to go into maximum overdrive. Using her long-honed softball skills, Jade pitched the stick across the lawn. With a happy woof, Frog leaped through the snow drifts. Jade watched the dog roll and tear around with her stick. Her anger and frustration melted. She laughed out loud as Frog trotted back over to her, completely covered in snow.

Frog dropped the stick at her feet and Jade picked it up.

"Get ready girl," Jade called out. "Go get it!" She unleashed the stick and Frog streamed off after it. She came bounding back through the snow in great leaps. Suddenly the dog stopped in her tracks. Her nose quivered, her eyes focused on something behind Jade. A low growl came from the dog's throat.

Jade whirled and stared up at the resort, straight at the window of the room she was sharing with Connie. The glass was black like a gaping maw into another world. A slow drip of black, viscous stuff seeped from the window and stained the outside wall like half-congealed blood.

Everything else was forgotten. Jade breathed a scorching stream of words on her frantic dash back inside. She blew through the lobby and took the stairs three at a time. She burst into the room and stood in the doorway for a second, chest heaving.

Connie was sitting on the bed, eyes blank. The novel was splayed open beside her, the middle pages bent as if it had fallen from her hands. The wall opposite her roiled with boiling black smoke, but it didn't stain across the carpet like it had before. It seemed frozen, stuck to the wall. Jade didn't need to wonder why. A fuzzy black cat was between Connie and the whatever-it-was. The cat's back arched, her tail puffed out to twice its size and she hissed, showing rows of sharp teeth. The black smoke shivered and shrank into itself some, but not enough. A few tendrils reached out, aiming for Connie. Jade grabbed onto all of her anger and shot a thought-needle to the black thing.

*Get out.*

Jade stood her ground, hands clenched into fists. The roiling smoke shrank into itself before it seeped through the carpet. The lights flickered and brightened, the freezing bite of evil in the air faded. The cat launched itself into the air and vanished.

The stricken look on Connie's face wiped all other concerns from Jade's mind. Connie had her arms wrapped about herself. Her face was white. Jade crushed the urge to reach out and gather Connie up in her arms.

"It wanted me," Connie's voice was a pale shadow of her usual cheerful tone. "It wanted to be *inside* me."

Bile rose in Jade's throat. She took a risk and touched Connie lightly on the shoulder. To her relief and surprise, Connie curled up against her. As Jade held her close, Connie shivered.

"It's okay, you're safe," Jade murmurred into her hair. "If it's not too hard, can you talk to me about it? Do you remember anything?"

"Nothing concrete, just feelings," Connie said. She burrowed into Jade's embrace. "I felt like after that night when I was in Gord's car. Like my body was used by someone, even though I don't remember it."

"Baby girl," Jade breathed. Her chest was a mass of pain. Connie didn't talk about the incident. And who could blame her? Connie had been attacked once, set up to believe she'd been sexually violated by her male coworker while drugged. The fact that it was all a horrible lie, perpetrated by someone Connie believed was her friend didn't come out until after she went through the medical and mental aftermath.

While Connie's shivers gradually quieted, Jade couldn't help but think back to their first encounter with the black shadow when it came rushing at them. A chill zinged through her. What if it was aiming for Connie and Jade jumped into its path? Although Jade was the only one to see and hear it, she wasn't attacked the way Connie was.

*It wanted me.*

Jade's muscles twitched with the urge to flee.

"We're ditching this case," Jade said. "It came after you and that's where I draw the line."

Connie disengaged herself from Jade and shook her head. "No, I don't want to leave this unfinished. Now it's personal. We can't let it win."

Jade paused at the fierce determination in Connie's eyes. Her face was set, her posture proud and strong. Jade's flight reflex melted. "All right, we stay and fight, partner." She held out one fist and Connie bumped it with hers.

"Thank you, partner," Connie said.

"For the record, it didn't get all the way to you," Jade said. "The cat held it off until I could get here."

"Cat?" Connie blinked and looked around.

Jade massaged her temples. A whisper fluttered through her mind. "Yeah, her name's Licorice. Looks like we got a haunted hotel with a ghost cat as a bonus. One who I owe a big favor to for putting herself between you and whatever that thing was."

Connie nodded. She gave Jade a weak smile.

"You know," Jade said in a light, joking tone, "It would be pretty funny if she followed us home. I bet Benny would just *love* to have a ghost in his bookstore again. And not one he can lure into his office with naughty audiobooks as bait, like he did to you."

Connie laughed. She retrieved her book and smoothed the pages with an apologetic expression on her face. She put it down on the bedside table, right beside the purple envelope. Connie held the envelope up and said in a bright voice, "I almost forgot about this. Let's do the second mystery question."

Jade swallowed her reluctant groan but couldn't deny Connie when she seemed so excited about the exercise. Jade lay back on the bed and laced her fingers together behind her head. "Okay, shoot."

Connie opened the envelope. "What's your favorite kiss of ours?" Her cheeks went pink in the cutest way.

"All of them," Jade said immediately.

"That's no fun," Connie said with a pout. She dropped down to the bedcover and snuggled up to Jade's side. "There has to be one that stands out."

Jade thought for a moment. "Yeah, there is," she said in a soft voice. She put an arm around Connie and pulled her close. Connie nestled against her. Their bodies fit together so naturally, as if they had always lain together like that. Jade pressed a quick, chaste kiss to Connie's temple. She spoke into Connie's cropped hair, "The first one. The first real one. That first time I saw you awake, in the hospital. You looked up at me and I was so fucking scared you wouldn't know me. Then you said my name and everything in the whole world just went right. Every single shitty thing that ever happened to me was worth that moment." The mental scene threatened to overwhelm Jade and she stopped talking. Connie's arm stole around Jade's middle.

"That's my favorite too," Connie said softly. "One of them, anyway. I remember it more clearly than anything else in my life. I was afraid too. Afraid I'd fallen in love with a dream."

"You were in love with me even then?" Jade asked in wonder.

"Uh huh," Connie said. She gazed up at Jade. "It took me a while to get up the nerve to actually say it, but at that moment I knew I loved you. I think I knew even before that."

As if a warm soap bubble popped inside Jade's chest, she was filled with a rush of emotion, which was the only explanation Jade had for what she said next.

"You know Connie, this week is going to be the longest we've spent together without any breaks. It kind of made me think," Jade said. "You know, about the future. You and me, together every day. Saying goodnight in person, not by text or phone. Like, what if we really could do this, live together? I wouldn't mind moving to someplace bigger, with more bedrooms and a yard big enough for a swing-set and a sandbox. Doesn't it make you think about it too?"

Connie was silent for a beat. She abruptly sat up and looked away. "Not really. What we have now is good enough."

There was a raw note in Connie's voice that stabbed Jade through the heart. All Jade could think about was somehow she'd seriously fucked up. She gnawed at her lip as the silence stretched out. Her mental turmoil was interrupted by a screech from the hallway.

Jade jumped to her feet. "Where there's screaming, it's probably got something to do with us." Jade met Connie's gaze.

Connie laughed. The strained air broke. "Or somebody saw a mouse."

"Well, yeah, that too. Come on, let's go check it out."

With Connie close behind her, Jade dashed out of the room. Garrett was standing outside one of the guest rooms. At his feet was a puddle of half-melted snow. Several more decorated the hardwood flooring of the hallway and a rather large pool was at the top of the stairway.

"Ruined! My slippers are absolutely ruined," Garrett said, gingerly lifting first one foot, then the other. He looked over his shoulder at Jade. His eyes narrowed accusingly as he gave her a scathing once-over. "I should have known. Were you born on a raft or something?"

Jade looked down. The cuffs of her jeans were soaked and she was still wearing her cowboy boots. Jade didn't particularly give a shit about either Garrett's slippers or the floor, she would track in much worse things than just snow if Connie was in danger, but she'd made herself look like an ass again and by association, Connie too.

"Shitface twat jockey," Jade growled. At least she was right about the fact she had something to do with Garrett's shriek.

Garrett covered his open-mouthed gasp with one hand.

"Looks like somebody forgot to put on their slippers," Mel said in a somewhat forced joviality. She had a sponge mop in one hand and a bucket in the other.

"Yeah, that was me, sorry," Jade said. She threw a glare at Garrett. "We're not too picky about footwear on my raft."

He tossed his head and mimed being hard of hearing. Shaking his head, Basil slipped past him and slunk down the stairs.

"Is everything okay?" Mel asked Jade under her breath.

"It is now," Jade replied.

Mel drew back. She started to mop up the spilled water, but Jade held out her hand. "Let me. I tracked it in, I'll clean it up. I bet you've got a bunch of things to do right now."

After a moment's hesitation, Mel handed over the mop. "You're right about that. When you're done, stow the stuff in the mudroom. It's by the back door."

"Yes, ma'am," Jade said. She grasped the mop handle and gave it an experimental twirl. It was a nice one, well-balanced. She was happy it wasn't one of those crappy stringy ones they used at Dorvelle. Mel cleared her throat and looked pointedly at Jade's offending boots. With another muttered apology, Jade kicked them off and quickly tossed them into her room. She gave up on her slippers and continued in sock feet.

Cleanup led Jade back down to the main lobby. By the time she demolished the last puddle and put the mop and bucket away, the other guests were in the dining room. Jade slouched in with her hands in her pockets. Connie was already seated with Garrett and Basil. She turned away from Garrett, who was monologuing about something, with a brilliant smile that eased Jade's surly feeling immensely.

"The prodigal daughter returns," Garrett said as Jade sat down. He waved his napkin at her and Jade clenched her hands together to stop herself from grabbing it and shoving it down his throat. Unaware of how close his life had been to ending, Garrett blathered on for the entirety of the meal. The food, which was served buffet-style kept Jade occupied enough so she managed to keep her temper.

After their bread pudding was finished, Doreen and her microphone addressed the assembled guests.

"I hope you enjoyed your dinner, let's give a warm thanks to the catering staff," Doreen paused as a small round of applause rippled through the room. "If you'll all follow me to the Wellness Room, we've got some fun icebreaker games planned."

Reluctantly, Jade abandoned her half-full cup of coffee and pushed her chair away from the table. She noticed Helen glancing at them as they went upstairs. Jade kept her eyes forward and told herself she didn't care. When they were all assembled, Mel took the floor.

"Okay people," she said and clapped her hands for attention. The buzzing chatter quieted down. "We're gonna start off with a fun mixer. Couples, split up and stand at opposite walls."

Jade left Connie's side and shuffled over to one wall. Across the room, Connie sparkled with excitement. She was so damned cute, so happy without reservation. Jade mentally dared Helen to try and find evidence Connie was being mistreated.

"Now we're in position, I'm going to hit the lights and you have to find your partner," Mel said. She held up both hands. "Speaking is not allowed. Keep things safe and polite, got it? Okay, here we go."

Jade had only a split second to meet Connie's mischievous glance before the room was plunged into darkness. Around her, Jade felt the subliminal buzz of people as they started moving around. Jade took a cautious step forward away from the comforting solidity of the wall. Even though there was a no talking rule, Jade heard a few coughs and nervous laughing. A Garrett-like *ooh!* filtered through the inky blackness.

Jade felt exposed. The air at her back was cold, like a breeze from outside got in. It twined around her body, spiraling around her like a living thing until it reached her knees where it vanished. Jade hugged her arms to her chest. She didn't like the game anymore. She reached out, trying to find her way back to the wall. Nothing met her frantically searching hands. It was as if the room had vanished.

A raspy breath reached her ears. Jade froze. Someone was behind her. She twisted away in panic. It wasn't Connie. She knew Jade's issues and would never come up to Jade like that. Cold hands rested on Jade's hips for an instant before they stroked up her back. Jade's breath caught in her throat. Her heart pounded. She couldn't get away. Fingertips trailed over the back of her neck, soft and gentle and icy cold. They circled around her throat in an almost tender gesture that ignited every survival instinct Jade had.

"Turn on the lights!" Jade shouted. Her skin crawled. She whirled and collided with someone who let out a gruff, "Oof!" before she dropped to her knees. The hands were still on her, they moved from her throat to dangle in the hollow of her collarbones. Jade scrubbed at the skin of her neck, but there was nothing there.

A breath hissed one word into her ear:

*You.*

"Shit-pile vomit stain!"

"What's wrong? Did you fall?" Mel's voice came through the darkness.

"Fucking lights *on!*"

A click and the room was flooded with light. The cold pressure of the fingers vanished. Left on her knees, Jade fell forward and caught herself with her hands against the floor. She tried to stop shaking. Her breath came in hard gasps. She was vaguely aware of worried murmuring. Pattering feet came to a stop beside her. A gentle hand touched her clenched fist.

"Breathe, Jade," Connie said in a soft voice. "It's okay. I'm here."

The words broke the shell of panic. Jade relaxed her tension-bunched muscles. She looked up at the ring of concerned faces of the people standing in a rough circle around them. Jade faked an anemic laugh.

"Just trying to see who's paying attention," Jade said.

"Are you okay?" Connie asked.

"Now I am," Jade said. She rubbed a hand through her hair and felt like a larger ass than usual. She gave Mel what she hoped was a reassuring grin. "Sorry about that. I'm good, really, but mind if I tap out?" Jade asked. She used Connie's willing shoulder to help hoist herself up.

"Of course not," Mel said. She looked as if she wanted to ask a question, but instead turned to the group and said brightly, "All right, how about we go onto the next activity?" She herded the remaining people into the middle of the room and waved a roll of toilet paper at them. Connie didn't move from Jade's side.

"You don't have to leave, too," Jade said. "If you're having fun, you should stay here. You know, get to meet everyone and mingle."

Connie wrinkled her nose. "The only person I want to mingle with is you. Plus, I'm at a good part in my book and I've got a bag of peanut butter M&Ms in my bag we can share. How about joining me for a read and snuggle party with snacks?"

"That's the nicest suggestion I've heard all day. Let's get outta here," Jade said. She reached out and very gently tucked a stray wisp of hair behind Connie's ear.

# Chapter Seven

"HOW GOES THE case?" Young asked. He set two paper cups of coffee on the desk before he stepped behind it and plopped into his chair.

"It goes," Jade said. She grabbed a packet of sugar from the pile on the table and dumped it into her cup. Beside her, Connie cradled her own coffee in both hands and blew across the top.

"Yeah?" Young leaned back and crossed one leg over the other with a slight grimace.

"You okay there, big guy?"

"Fine, just getting a bit rusty in the joints," he said. "So, do I owe this visit to the fact you two got something?"

"Maybe we do. Maybe we just wanted to hang out at the station with all you good-looking people and score free coffee," Jade cracked. She tensed. One of the younger officers who bothered her, a guy named Becker, wandered over to them. Jade didn't like the slow, appreciative once-over he gave Connie.

"Hey Spooky," he said. "I see you got yourself a sidekick."

"Somebody's gonna get a kick all right," Jade growled low in her throat. "Keep ogling my girlfriend like that and you'll find out who."

Becker held up both hands and stepped back. "My apologies," he said. He tipped an invisible hat to Connie. "Didn't mean to be rude, miss. Don't know how you put up with Spooky, but good luck to you."

Connie just blinked up at Becker until he left. While Jade scowled at his back and tried to drown the swear words that wanted to explode from her mouth with gulps of sweet coffee, Connie took the folded article from her pocket and spread it out on the desk.

"Jade found this article," Connie said. "We think it may be a key to understanding what's going on, but there's not really enough here to know for sure. That's where you can help us out. We need to know more details, maybe who else was involved, or someone who can give us some insight into what happened." She smiled at Young and Jade could practically see the older man's heart melt. Jade understood completely. She had been on the receiving end of that smile more than once. Although Connie didn't seem aware of her superpower, Jade couldn't refuse any request accompanied by it.

"Say no more, I'm on it," Young said. He picked up the article in one hand and tapped away one-fingered at his computer keyboard with the other. Jade stifled her grin and gazed over the rim of her cup at Connie, who leaned forward over the desk with a look of interest.

After a few decisive taps, Young sat back in his chair and said, "How about I send you the details when I get some?"

"That would be great," Jade said. She got to her feet, more than ready to be somewhere else. The heat and bustle of the station always made her antsy, not to mention the added punch of the raucously cheerful Christmas decorations all over the place. If Jade never saw another ropy string of silver garland again, she wouldn't be upset.

"Thank you, Detective Young," Connie said.

Young waved her off with a brusque air Jade knew was fake. Jade gathered up their empty cups and chucked them into the trash on her way out. Once they were in the truck, Jade breathed easier and the tension eased from her shoulders.

"Next stop, Britt's place," Jade said. She poked at the navigation for a moment and called up the address Mel had given them. Jade got a cold feeling in her gut when she saw the suggested route. Connie was still and silent in the passenger's seat. "We can go around," Jade said quickly. She reached for the screen again, but Connie's fingers on her wrist stopped her.

"It's okay," she said. "Driving around the harbor will take ages. Take the bridge. I'll be all right."

"If you're sure," Jade said.

"I am," Connie replied. Her eyes crinkled up at the corners with her mischievous smirk. "Don't worry, I won't toss myself over the side again."

Even though her heart gave her a jab, Jade breathed out a chuckle. She started the truck and pulled into traffic. While she drove, Jade mulled the night she would never forget. The night she stood on the Maria Louisa Angwin Bridge and watched Connie—actually, an echo of Connie's spirit—jump to what was supposed to be her death. Her hands tightened on the steering wheel.

That was also the night Connie had come to her, brought her back when Jade was exhausted and on the edge of despair herself. It was the first time Jade knew a true, loving touch. She shifted in her seat as her body remembered how Connie's ghostly fingers had given her such pleasure and how they had lain together that night, neither in this world or the next but somewhere in between. A damp warmth seeped from her crotch. Jade bit the inside of her cheek to try and distract herself before her overeager sex soaked another pair of underwear.

Cheerful tunes from the stereo provided background music as they went over the bridge from Traynor's Port to Portsmouth. The tires hummed over the steel-supported suspension bridge. Jade kept her eyes fastened to the road ahead. In the daylight, with the sky wan and overcast with the premonition of snow, the echoes that haunted the walkways were hidden. But that didn't mean they weren't there.

On the other side of the Angwin, the classic stone buildings and towering offices of Traynor's Port gave way to a grey, industrial urban landscape. When the bridge shrank out of sight in the rearview mirror, Jade's feelings lightened considerably. She hummed along to the music from the radio and even tapped her fingers on the steering wheel. She glanced over to Connie, who leaned her cheek on one hand, enjoying the drive.

Britt's apartment was a blocky monolith with visitor parking conveniently located in front of the main entrance. The lobby was small and halfheartedly decorated with red and green foil cutouts of stuff like snowmen and stars. At one point, someone had sprayed fake snow into the corners of the windows, currently it looked like dried-out cottage cheese. Jade shifted her weight from one foot to the other while she and Connie stood in the lobby, waiting to be let in.

"Feels like a first date," Jade said. "A bit nervous, kinda excited. You know, what if she doesn't like us, or what if we hit it off really well and get what we came for? Maybe more than we expected."

Connie sputtered and her face went pink. "I hope you remember your manners."

"Always," Jade replied with a smirk.

The door buzzed open.

Since Britt's room was on the seventh floor, Jade called an elevator. She was glad they avoided the stairs because Jade didn't think she had the willpower to watch Connie's cute butt wiggle all the way up without tackling her on one of the landings.

Jade knocked and the door creaked open a bit. Bleary eyes peered out at them. Jade aimed her best non-threatening grin at the young woman.

Jade quickly introduced herself and Connie, finishing off with, "Mind if we come in?"

The smallest grunt of what Jade deemed assent came back at her before the young woman disappeared from the crack. Scuttling footsteps and the creak of sofa springs followed. Jade shared a look with Connie before she eased the door open. The apartment was just the right size for a single person. It would have been a nice place to live if it didn't look like the inside of a bear pit at the end of winter.

The coffee table was piled with dirty dishes and instant noodle cups. The small kitchen corner was filthy as well. Every light was on, even the bathroom, and every curtain was pulled shut, with clothes pegs holding the middle edges together as if to shut out even the smallest hint of the world outside. The air was stale and a rank odor caught in Jade's throat as she drew in a breath.

Jade turned her attention to Britt, who sat at one end of the sofa, hugging her knees to her chest and rocking slightly. The incident at the resort was almost two weeks ago. By the looks of things, Britt had been holed up in her apartment all that time.

She shared Doreen's fair coloring but that was where the resemblance ended. Where Doreen was sturdy and full, Britt was fragile. She seemed drained and brittle, like a tap would crumble her. Britt's face was pale and her lips were chapped. She repeatedly gnawed at them. Britt's hair was matted and greasy. She was in pajamas that hung off her as if they were slowly melting with every passing day they didn't see the inside of the washing machine. Her face was sallow and she had purple smudges under her eyes like she hadn't slept in days.

She looked like shit. Connie hung back, tacitly giving Jade the lead. Jade awkwardly sat down at the other end of the sofa.

"Sorry to barge in," Jade said in a jolly tone that took a whole lot of effort to maintain. "Were you taking a nap?"

Britt shook her head. "I don't sleep," she said. Her voice was harsh. She cleared her throat and coughed. The hand she pressed to her mouth shook. Connie leapt from her post at the door and pattered into the kitchen corner. Jade glanced at her gingerly moving a pile of pizza boxes that were blocking the fridge before she opened it and peered inside.

Connie came over with a mug of something. She handed it to Britt, who flinched and pulled away.

"It's just water," Connie said, a little apologetically.

Slowly, Britt curled her fingers around the mug, then raised it to her lips and drank.

The silence dragged out. Jade clasped her hands on one knee and studied the young woman. The way she clutched at herself and kept her head down pulled hard at Jade's memory. She'd seen people like that on the inside, who had something so bad happen to them they retreated inside themselves.

Jade bit her lip. That could have been her. She learned the hard way never to let down her hyper-vigilance. Jade knew what it was like to be beaten down, but she also knew how to get back up. Jade didn't think a prison welcome had happened to Britt. Jade's gut twisted. Something worse had. She needed to find out what. Jade knew from experience, the girl wouldn't talk until Jade had her trust.

Jade leaned forward and rested her elbows on her knees, her fingers laced loosely together.

"Do you know who we are?"

"Yeah, Mom texted me you were coming. Mother said you were some sort of, like ghost hunters."

Jade mentally cursed. "Mother" had to be Doreen. Just great.

"I'm a licensed private investigator," Jade said. "Connie and I specialize in solving paranormal-influenced cases."

Britt didn't stop rocking, but she raised her head and studied Jade. "So are my moms paying you?"

"Nope," Jade said. "I'm not doing this for them. I was asked to check things out by the police. My focus is bringing closure and justice to whatever it is that's stirring up shit at the resort."

Britt jumped. Her sickly-pale face went almost grey. Jade tensed in case she pitched over.

"Hey Britt," Jade said in a soft voice she kept in a special place and only pulled out when she really had to. It seemed to work. Britt let out her breath and blinked a few times. Her eyes were glazed over with tears. "Are you okay?" Jade asked.

She shook her head.

"Talk to me, Britt."

"I don't know what happened," she said at last. "You're going to think I'm crazy."

"Britt, honey, you're safe to tell us the truth," Jade said. "Look at what we do for a living. We're prepared to believe you. Nothing of what you say leaves this room, either. You have my word as a PI, and also as a person who's seen shit nobody else would believe too."

Britt went still and silent, her eyes were unfocused as if she was watching something only she could see. Connie nudged aside an overflowing wastebasket and sat down on the floor next to Jade. Her arm pressed against Jade's leg. The softness and warmth was welcome in the face of such a tortured soul.

"Okay," Britt said in a whisper. Her eyes were haunted. She repeatedly wrung her hands. Her lower lip trembled. "You're not going to arrest me or put me in a mental hospital or anything like that?"

"No, of course not."

As if she couldn't hold the words back anymore, Britt said, "I did it. It was me." She buried her face in her hands. Her shoulders heaved. Jade froze in indecision but Connie was on her feet in an instant. She gently laid a hand on Britt's arm.

Without raising her head, Britt said, "I didn't know until the last one, I didn't remember anything, just the horrible nightmares with all the screaming. Then it got—worse. The last time, I woke up with my hands full of plaster dust and a broken knife under my bed." This time she looked up. Her face was wracked with pain and panic. "Once I realized, I started to remember bits of it. It was like something took over my body. Something controlled me from the inside, making me do stuff I would never do! I felt...raped. So many times."

"Clam-packing jizz dog," Jade breathed. Britt's story corroborated Connie's experience. Only Britt had been used fully multiple times. No wonder she was a mess. Jade leaned back into the sofa in shock. A discarded instant noodle cup crumpled behind her. She asked, "This happened only when you were asleep?"

Britt nodded. She blinked sleepily then shook her head and

bit her lip violently. Jade winced.

"Don't do that," Jade said.

"I have to," Britt said. Her lip was bleeding, a red streak on her face. She rubbed the back of one hand over her mouth and the streak became a smudge. "I can't sleep. Not even a second. What if it takes me over again? No, I can't. I'd rather die."

"It's not here," Jade said. She leaned forward. "It's in that house, in that room. I saw it too."

"You did?"

"Yeah," Jade said. "What it forced you to do wasn't your fault. It's pretty pissed off and unfortunately it chose you as a tool."

Britt sagged back into her chair with a look of raw relief. She dropped her face into her hands and started to sob. Her shoulders shook.

"Aw fuck-barrels," Jade muttered. She had no idea what to do. Connie kept her hand on Britt's shoulder and sat down beside her.

"It's okay," Connie said. "You're safe. We're going to make sure that thing goes away and never bothers anyone again."

That seemed to set off something inside of Britt. She barfed out a bunch of words, the gist of them were along the lines of: "going crazy" and "couldn't tell anyone." There was a small aside about her mother that Jade didn't really follow. Connie spoke soft words of comfort and provided a series of tissues. Needing to do something, Jade jumped up and went into the kitchen. She dragged a few garbage bags out from under the sink and pitched most of the delivery food boxes into them before she plugged in the kettle and scrubbed out the least gross mug from the collection in the sink. Most of them had instant oatmeal residue caked inside them. Jade's nose buzzed from the fake sugary cinnamon smell that rose up from the sink as she set them in water to soak.

Under Connie's patient nursing, Britt managed to get herself under control and eventually sipped at her mug of tea.

"I guess whatever it is doesn't like us poking around and renovating," Britt said.

"It doesn't like something," Jade said. She got an idea and decided to go with it. "Are you seeing anyone?"

"What?" Britt's head snapped up. She looked like she was on

the verge of bolting. "Um, yeah, kinda," she said. Her face went red.

"Your parents don't know about...her?" Jade took a chance.

Britt flinched. "Oh shit, how did you know?"

Instead of answering the question, Jade asked, "Why didn't you tell them? It's not like they're not going to understand."

Britt shook her head. Ropy locks lashed her face. "I think they'd be disappointed if they found out I'm bi. They were so relieved when I started dating guys. They're from a different generation, they had it tough and I felt they always wanted me to have it easier than they did."

Connie asked, "How long have you been together?"

"We've known each other for about a year, and started going out about four months ago." Britt's face relaxed into a smile, small and anemic, but it was a start. "It's been really great with Wendy. I mean, not at all what it was like with guys. I feel such a deep connection with her, you know?"

Jade exchanged a quick glance with Connie. They had a time frame, Jade needed to find the trigger. She asked, "Did you ever sneak her into the resort, you know, for a bit of fun?"

"No, I'd never do that." Britt looked aghast.

"But you did do something," Jade said. "What's haunting your parents' resort hates girl-on-girl. Something set it off. Think about the first incident. Did you do anything the night before?"

"Oh God," Britt said. She pressed a hand to her face. "Okay, yeah, we um kind of sexted. Now that I think of it, every time we either sexted or, you know, did it over the phone, something would happen." She let out a shaky half-laugh. "I can't believe I'm telling you this stuff."

Connie tilted her head with a little quirk to her lips. She said, "Don't be embarrassed. Being intimate with someone you love is natural and fun. We get it. And it's relevant to the investigation."

"Call her," Jade said firmly. "Get her over here, you shouldn't be alone right now."

Britt looked down at herself, as if for the first time realizing her unwashed state. She shook her head. Her face crumpled and she looked on the verge of tears. Jade breathed a sigh of relief when Britt's face went back to normal and she spoke again. "I've been avoiding her texts and I didn't answer the door when she knocked. I bet she's pissed at me. A-and I can't let her see me like this. But I can't—not the shower. I can't go in there. I feel so—defenseless. No."

"It's all right, you're safe here," Jade said. Britt just shook her head and looked miserable. Jade let out a long breath. "Okay, I'll make a deal with you. How about I stand guard? I'll be your guardian angel of the bathroom." Over Britt's shoulder, Jade met Connie's eyes. Once Connie had been that for her, although this shower was not going to end up the way theirs had.

Britt pulled her pajama top away from herself and made a face. "Ugh, I can't stand myself," she said in a defeated voice. "Um, if it's not weird, that would actually be really great."

"Don't worry," Jade said with a slow grin, "I'm not gonna peek. Deal?"

Jade got to her feet and held out her hand. Slowly, as if her knees hurt, Britt rose from the sofa. She took Jade's hand and shook it briefly. She retrieved her hand and pointed. "The bathroom's over there," Britt said. She looked around sheepishly. "At least it's not as much of a pigsty in there as it is out here."

Jade shrugged on their way to the bathroom. "It's no big deal," she said. Jade didn't add that she'd gotten used to much worse in her twenty years in prison.

True to her word, Jade stood guard at the door while Britt stripped. Once she heard the shower start, Jade ducked into the bathroom. The shower curtain was opague and Jade was glad for that. The situation was already awkward enough without Jade trying to avoid looking at stuff she shouldn't. While Jade's heart belonged only to Connie, sometimes her eyes took little side-trips.

Over the sound of falling water and the few stilted attempts at small-talk, Jade heard the vacuum cleaner going. She stifled a grin. Mason and Mayflower, paranormal investigation plus house-cleaning.

# Chapter Eight

BRITT'S APARTMENT SANK into the background. "Last Christmas" came on over the stereo and Jade tapped her fingers on the steering wheel while her mind whirled. Something nagged her about Britt's story. Jade felt sick with unease. She didn't want to think about what it meant just then. Jade glanced over to Connie, who was nodding along with the melody.

"Gay Christmas," Jade announced.

Connie giggled. She sobered and said, "One mystery solved, at least."

"Yeah, and Britt seems like she'll be okay. We left her in good hands."

"Wendy's nice," Connie said. "She seems very easygoing."

"Good thing too, after enduring a silent treatment like that."

"Don't ever do that to me." Connie turned in her seat and faced Jade. "Even if I do something awful and you hate me, find some other way to punish me. Don't do the radio silence thing."

"Sweetheart," Jade said. She took one hand off the wheel and placed it over Connie's. "You have my word. I can't imagine ever hating you, no matter what you do. I don't like the idea of punishing anyone, especially you."

"Thanks," Connie said. She squeezed Jade's hand once, then let her go.

Outside, the last dregs of Portsmouth streamed by, blocky warehouses and a few scattered clusters of suburban homes. The trees on either side of the highway got thicker the longer Jade drove. In the back of Jade's mind, an idea had been growing for some time. She didn't know how receptive Connie would be, but unless Jade put the idea out there, there was zero chance of it becoming reality.

"You ever think about those hotels?" Jade asked, breaking the comfortably, slightly sleepy silence abruptly. Connie sat up and tilted her head in question. Jade plowed on, "The kind you can rent a room for a couple hours?"

"Yes, a couple of times," Connie said. She leaned closer to

Jade, interest on her face. Inwardly, Jade cheered.

"So, if there's one between here and South Aisling, would you be interested in making a brief pit stop and maybe indulging in a bit of daytime fun?"

Connie sat still and quiet in thought. The silence stretched out. Jade started to feel worried. Then Connie's dimple appeared and she said, "Absolutely." Her lips quirked up and she got a naughty look on her face. "I always thought that type of hotel was for people on those sites where you can find a partner, you know, to hook up or whatever."

Jade grinned. Would Connie go there? One way to find out. She glanced sideways and caught Connie's eye when she looked up from her phone screen. "Wanna do something like that?"

Connie raised her brows in a question.

Jade turned her attention back to the road. She licked her lower lip. "You know, pretend like I messaged you, looking for someone to show me the ropes when it comes to getting naughty with a woman. Not really a toaster-oven thing, but like I've led an extremely virtuous life until now and finally reached my limit of being celibate. Think you'd be into doing something like that?"

Connie hummed, low and thoughtfully. "That sounds really hot. Tell me more."

Jade relaxed. She pressed her shoulders back into the seat. An excited, warm feeling bloomed deep in her belly. "We'd meet up at the hotel, and you'd teach me how to please you. You'd tell me exactly how to get you off and I'd do anything you want."

"Ooh," Connie said. Her cheeks went pink. "Yeah, I could do that."

Jade smirked. "Cool. Now get on that phone of yours and find us a place."

Connie worked industriously for a few silent minutes. Jade tried to calm her roaring hormones by paying very close attention to the sparse traffic and infrequent road signs that dotted the landscape.

"Got it," Connie said. She waved her smartphone in the air. "I just made a reservation for us at the Lighthouse Motel. It looks shady enough to be perfect. Is three hours okay?"

Jade glanced at her watch. "That's fine, we'll be back in plenty of time for dinner."

"Good, because you're going to be hungry after the workout I give you." Connie gave Jade a slow, naughty grin then fell into thoughtful silence.

JADE STOOD IN the bathroom of the suitably shady motel. She shook out her hands and let out a breath. Shit, she was nervous, but in a very good way. She stood at the door and went over the details she and Connie discussed in the truck before she lifted a hand to knock. Jade didn't want to start the scene standing outside, plus she could wash up from the drive, so the one deviation from reality was to start from the bathroom. Connie's voice called out and Jade eased herself into the room.

It was pretty standard, just shabby enough for the deliciously illicit air to push Jade's body into readiness. The bedcover was thrown back and Connie sat on the starched sheets of the double bed that took up most of the room. She was barefoot and looked seductive and alluring in the low light from the single pea-green shaded lamp. She met Jade's eyes with a smoldering gaze full of promises.

Jade swallowed hard and rubbed her sweating palms on her jeans. Her clit jolted. Her breath came faster. Just from one look, Connie got her going. It was going to be a fucking fun afternoon, that was for sure.

Connie gave her a slow once-over, then leaned back on her hands. She lowered her head, licked her lips and said, "I wasn't sure you'd come."

"I had to meet you. Whether I come or not is up to you," Jade replied. The tiny chuckle Connie gave set Jade's body into high estrus. Her nipples tingled and her cunt got hot and juicy.

"No second thoughts?"

"None. I'm yours," Jade said. She shivered under Connie's searing scrutiny.

Connie pursed her perfect, cute lips. She slowly sat upright, then leaned forward. "Strip for me," she said.

Extremely aware of Connie watching her every move, Jade shucked her plaid flannel shirt and T-shirt. Even though the room was toasty warm, her nipples were hard points under the grey fabric of her sports bra and goose bumps shivered over her skin. Her entire body ached for Connie's touch. When she was in nothing more than her boxer briefs and sports bra, Jade paused.

"I didn't tell you to stop," Connie said in a dangerously sexy voice.

Jade bit her lip to keep from groaning. She slowly lifted her sports bra. She didn't break eye contact until she pulled it over her head. She hooked her thumbs into the waistband of her briefs and slipped them off. Jade kicked herself free of them and stood, bare as the day she was born in the middle of the seedy motel room.

Connie took her time and gave Jade another leisurely look-over. Connie's eyes got glassy with arousal. Under her top, her breaths got faster, her breasts rising and falling. Jade had never felt so powerful. She had been a victim, under someone else's control, and it made her a survivor. Now, willingly surrendering herself to Connie made her feel more powerful than she ever did before. No longer a survivor, she was a warrior. They both were.

"Come over here," Connie said. She slipped back and patted the space beside her. "I'm going to show you how to fuck like a real woman."

Jade's knees nearly gave out at the hungry tone. She didn't need to be asked twice. Jade crossed the room and took her place next to Connie.

Jade swallowed. "What do you want me to do first?"

"Let's see how you kiss." Connie held still and Jade carefully put her hands down on either side of Connie's hips. She leaned in close, then gently brushed her lips over Connie's. Jade closed her eyes and opened her mouth. She could hardly control her shiver when Connie responded to her and kissed her back. Connie's lips held her and Jade eagerly leaned into her. Jade's nipples brushed the soft material of Connie's top.

A shock of arousal lanced through her, resonating in her core. Jade shifted her weight, desperate for relief. Connie drew back. Jade was at once intensely aware of her nudity. She felt like her pussy was drowning. Her belly hummed with pent-up desire.

"Was that okay?" Jade asked.

"It's a start. You're a quick study," Connie said. She got to her feet and stood in front of Jade. She quickly, almost perfunctorily, pulled off her top and bra. Jade gazed at her breasts. The hard, cherry-kissed tips enticed Jade, the tight little aureoles called to her to taste them. She ached to cup and squeeze the creamy fullness in her hands. They swayed with the motion of

Connie getting out of her pants and underwear. When she was bare, Connie stood still in front of Jade, echoing when Jade undressed for her earlier.

Unable to help herself, Jade's attention drifted down and she focused on the softly full lips between Connie's legs. Her face heated up. Jade knew she was busted when Connie let out a chuckle and reached down to gently part herself with her fingers. Sleek pink inner lips peeked out, deliciously wet. Connie brushed her fingers over her clit, rocking her hips ever so slightly.

"Oh fuck," Jade gritted. She squeezed her thighs together. Jade felt like she had a ticking timebomb tucked into her crotch. She sucked in a lungful of air and tried to get herself calm. It didn't work. Jade's heart thundered. She knew exactly what she wanted to do to that gorgeous, pouty pussy in front of herself, but it was Connie's move to make. "Tell me what you want me to do," Jade said. She held her breath and hoped.

"I want you on your knees," Connie said. She stroked her inner folds again, pulling the hood back to reveal the hard, pink pearl nestled inside. "Let's see if you're good at kissing me here too."

Connie's eyes were bright and her expression one of sultry anticipation. Jade stifled the happy yell of triumph that would spoil the mood. Instead, Jade slipped from the bed to the floor. She followed when Connie backed up a step to lean against the padded headboard of the bed. Every movement was delicious torment of Jade's soaked and throbbing sex. Experimentally, Jade let one hand trail down her own belly, moving toward the ache that she couldn't ignore. She spread her knees.

"May I?" Jade asked.

"No," Connie said. Her lids drifted half-closed and she looked down at Jade, at once beautiful, sassy, and powerful. "Tonight, that, and the rest of you, belong to me."

"Sweet Jesus," Jade breathed.

Connie parted her thighs and leaned back slightly, opening herself with her fingers before drawing her hand away. The message was clear. Jade scooted forward on her knees and reverently took Connie around the hips. The musk of Connie's arousal was intoxicating, at once so familiar and new. Jade gently nuzzled into the trimmed curls, then pressed a hesitant kiss to the swollen bud. She struggled to keep in character, like she'd never done

that before. The role was just too enthralling for her to drop it.
More than that, Jade felt like she was being made anew, reborn
into the person Connie believed her to be.

Jade's heart soared with the tiny gasp Connie let out at the
first stroke of Jade's tongue over her slick folds. Jade felt a hand
on her head, pulling her closer. Jade eagerly complied. She got
into a good rhythm, licking and sucking in good measure. Above
her, Connie's breath came out in hard pants, her hips rolled in
counterpoint to Jade's loving caresses. Jade's thighs were wet, her
inner muscles squeezed every time she flicked her tongue over
Connie's clit. Connie's breaths were punctuated by moans that lit
a fire in Jade's crotch.

Connie drew her hand through Jade's hair, then tugged
lightly. "God, I want you, Jade. In me."

Jade didn't need to be told twice. She brought one hand to
Connie's waiting sex. Still teasing the delicately firm clit with her
tongue, Jade pushed two fingers into Connie. Her entrance was
met by a low moan and a shudder. Jade let Connie set the pace;
she sank deep into Connie and out, urged by the motion of her
hips.

With a strained whimper, Connie guided Jade off her clit.
Jade soon forgot the momentary flash of disappointment when
she took in the delectable sight of Connie's pussy split by her fingers. The rhythm picked up.

"Like that, yes, like that," Connie moaned like a mantra. Jade
glanced up. Connie's head was thrown back, her eyes closed and
cheeks flushed. She looked like an angel in the grips of unholy
passion. Her breasts swayed with the pump of her hips. She hung
onto the headboard of the bed as if it were the only thing anchor-
ing her from flying off into space. Suddenly a tremor rippled
through her. "Coming," Connie gasped out. Her inner muscles
grabbed Jade. She let out a short cry that cut off with a sharp,
final thrust that left Jade fully sheathed in her.

Jade held Connie steady throughout the juddering cascade of
tremors. Even as the waves of climax broke over her, Connie kept
thrusting hard onto Jade. Her slick lips glided over Jade's skin,
hungrily pulling at Jade's fingers when she drew out. Jade bit her
lip. She loved being fully locked into the hot, tight channel.

The sight of Connie lost in climax was almost enough for Jade
to forget her own clenched pussy. Almost. Finally, the shudders

quieted and Connie allowed Jade to withdraw. Connie stretched, sighed in contentment and opened her eyes. Jade gulped. She could barely wait for what was coming next. After a moment when they both caught their breaths, Jade decided to move things on to the next stage. Hopefully it was one with her on the receiving end of Connie's fingers, tongue, or anything else she wanted to give her.

"How was I?" Jade asked.

"You did very well," Connie said. "And I think it's time I give you your reward. Get on the bed and get ready for me."

Jade staggered when she got to her feet. She shivered. She had never been that turned on before. She collapsed gratefully onto the bed and leaned back against the pile of pillows, noting with amusement that Connie had already put down a folded towel on the sheet. Jade parked her butt on the towel and waited for Connie to move, but she stood still. One finger tapped on her sweetly flushed lower lip. Her eyes roved over Jade's form.

In response, Jade drew up one knee and spread her legs. "Like what you see?" she asked with a challenging raise of one brow.

"Oh yes," Connie said. Her angelic dimple did nothing to hide the wicked light in her eyes. She crawled onto the bed and knelt between Jade's thighs. She bent Jade's other leg, spreading her wide. Jade's heart thundered. She felt extremely exposed and unbelievably aroused. She couldn't help but shimmy her hips, silently begging for something, anything that would ease her clenched torment. It didn't come. Connie raised her eyes to Jade's face. "Touch yourself for me. Show me how you please yourself."

Jade nodded, unable to speak. She felt a flush spread over her chest and throat. She reached down and drew two fingers through her slit. Her hungry pussy welcomed the touch. Jade's head went back into the pillows and her hips thrust automatically. Waves of pleasure zinged through Jade. Her rigid clit slid between her fingers. The muscles in her thighs shook. She loved the fact Connie was watching her partake in that secret, intimate moment. Jade had never shared that with anyone before.

"Tell me before you come."

"Oh fuck," Jade said through gritted teeth. "I'm really fucking close."

"Stop," Connie commanded.

With a groan, Jade pulled her hand away and was rewarded by Connie's soft body coming down over hers and her lips meeting Jade's in a hungry kiss. Connie's hands claimed Jade's breasts, her thumbs teased her nipples. Jade couldn't help but slip her hands over the smooth swells of Connie's backside. Connie wriggled her hips in response and gently pressed herself into the cleft of Jade's legs. Connie's pussy lips slid into Jade's, rubbing up and down her spread opening. Jade broke the deep kiss and gasped into the air.

"Fuck, that's good," Jade said. Her breaths got hard and fast. Connie replied by kissing her neck, then trailing to one breast. Jade gazed down in bleary euphoria. She whimpered in pleasure when Connie's lips closed over her nipple. Her talented tongue circled Jade's aureole like she was enjoying a candy. Connie kept up a steady pace between Jade's legs, the burning urge to come rose with each thrust. Jade kneaded Connie's firm ass, rocking them together in a harsh, wet rhythm. Their roles slowly eased off, but Jade didn't have the mental wherewithal to keep it up anymore.

"God, I need to come," Jade said between quick, gasping breaths. "Please, baby girl."

Connie let go of Jade's nipple and looked into her face. She was pink-cheeked and breathing hard. Her lips were wet and swollen from their heavy kissing.

"All right," Connie said. She hoisted herself up enough so her breasts swung free. She scooted back a fraction. At the loss of contact, Jade grunted in protest and canted her hips in a silent plea. An instant later, Connie slipped two fingers deep into her. She pulled out, thrust hard again. Jade arched back, spreading her legs even more, welcoming Connie. Her eyes fluttered shut. Connie's slick fingers found her clit. She drew quick circles over Jade's throbbing nub.

"Oh fuck," Jade gritted. She wasn't going to last. "Connie, baby, please—"

"Come for me, Jade."

Jade let go. She was beyond words, she existed only to serve and please the woman who echoed her harsh cry with a soft, sympathetic hum. Jade was complete in that instant. The shuddering waves seized control of her. Hot juice ran down her slit. She came back down several long heartbeats later, curled up sweat-damp and shaking in Connie's arms. When her breathing got back to normal, Jade stretched out and flopped over onto her belly.

She looked up at Connie, who smiled back.

"Good?" Connie asked.

"The fucking best," Jade replied. She grabbed Connie around the waist and nestled into her bare lap. Connie's trimmed bush tickled her breast. Jade dropped a kiss to the soft, bare skin just under her bellybutton. "I'm almost ready for round two."

Connie laughed and brushed Jade's bangs back out of her face. "That would be nice, but we have to get going soon. How about a shower? I can wash your back."

Jade pretended to think about it, when she was actually picturing how the soapy bubbles would run down Connie's breasts and Jade would follow them with her fingers until she reached that sweet little peachy mound she was dying to tease into pouty wetness again. Jade swallowed her lascivious smirk. "Sounds good," she said. "Lead the way. I'll be right behind you."

"That's because you want to look at my butt," Connie said. She jumped up and wiggled her backside.

"Hell yeah, glad you figured that out," Jade said. She hurried through the obstacle course of discarded clothing, following the cutest backside in the entire universe.

# Chapter Nine

THEY ARRIVED BACK at the resort when the afternoon was already darkening into early evening. Jade was in such a good mood, she thought she could hang out with both Garrett and Helen and not want to throttle either. Unfortunately, the other guests were absent so none of them could benefit from Jade's cheerfulness.

Doreen was supervising some of the catering staff in the dining room and Mel and the dogs were nowhere in sight. The other guests were possibly hanging out at the Tourist Information Center and giving Percy an aneurism. Connie suggested they hang out in the reading room until dinner, and Jade readily agreed.

Like the rest of the resort, the small but well-stocked room was devoid of people. Jade sprawled out on the large, comfy sofa with her phone. While Connie explored the various shelves and cabinets, Jade swiped through the old photos Connie sent her. Nothing really stood out. She turned off the display and put the phone down on the low table in front of her. Connie turned from the board game cabinet and trotted across the room. She sat down on the sofa next to Jade and kicked off her slippers, then crossed her legs and sat with her chin propped up on one fist, regarding Jade with a sparkle in her eyes.

"What do you think, partner?" Jade asked. "What's our next step?"

"We need to check out the boathouse," Connie said.

"I agree," Jade said. "What happened there may or may not have any connection to what's going on here, and I want to get that possibility out of the way ASAP. I'll go out there tonight after dinner."

Connie nodded. "I'll go with you for backup."

The offer struck a cold nerve. Jade's particular ability wasn't limited to only seeing ghosts, her presence drew them out and made them stronger, which was fine if they were dealing with someone's Great-auntie Martha who wanted to share her secret shortbread recipe from beyond the grave. Not so much with a murderer.

If the boathouse yielded more than an echo, Jade wanted Connie as far away from there as possible. The similarities between Connie and Britt — and Teresa — worried Jade. A lot.

"Actually, I should do this alone," Jade said. She reached over and gave Connie's hand a quick squeeze. "I appreciate the thought, but I'm going to need to concentrate and you're far too cute and distracting."

"All right, but I want you to come back to me quickly, and in one piece," Connie said. She squeezed Jade back and softly ran her thumb over the back of Jade's hand in a way that had Jade's entire body heating up.

"I won't leave you for long, that's a promise," Jade said. She couldn't sit still anymore, and she couldn't ignore the uncertain expression on Connie's face. Jade opened her arms. "Come here, sweetie."

Connie didn't even hesitate before she curled up on Jade's lap and twined her arms around Jade's neck. She nestled against Jade with a little sigh and a wiggle that was probably not meant to turn Jade on as much as it did. Jade tried to ignore the insistent pulsing heat between her legs. Connie's soft lips pressed against her neck in a series of kisses that didn't help one bit.

For a moment, Jade just leaned back and enjoyed the affection. They weren't doing anything too bad, she reasoned. Nothing they couldn't stop in a moment if anyone came into the room. They weren't even in direct line of sight from the door, and all was quiet on the supernatural front as well. Jade's mind got fuzzy as Connie's breaths grew fast and hot, the kisses on her neck wet and demanding.

Jade bit off a whimper as Connie cupped her breast. The pressure was too light for Jade, who put her hand over Connie's and held her closer. The heat of her palm radiated through Jade's entire body. Jade arched her back in an involuntary motion when Connie ran her free hand down over Jade's body, down her side to her hip.

"You're getting me going," Jade whispered.

"I know," Connie said. Her voice was soft and breathy. She drew back and looked at Jade. "Too much?"

"Maybe." Jade shifted. Inside her briefs, she was already wet and throbbing. She resisted the urge to buck her hips up to try and get some friction. It was going to be a long night. Jade swallowed her groan and said, "Whatever's haunting this place seems strongest in our room, but it got me in the Wellness Room so I think we should probably assume it can go anywhere in the resort."

As if in response, the lights flickered. Jade sucked in a breath and very gently eased Connie off her lap. Even though she looked disappointed, Connie soon brightened up. She dragged over a stool, ensconced herself on the chaste side of the coffee table, and convinced Jade to join her in a card game she pulled from the cabinet.

They played fiercely for a while. Jade was in the middle of gloating about a particularly good trick when Mel came into the room like a steamboat on a mission.

"There you are," Mel said. "I saw your truck in the lot and I wondered where you two were."

"Yeah, we're here all right," Jade said. "Anything you needed us for?"

Mel hesitated. She dragged a hand through her brushy hair. "You talked to Britt today, right?"

"We did," Jade said. "She's okay, that much I can tell you."

"Thank goodness," Mel said. She let out a long breath and looked relieved. "I don't suppose you could tell me anything else? Like, why the radio silence?"

"No, sorry, but it's nothing to do with you or Doreen." Jade held up a hand. "I'm not going to spill any more details. That's my code. It's like I'm a doctor, got it?"

"I figured as much," Mel said. After a beat of uncomfortable silence, she leaned over the table and studied the spread-out cards. Mel met Jade's questioning look with a smirk. "I didn't come in here only looking for secret information. I also wanted to let you know the bath's free right now. I just dropped off a load of fresh candles and refilled the bubble bath dispenser. Perfect for a party of two. Interested?" She waggled her eyebrows.

"Uh," Jade said, caught off-guard by the wave of hungry arousal that swelled her clit and sent little jolts of electricity up and down her thighs. She cleared her throat and crossed her legs in what she hoped was a casual way. Jade did not need the image of Connie's wet, glistening skin in her mind. She did not want to picture how the droplets of hot, scented water would course down the inner curves of Connie's breasts in sparkling bursts as she rode Jade like a racehorse. Sweating, Jade forced out a fake laugh. "Tempting, but Connie's gonna have to enjoy it by herself. I'm on the rag." Jade shrugged and made a "what can you do?" face.

"That's too bad," Mel said. Her eyes narrowed and she looked at Jade shrewdly for a moment before her usual host's cheer returned. "If you need supplies or anything, just check the amenity box in your room. It's all on the house."

"I'm fine," Jade said. She grimaced and tried to turn it into a smile. Beads of sweat tickled her temples. "In fact, I'm just about done anyway. You know how it is when you hit forty. All that girly shit kind of goes to rust and dust, am I right?" Jade clenched her hands into fists and willed herself to shut the fuck up.

Mel surprised her with a genuine laugh. She stuck her hands in her pockets and rocked back on her heels. "If you say so. Everything I've got is still in tip-top working order." She suddenly pulled a hand from her pocket and shook back her cuff. With an apologetic look, Mel said, "Sorry, wish I could chat more, but I'm expecting a cheese delivery right about now. Have fun kids, and play nice." She didn't wait for anyone to reply. Mel turned on her heel and strode out, just as purposeful as she entered.

"On the rag? Seriously?" Connie asked. She sputtered and clapped a hand over her mouth.

"What?" Jade asked. "It's as good excuse as any."

"Yes, until Mel or Doreen goes to empty the corner box in our bathroom."

"Fudgetits," Jade spat. She blew her bangs out of her face in an aggrieved huff. "Jigger nuts, I didn't think of that."

"It's okay," Connie said. "I don't think she believed you anyway."

"That makes me feel better," Jade said through a scowl. She leaned back and addressed the ceiling. "Helen thinks I'm beating you and I just gave Mel another reason to think we're not actually together. Fucking hell, why don't I just go fuck up some more?"

"None of that matters," Connie said.

She abandoned her perch on the stool and curled up beside Jade on the sofa. At the sudden company, Jade hauled herself upright.

"The only thing that matters is we're in this together and we're going to put this situation right," Connie said. She tucked her feet beneath herself and snuggled under Jade's arm. Her head rested in the hollow under Jade's collarbone like it was designed for her. Hell, it probably was. Jade's entire body, heart, and soul fit with Connie's in a way that nothing ever had before. Jade closed her eyes and felt the tension bleeding from her muscles.

"Thanks baby girl," Jade said. She dropped a kiss to Connie's temple and murmured into her hair, "You know what would make me happy? You calling me honey-butt again."

Connie gasped out a laugh. "You liked that?"

"Sure did," Jade said.

"Okay honey-butt," Connie said in a challenging tone. "How about we finish our game? Your last turn was pretty good, but I'm still in the lead by about a hundred points. And I believe the loser has to give the winner a massage."

Jade hastily rearranged the cards in her hand and shot a grin across the table. "Don't get too comfortable, Connie. I'm just getting started. It's gonna be me under you tonight."

"You think so?" Connie arched a brow and pursed her lips. Jade had to focus on the array of cards spread out on the table to keep from throwing herself across it and into Connie's arms to claim those perfect rosebud lips.

"I know so," Jade said. She made a gun with her fingers and pointed it at Connie. "So let's play."

For the rest of the game, Jade struggled to keep X-rated images of Connie straddling her hips while her hands worked over Jade's back muscles from taking over the logic part of her brain. She didn't succeed very well and ended up making a series of mistakes that cost her the game, as well as her massage.

"Turd-wads," Jade muttered while Connie gleefully counted up her points. Jade put on a show of sulking, but Connie's sweet smile melted her small twinge of negativity. Jade leaned forward and swept the cards into a huge, unruly pile. "Okay, sweetheart, you're getting the massage of your life tonight."

Connie raised one eyebrow. Her reply was interrupted by the chime of the clock for dinnertime.

"You go ahead, I've got this under control," Jade said. "Loser's duty."

"Okay, thanks," Connie said. She jumped up and trotted over

to the door. Cleanup efforts suffered a short hiatus during Connie's walk. In the doorway, Connie paused and turned around, totally catching Jade checking her out. Connie smirked then shook her head when Jade answered with an elaborate shrug.

After Connie and her distracting curvy tush left, Jade got the cards into enough order to shove them back into their box.


OUTSIDE THE DINING room, Jade paused and took a breath. She shook out her hair and stuffed her clip into her pocket. The voices inside the room were jovial and bright. She could do this. Jade plastered a fake smile on her face and stepped through the doorway.

Jade's entrance was marked by a sudden drop in volume. She forced herself not to react to the calculating way Helen looked Jade up and down as she passed. Years of practice in the prison cafeteria came back and Jade put on her "I don't give a shit" look with ease. If only she could extinguish the rage. She wanted to grab Helen by the collar of her plaid flannel shirt and tell her exactly what she could do with her stupid superhero complex.

In the interest of not getting her ass kicked out of the resort, Jade's trip to her table was singularly uneventful.

"Have you been into town yet?" Garrett asked as Jade took her place next to Connie. He didn't wait for an answer before he plowed on, hands a-flutter. "Basil and I went around this afternoon, looking for some antiques to compliment our living room décor. And that man in the tourist information bureau! I thought places like that were supposed to be nice to visitors. At least I gave him a piece of my mind. Honestly, being a homophobe in this day and age?" He huffed and shook out his linen napkin.

Basil looked like he wanted to sink into the floor and disappear.

For a moment, Jade pictured the scene of Garrett inflicting himself on Percy. She pressed one knuckle to her upper lip and tapped Connie's shin with her foot.

"Yeah, we met Mr. Havarth," Jade said when she could keep a straight face. "A bit old-school if you ask me."

"*That's* for sure," Garrett said. Mel came over and placed an opened bottle of red wine on their table. Jade looked up, puzzled. Garrett beamed. "A little drinky-poo courtesy of *moi*. I thought we could all toast to a lovely rest of the week."

"Thanks, but I'll pass," Jade said. She didn't want to even pretend to drink that night. Her head needed to be as clear as possible for what was coming.

"Oh?" Garrett raised both brows. "And why would you be abstaining, hmm? Don't tell me you have some good news for all of us."

"What the fuck are you talking about?"

"So you're not, ahem, in the family way?"

"The fam—Jesus Christ, Garrett," Jade said. "As if I'd let some fuckhead guy jizz in me."

"There are other ways to achieve the same outcome," Garrett said and rolled his eyes. "You'll indulge, won't you Connie? You *are* of legal drinking age, aren't you?"

Jade's fingers reflexively curled around the handle of her knife.

"Jeez, Garrett. Let it go," Basil muttered.

"Just a friendly quip," Garrett said breezily.

"I'd love some. That's very kind of you," Connie said. She handed over her glass and accepted the gift with her usual effortless smile. Jade gritted her teeth and loosened the death-grip on her knife enough to snatch up her water glass to join halfheartedly in the toast.

Garrett said, "By the way, Basil and I have signed up for the flower arrangement and hula dance workshops tomorrow. Is it safe to assume we won't have a scheduling overlap?"

Jade was tempted to brave one or both, just to see the look on Garrett's face, but she decided to go with the option that had the least chance of permanently revoking Jade's butch card.

"We're cool," Jade said.

Garrett nodded and sashayed off to the buffet table with Basil following.

Once they were relatively alone, Jade relaxed. She stretched out her legs and looked over to Connie, who was sipping her wine, looking cute and amused. "Speaking about schedules, what are we doing tomorrow, babe?"

Connie absently licked a drop of wine from her lower lip and tilted her head in thought. Jade tried not to drool. *Fuck.* She swallowed hard and surreptitiously adjusted her jeans so the seam wasn't digging into her clit so hard.

Connie moved closer to Jade, almost snuggled up against her. She said softly, "Until we hear from Detective Young, there's not much we can do." Connie straightened up, pulled away and continued at normal volume, "How about I sign us up for a workshop or two tomorrow?"

"Sounds good," Jade said.

"I bet there's still space in the pole dancing class."

Jade nearly backwashed her gulp of water. "Anything but that. I'd even arrange flowers with Garrett."

Connie laughed out loud at that. Basil and Garrett returned with their plates. While Garrett looked askance at Connie's outburst, Basil gave her a smile and passed Connie a basket of rolls for them to share.

At the end of the meal, Connie scampered over to the activity table and Jade went back to their room. She brushed her teeth, then wandered out of the bathroom and stood still in front of the window, calming her mind. Even though the crime was over a decade ago, if an echo remained, it would hover untouched in its own little time loop. Jade grimaced. Two murders had actually taken place in that boathouse. Both perpetrated by the same man, the second victim being himself.

The sound of the door closing brought Jade back to the present. Connie crossed the room and softly wrapped her arms around Jade's waist. She rested her head on Jade's chest.

"I want to tell you not to go without me," Connie said in a small voice.

"It's gonna be okay," Jade said. She stroked a hand over Connie's hair.

"What if..." Connie trailed off. "What if he's still there? What if he's like Gord? If I'm not there it could be really bad for you. I mean he almost killed you."

"Sweetheart." Jade dropped her head to press a quick kiss on the top of Connie's head. Her body tensed as she dredged up the memory of being in Gord's room and being attacked by his vengeful spirit. "Rule one of ghosts is they have a fucking hard time physically affecting things. He didn't actually have his hands around my throat, he got into my head and fucked me up that way."

"So even if I wasn't there, you'd be okay?"

"If I couldn't shut him out and you didn't show up to save

my ass," Jade said, choosing her words carefully, "I would eventually black out, which would be an extremely shitty thing to happen. So you did save me and I was really lucky you were there."

"But not this time?"

"This one's different. It's not personal." Jade was silent for a moment before she said, "And I think I'm out of the age bracket for this guy. Don't worry, sweetheart. I got this."

"Oh." The one word held volumes. Connie drew away and looked up at Jade. She was calm and seemed reassured. "Thanks, Jade."

"For what?"

"For everything." Connie sparkled. She took one more step back. "All right, go out there and bust some ghosts. And then come right back and claim your massage."

"Aw shit, that's awesome, but I lost fair and square," Jade said.

"Don't worry, you can make it up to me somehow."

"You bet I will," Jade said. She flashed Connie her best rakish grin, then turned and headed out.

# Chapter Ten

THE NIGHT AIR was dark and biting. A silent chill hung over the grounds. Jade's warm breath came out in soft, puffy white streams. She shoved her hands into her pockets and turtled her chin into the raised collar of her jacket. Once she left the comforting light bleed from the resort, Jade felt the cold even more keenly. She shivered. More than the low temperature, she sensed something dark just beyond the scope of her vision. She left the footpath and waded into the pristine snow. Jade grimaced and made a mental note to avoid tracking half of the yard through the place the way she did the day before.

The moon lit the sprawling grounds well enough Jade didn't need the penlight she stashed in her pocket. The shadows were thick and looked hungry. Unconsciously, Jade stuck to the silver-glowing areas. The boathouse was huddled among scraggly pine trees, the sparse needles were rusty with disease. Jade paused outside the door. The hairs on the back of her neck prickled. She took a quick look over her shoulder. The pond was frozen over and hidden under drifts of snow. The posts of the dock stuck up under the thick blanket, with naked wood peering through here and there like the bones of some decaying animal. She shrugged off the nagging unease and turned her attention to the boathouse.

Unlike the resort, the small outbuilding was left unrenovated. Possibly due to budgetary restraints, or simply being lower on the priority list than the main house and "event space" barn. The building was shingled, but so many had fallen off that the black strips of weathered tarpaper outnumbered the ones that remained. Jade stood outside the door for a moment, just breathing and waiting.

She steeled herself and slowly pushed the door open. The inside was just as frigid as the outside, but the sudden absence of the small noises of dead trees rustling thickened the air. Moonlight streamed in through the windows, illuminating the aged walls. The bare boards were decorated with a few fragile pinup posters and a calendar showing a date some twenty years ago when time apparently stopped there. Lighter strips on the wall to Jade's right indicated at one time massive shelves had been there.

Jade took a few steps into the boathouse. Underneath her boots, the aged floorboards creaked and popped. The still air seemed even colder than outside. It was heavy with darkness. The shadows were viscous. Then she heard it. The sigh. The creak of rope and the soft burr as it rubbed against the wooden beam. Jade didn't turn around.

"You've been here all this time," she said.

The only answer was a low moan that choked off like a sob. Jade closed her eyes. She fought the rage that bubbled up from her gut. She didn't want to think about Teresa, the original victim. She'd been the same age as Britt and Connie, young women with their entire lives in front of them. Whether that meant a brilliant career that saved lives, a love that changed the world, or the start of a family line that rang with truth and acceptance, it didn't matter. What was to be never came to pass. It had been cut off brutally by a man who thought he knew better, who thought he had the right to judge and convict. Jade clenched her fists for a moment, then let go.

She turned around.

It wasn't an echo. It was him. Link Porter. The man hung from the rafter, his body gently swaying back and forth. His face was the bulged purple monstrosity of strangulation Jade had seen before. His eyes were just as goggly as she expected. His bloated tongue hung from his mouth. If he was corporeal, the next step would be his head rotting off his body, both pitching to the floor in a wet symphony of meat.

"It wasn't enough," he said. His voice was bubbly and raw, like he was breathing the words through a slushy mixture of vomit and phleghm.

"What wasn't?"

"Sixteen months. It wasn't enough. I took a life. I ended her. I deserved more punishment. I was wrong, I know that. Nothing I suffered could undo that. Nothing I did could make it right. I should have been there for my entire life. I didn't deserve freedom."

"Prison is hell," Jade said. She grit her teeth. She didn't want to say any more, but she couldn't help it. "It's a fucking broken system. It takes people and makes them into monsters."

"I was already a monster." The words were soft, mournful.

"Ease it off," Jade said. She blinked and shook her head. She wasn't supposed to feel like that. Like she had something in common with that homophobic piece of shit. But she did. "Link," Jade said and the head rose, the squashed-out eyeballs focused on her. "Pick up your hands and ease the noose off. You'll fall gently to the floor. Come over here and sit with me."

A wave of sadness hit her. Guilt and regret threatened to swallow her. Jade's knees buckled. She eased herself down onto a pile of tied-together planks. The aged wood was icy and wet under her butt. Everything Jade was afraid of became sharper. She wasn't good enough for Connie. Her issues and fucked-up life were too overwhelming for someone as sweet and caring as Connie. Jade would drag her down and drown her. Connie would have a life without her. She'd find someone better, more worthy, more stable and normal.

Jade pressed her palms into her eyes but she could still see him. Link reached up and spread the noose. He fell awkwardly to the ground and took a few steps in her direction. A spear of moonlight showed he was significantly recovered, almost normal in appearance, except he was mostly translucent.

"Why didn't they let me stay longer?" he asked. He held out his hands and looked at them, as if expecting blood to be still on them. "I did something horrible. I took a life. I should have suffered more. It should have ended when I gave my life in return, but it didn't. I'm stuck here. I can't leave."

"I know," Jade said. Her voice cracked. The despair that filled every crevice of the room pushed into her mind. It dragged at her, threatening to pull Jade down into a bottomless black sea. She had to break the downward spiral. She had to shock him out of it. Jade bit back the sadness the only way she could, with anger, of which she had an endless supply. Fuck him. Fuck Link Porter and his pathetic self-pity, his misery that stained the entire place.

She stood and was seized by an urge so strong she couldn't do anything but strip off her jacket. She glared Link right in the eyes as she ripped her flannel shirt open and whipped her undershirt and sports bra over her head. She stood, bare-breasted and proud in the sudden freezing air. Link averted his eyes, either because he was a gentleman or the sight was too gory for him to process. The remains of the numerous skin grafts covered her arm and spilled across her back, a stark reminder of the agony Jade endured.

"Look at me," she commanded. He raised his head. Jade said in a low, controlled voice, "Pain is not a currency. You can't use it to erase the past. It only fucks you up and fucks up your life. I've been through enough to know. You made the choice. You killed Teresa Kendall and you killed yourself. Two lives ended because of you. There is no going back from that."

"What can I do?" he asked.

"Go," Jade said. The burst of rage-energy kept the chill at bay. She wasn't even shivering. She stood with her hands on her hips, her shoulders thrown back. "Leave here. Don't come back."

"But I want to say I'm sorry. I am so sorry —"

"Sorry never won any wars," Jade spat.

"I am. Every day I wish I knew what happened next. How everything turned out."

"No," Jade said. "It ends here. You don't have the right to know. It's not your concern anymore. Leave this place."

He wavered. His form flickered. Jade focused her energy on him. Once more, she felt the pull of kinship. This time, she didn't allow herself to hate it.

"Don't be afraid of what lies beyond," Jade said gently. "Everyone goes to the same place; you're going home."

Something changed. The air or the stuff holding the fabric of the universe together sighed, let go for a moment, then recovered. Jade breathed again. A weight she didn't know she was carrying lifted off her shoulders. Jade let her head fall forward. She didn't often indulge in self-doubt. She didn't have any immunity to it. The emotions were raw and left Jade feeling vulnerable and extremely alone. She relaxed her bowstring-tight muscles. The subzero air burst over her skin. Jade bent down and grabbed her discarded clothes. She roughly pulled them on.

Her footsteps sounded very loud as she crossed the empty boathouse and closed the door behind herself.

Jade stood in the snow. An errant thought whispered to her, run away. You are flawed and broken, just like him. You'll harm everyone you love, drown them with your sorrows. Leave, don't look back.

A crushing feeling of loss grabbed Jade's chest. She couldn't breathe. A flicker of movement caught her eye and Jade nearly fell to her knees. The sadness broke. Jade kicked up an avalanche of snow in her dash to the path where the small figure stood, mittened hands clasped worriedly. Jade grabbed Connie in a fierce hug. Connie wrapped her arms around Jade's neck and nuzzled her the way she always did, the way that made Jade feel complete.

"I didn't want to intrude," Connie said. "But I couldn't just let you go out here alone. I hope that wasn't overstepping."

"Not at all. Sweetheart, God I needed to see you and there you were," Jade murmured. She freed a hand to swipe at her eyes.

"Tough case?"

"Yeah," Jade said. She released Connie, took a shaky breath, and looked up into the night sky. "He was there, Link Porter. He's gone now."

"Good," Connie said. She slipped her arm through Jade's and guided her back towards the brightly-lit mansion. She didn't ask for details, and Jade didn't give any.

They climbed the steps up to the front door. Jade didn't register the babble of cheerful voices and Christmas music until she was standing in the entrance hall.

"What the fuck's going on?" Jade asked.

Connie leaned into her, eyes bright. "Wow! It's a slumber party."

Jade gave the room a slow, disbelieving survey. Instead of the small army of overstuffed sofas and displays of information pamphlets, the entire lobby was a mass of small blanket-covered dwellings. Garrett could be seen in the entrance of one, clad in floral-print pajamas, directing Basil who had a bunch of what looked like sofa cushions under his arm.

"Absolutely not," Garrett said. "Those do not match our color scheme at all. Honestly! Just put those back where you got them." With a sigh and a toss of his head, he disappeared into the blanket fort.

Basil started back toward a gigantic pile of various cushions, pillows, cardboard boxes, and folded blankets. On his way, he passed Jade and Connie and stopped.

"Hi there. Want to join us?" He bumped up the cushions that hadn't passed Garrett's muster with one knee. "There's plenty of materials left for your very own fort. We're making s'mores later and I heard the movie pick is a double feature: *Mister Amaze-a-tron* and *Charlene's Angels*. What do you think? Up for a pajama party of the finest kind?"

Jade glanced at Connie, who aimed puppy-dog eyes back at her. The decision was made.

Jade kicked off her boots, got into her slippers, and held out her hands. "Pass those over, Basil. We're moving in next door."

He laughed. "How about I just keep them here for you? FYI, we have a dress code and you two are in violation."

Jade glanced around at the other people, who were all in various styles of fuzzy nightwear.

"I guess we are," Jade said. She backed up with a quick salute and, with Connie bounding along next to her, went upstairs to change.

"Thanks for doing this with me," Connie said. She glanced down, the sparkle left her eyes for a moment. "I was never allowed to stay overnight anywhere when I was a kid. My mother didn't like it when I had friends or did stuff she couldn't control."

Jade bit her lip. Connie rarely spoke about her family or home life, but when she did, it was always bleak.

"Now you can do anything you want," Jade said. She grinned and bumped Connie's shoulder with hers. "Even stay up late and have a slumber party with blanket forts."

Connie's smile lit Jade's world.

They quickly descended to the lobby where Jade staked out the area for their blanket fort while Connie and Basil ferried building materials back and forth. The fort was constructed forthwith and Garrett sent Basil over with a housewarming present of a bottle of wine from the ample stock at the open bar Mel was overseeing. Jade opted for hot chocolate and let Mel indulge her with a handful of mini-marshmallows on top. They gathered for a toast on a braided rug between their two forts that Garrett declared was "the neutral zone."

"So, ladies." Garrett slung himself down on his side and propped his head up on one hand. "Know any good ghost stories?"

Jade met Connie's gaze for a telling moment before she turned back to Garrett and said, "Nope. I hate that spooky shit. How about a dirty-joke telling contest? Guys versus gals, the most perverted wins."

Garrett rolled his eyes, but Basil held out his fist for a bump. "Challenge accepted. Bring out your worst, Mayflower."

# Chapter Eleven

"FUCK ME, THIS is no fun," Jade groaned into her pillow. Lemony sunlight filtered in through the gaps in their blanket walls. Sleeping on the floor seemed like a good idea the previous night, but that morning her back assured her it actually wasn't. Next to her, Connie rolled over and sat up. She stretched with an ease and elegance that Jade would have envied if the view wasn't so appealing.

"Sleep well?" Connie asked.

"Yeah. Pretty well," Jade said. She rolled over and couldn't hide the wince in time.

"No you didn't," Connie said. She crawled over the rumpled mounds of bedding and plopped down next to Jade. "Are you okay? I should have gotten more padding on the floor."

"Nah, I'm cool," Jade said. "As long as that offer of a massage still stands."

"Definitely," Connie replied with a decidedly unchaste gleam in her eyes.

"What are you thinking, baby girl?" Jade murmured. She reached out and twined her fingers with Connie's. Connie's thumb lazily caressed Jade's hand up to the sensitive hollow of her wrist.

"Just that he's gone," Connie said. "Link Porter. The rest of this retreat belongs to us."

Jade's lips pulled into a smirk. Her heart thudded and a tingle of arousal bloomed at Connie's tone. Besides the lingering self-doubt, which was her own damn problem, the encounter with Link the previous night was fairly standard.

Jade said, "For what I was expecting, it was almost too easy. He didn't fight me or anything, he just went when I told him to go."

Jade's intuiton prickled. She pressed her free hand to her lips.

"What is it?" Connie asked.

"It really was too easy," Jade said. She turned her thoughts inward. "He wasn't angry, just sad. Really remorseful. Maybe..." Jade trailed off. She shook her head. "No, I mean I got him. There can't be two ghosts haunting the same place, can there?"

Connie sat back on her heels. "If there's anything I've learned since being with you, it's that anything is possible. How about we wait and see before declaring our mission officially over?"

"Good idea," Jade said.

The sounds of fellow wakers rustled around them. Jade peered out of the makeshift doorway. In front of his own fort, Basil straightened up with a groan and a hand on the small of his back. Jade winced in sympathy.

After cleanup and a hot shower, a revitalized Jade took her place at the breakfast table.

"How are we feeling this morning?" Garret asked Jade over the rim of his latte. "None the worse for wear after your wild night out?"

"Not bad," Jade mumbled. She made a face and put down her fork. "I certainly feel better than these eggs taste, but I'm a bit spoiled for breakfast."

Under the table, Connie's thigh pressed against hers. Jade tried to keep her expression nonchalant, but it felt like a hundred canaries woke up in her boxer briefs.

"Of course you are," Garrett said snidely. "I, for one, am glad I decided to retire halfway into your filthy joke contest and return to my room, where I assure you, I spent a most restful night." He glanced over to where Basil was demolishing a stack of French toast. "Not having to deal with a snorting warthog may have had something to do with it."

"It's not that bad since I got that nose thingy," Basil said. He looked crestfallen for a moment, then rallied. "At least I didn't have to fight for the blanket or put up with someone's cold feet on me."

"Thanks for airing our private information," Garrett shot back. "I am tired of you and tired of pretending this whole resort isn't some sort of scam. I'm packing my things and I'm going home."

He stood and threw down his napkin before he whirled and stalked out of the room, still managing to keep his slippers from flapping about madly. The other residents of the tables watched the spectacle. Jade was glad for once it wasn't her causing the scene, even though she was still in the middle of it. Uneasily, she looked over to Basil.

"You okay, bro?" Jade asked.

"Yeah," he replied with an apologetic shrug. "I'll let him stew for a bit then go up and talk to him. Don't worry, things are cool. Or they're going to be. Sorry about the fuss."

Connie piped up before Jade could. "So he's not going to leave?"

"No, he likes a bit of drama from time to time."

Jade raised her eyebrows and went back to her breakfast. "That certainly was dramatic."

True to his word, a few minutes later, Basil collected his and Garrett's dishes on a tray and excused himself from the table.

Jade and Connie did too, and soon Jade was facedown on the floor of their room with Connie industriously working her shoulder muscles. She dug her thumbs under Jade's shoulder blades. A shock of pain lanced through her.

"Aw bullocks felcher," Jade gritted. She buried her face in her arms.

Immediately Connie stopped. "Did I hurt you? I'm sorry, it's just you're so tight."

Jade cracked a leer at that. Quickly, she coaxed her face into a more suitable expression. "It's okay," Jade said. "It feels good. You're hitting me right where I need it."

"Okay," Connie said, and continued the massage.

"By the way," Jade said. "What are we doing today? I forgot to ask last night."

"Well, *you're* doing a holiday extravaganza workshop in the arts and crafts room."

"Me?" Jade closed her eyes as another knot in her back loosened under Connie's talented fingers. She bit back the groan of satisfaction. For once, Connie's hands on her made her more relaxed than horny. Jade asked, "What are you doing, babe?"

"I, um, signed up for a private lesson." Connie's tone was just a bit too casual, the stutter of shyness colored the words. Jade's curiousity was piqued.

"Really," Jade drawled. She was on the verge of asking for more information, but decided that if Connie wanted her to know, she would tell her. Jade relaxed into her crossed forearms and let out a long breath. "Okay, I think I'm all recovered from sleeping on the floor. Thanks, babe. You have magic in your hands."

The weight of Connie's body left Jade's back and she felt cold and alone without it.

"I'm glad I could help," Connie said.

Jade rolled over and looked up. Connie's cheeks were pink and she nervously checked the time on her phone.

"Um, I have to go," Connie said. "Are you sure you're okay?"

"I'm good," Jade said. To prove that, she hauled herself to her feet and gave a stretch. Her shoulder popped, but everything else was in order. She leveled Connie with an affectionate look. "Go kick ass at your lesson. I'll do the same." Jade held out a fist and received a prompt bump from Connie.

"I'm getting lunch there, so I'll see you later on this afternoon," Connie said. She turned to leave, then whirled back around. "I nearly forgot, we have an appointment at the Yule-Timey Photo Booth at one-thirty. I'll be back in time."

"Cool. I'll be there," Jade said. On impulse, she leaned forward and kissed Connie briefly on the cheek. She whispered, "Love you, baby girl."

Connie immediately flushed bright pink and looked most pleased. She nodded and left the room, which didn't seem to take offense at the small display of female affection. Jade checked herself in the mirror. She tucked her plaid flannel shirt into her jeans, then hauled it back out. She was still pretty clueless about dyke fashion, but she had to admit she rocked a plaid flannel shirt. Jade dug a plastic clip out of her bag and twisted her hair up. If she was going to be doing extravaganza worthy things, she needed to be ready.

The Arts and Crafts Room was on the first floor, off the lobby. Even though her chest was tight and her palms were damp, Jade walked in like a boss and swaggered up to the long table that was filled with leaves and covered bowls. Two couples were already there, Helen and Lisa were one of them. Jade had never felt so judged in her life as the row of sixty-something lesbians raked her from head to toe.

As if she didn't give a single shit, Jade pulled out a chair and draped herself over it. Instead of asking the other people in the room what their fucking problem was, she looked at the supplies on the table and tried to figure out what the hell they were supposed to be making. Jade was pretty good in the wood shop and kitchen from her twenty years on the inside, but crafty stuff was never really on her radar. Before Jade figured anything out, Doreen came into the room. She had an apron on over her clothing, with scissors and stuff sticking out of the front pocket, and looked very handy. Jade shifted uneasily in her chair. What had Connie signed her up for?

"Good morning ladies," Doreen said in a businesslike voice.

"Morning ma'am," Jade replied automatically. She bristled as everyone glanced at her, but kept her eyes front.

Doreen said, "Welcome to a special one-time-only workshop. As you know, this is a holiday extravaganza, and to that end, I've prepared a number of festive materials. Feel free to make anything you like. She indicated a well-laden end table. "Over here are the glue guns and gloves. If you need assistance, don't hesitate to give me a shout. All right, have at it!"

After mulling things for a while and checking out what everyone else was doing, Jade settled on making a kind of wreath-thing out of sticks and bits of ribbon.

For some reason, Helen kept glancing at her and smirking.

The twig in Jade's hand snapped.

"What?" Jade asked.

"I saw the private lesson Connie signed up for," she said. "Lucky you."

Jade shrugged and returned her attention to trying to get the wreath to stay in a somewhat round shape. She wasn't interested in hearing what Helen had to say, particularly if it was about Connie.

"She didn't tell you what it was, did she?"

"Nope. That's her business, so don't spill it, I'm not listening," Jade said. The ribbon she was using to tie together a bunch of sticks slipped open and the entire thing fell into a pile. "Jackoff cockwhore," Jade muttered. She blew her bangs back and slouched in her chair for a minute until her frustration eased. Jade rolled her sleeves up for a second try, damned if a bunch of sticks could get the best of her.

A glue gun and a bunch of zipties later, the wreath looked passable, if not exactly festive. Jade found a tube of glitter and liberally coated the less-than-aesthetically pleasing bits with rainbow sparkles. Jade hummed tunelessly as she worked. A shadow fell over her workspace.

"That's shaping up nicely," Doreen said. She passed over a box of silver bells. "These might make a good accent."

"Thanks," Jade said. "I think I'm getting the hang of this crafty bullshit—uh, stuff."

Doreen just chuckled and moved on to help Lisa secure the lid of the snowglobe she was working on.

"So you served?" Helen's sudden question startled Jade. The bell she was trying to secure to the wreath with a length of wire fell from her fingers to the floor.

For a moment, Jade held herself still. She didn't want to lie. If Helen was asking the question it meant she'd figured Jade out already. Hell, she was old enough to remember Jade's original trial. Not that many out lesbians had massively public murder trials, and as a lesbian herself, it was more than possible Helen followed Jade's dive into infamy. Whether she was Jade or Janebeth didn't matter. Someone who knew her case would be able to figure it out.

"Yeah, I did," Jade said. She scooped up the fallen bell and focused on threading the wire through it. "Twenty damn years."

"May I ask which branch? I have a brother in the Navy."

Jade stopped messing around with the bell and stared at Helen for an instant before she dropped her eyes to the table in front of herself. Fuck. Jade tried to keep her tone as light as possible. "Oh you meant in the military." Jade faked a laugh. "Then, no."

Dead silence met her answer.

"Don't worry," Jade said. "I'm not going to pull a shiv on anyone. And I don't give a fuck if you drop the soap or not. For the record, yes, I have a counselor and I would rather spend the rest of my life rotting away back in that cell than hurt Connie in any way."

"Glad to hear that," Helen said. Jade didn't miss how she edged her chair away.

As if a few centimeters of distance would really make a difference. If Jade wanted to put some damage on Helen, not even an entire cafeteria of distance would be enough. It was all in timing and opportunity. Never in front of the guards. Strike fast and hard, then get the fuck out of there. Primal reflexes snapped into place. Blood pounded in Jade's ears. Her vision narrowed. The metallic tinkle of the bell falling from her fingers yet again brought Jade back. She consciously lowered her shoulders and took a few deep breaths.

Doreen fixed Jade with a long, calculating look. Jade fought the wave of despair. If Doreen thought she was a couple sandwiches short of a picnic before, Jade just proved it without a doubt.

Even though Jade wanted to stuff her half-decorated wreath into the nearest trashcan and walk out, she didn't. She fought with it until twelve o'clock loomed and Jade excused herself with a feeling of great relief. She swiped a packed lunch from the inviting display in the dining room and took it up to their room.

Jade eased herself down onto the bed and set the wrapped pack of sandwiches and bottled water on the bedside table. She held herself still, listening for something outside the audible, for some kind of subliminal hint of a presence beyond sight. Nothing. The only thing Jade registered was her own breathing, the ever-so-slight rattle of the old glass in the window from the wind outside. The fact that nothing was there now didn't mean much. Jade gave up and sprawled out, propped up against the pillows. She stretched back and laced her fingers together behind her head. On her own, Jade didn't have any options to call up the homophobic whatever-it-was. Even with Connie there, she still wouldn't. Jade would be damned if she purposely tempted the hate-spewing *thing* back. The one time it invaded her mind was more than enough and Jade wanted to keep Connie off its radar as much as possible.

Lunch and a book occupied Jade until the appointment Connie set up loomed. The Yule-Timey Photo Booth was stationed in a curtained off corner of the lobby, so Jade didn't have far to go. She tromped down the stairs and entered the lobby with a mixture of curiosity and nerves. Connie was nowhere in sight. Jade shrugged and went to the booth.

"I'm here for the one-thirty appointment," Jade said to the slim fellow in stylish jeans and chunky-knit sweater who turned from his laptop. A spill of photographic equipment was next to him on a tall trolley.

"Let me guess, you're Jade," he crooned and held a hand out as if expecting a kiss on his knuckles. Awkwardly, Jade shook it. "I'm Reginald. Pleased to meet you, I'll be your personal photographer today. Feel free to avail yourself of any and all props for a photo session fit for the season. We can get underway as soon as your adorable girlfriend gets here."

"Sure thing," Jade said. "So tell me about the options."

"We have a few paid packages which will include both digital and prints, or I can do you for free on your smartphone. The choice is up to you."

"You'll do me, huh?" Jade snickered and Reginald smirked back. Trust Mel and Doreen to find the gayest photographer in the province. She liked him already. "I'll see what Connie has to say, but I'm not opposed to splurging on some pics."

"Wonderful," he said.

The booth featured a printed backdrop of a snowy meadow, a decorated fake Christmas tree, and a wooden bench that looked swiped from a vintage movie set.

Jade went over to the prop box and rummaged through it. She found a fun woolen cap with felt reindeer horns on it and tried it on. She was debating between two different scarves when Connie pattered into the booth. Her cheeks were pink and her hair was tousled.

"Sorry I'm late," Connie said. She was breathless as if she'd sprinted from wherever she was. She had her slippers in her hand, but quickly dropped them and put them on.

"Don't sweat it, babe," Jade said. She pointed to the hat. "What do you think, is it me?"

"Very," Connie said. "Okay, how about me?" She picked up a white knit toque with panda ears and stuck it on her head, then whirled a holly print scarf around her neck. Connie dove into the prop bin one more time and came up with a pair of fur-trimmed red panties. With a mischievous grin, Connie posed with them and Jade swallowed the rush of desire.

"How about these?" Connie asked.

"Fuck me," Jade murmured under her breath. How could one person be so cute and so sexy at the same time? She gazed at Connie, unable to stop the image of Connie sprawled out on a blanket in front of a roaring fireplace, wearing nothing more than that silky bit of lingerie. She could picture exactly how the firelight would play over the soft curves of her breasts and belly, leaving the sweet little triangle between her legs in shadow. Jade's inner muscles clenched and she surreptitiously squeezed her thighs together.

Connie crinkled her nose and tossed the panties back. She leaned over and whispered in Jade's ear, "If I ever wear something like that, I don't want anyone to see except you."

Jade could only reply with a strangled whimper.

"Are we ready to start?" Reginald popped up in front of them, startling Jade out of her brain-stall.

"Yeah, let's get this show on the road," Jade said. She shoved her hair back over her shoulders and fanned herself with one hand. "Can we do this outside? It's a bit hot in here."

Reginald just regarded her with a raised eyebrow. He produced a list of various photo packages. Initially, Connie balked at the price, but Jade insisted and they agreed on one of the more generous packages that featured both indoor and outdoor shots, which Reginald promised them would kick Christmas in the ass and make it their bitch.

Reginald started them off on the bench, sitting back-to-back with colorful buckets of candy canes in their hands.

"Oh yes, give me Christmas, warm and fuzzy, ooh like that," Reginald coached them. He jumped around, snapping pictures. He really got into it and Jade had to swallow laughter a few times at his enthusiastic stage directions. At one point he was lying on the floor with Jade and Connie holding heavily decorated pine branches between them. While Jade wasn't all that fussy about getting her picture taken, Connie glowed with excitement. After three separate outfit changes and numerous props, Reginald ushered them outside, draped in woolen scarves. They found a nice spot behind the resort, just off the path where the snow was still pristine and sheltered in a small crescent of pine trees.

Until then, the mood of the shoot had been festive and fun. Once they were outside, away from the somewhat oppressive fragrance of candles and potpourri, in soft silence, Jade felt the scene was at once more introspective and intimate. The wind rustled through the branches, dislodging a dusting of snow in a sparkling curtain. Connie turned away to look with an entranced expression on her face. Jade's vision was filled only with Connie.

Without thinking, Jade stepped into the snow and enfolded Connie in her arms from behind. She lowered her head into the crook of Connie's neck and breathed in her scent. Her chest got hot where Connie pressed against her.

"Oh my, now that's more like it," Reginald exclaimed. "Get

cozy, gals."

Shit. She forgot about Reginald in the moment. Jade nearly let Connie go, but decided to go with it. She very gently spread her hands over Connie's midriff and held her close.

"Are you okay with getting cozy?" Jade asked softly.

In response, Connie closed her eyes and lifted her chin. Awareness of everything else vanished. Jade's entire world was the young woman in her arms. Jade couldn't hide her slow, lascivious smile when she nuzzled her face up to Connie's short golden curls. She pressed a kiss just behind the perfect pink shell of one ear and was rewarded by a little gasp and chuckle from Connie. Jade didn't even register the sound of the camera. She was focused completely on how soft and warm Connie's skin was under her lips, the silken strands of hair against her cheek. Jade drew her hands apart and rested them on Connie's hips.

Her knees nearly gave out when Connie rocked her hips back, pressing her firm ass hard into Jade.

"Is this okay?" Connie asked in a bare whisper.

"Fuck, yeah. God, keep doing that," Jade said with a groan. There was nothing she could do about how wet she got from that small pressure. She spread her legs slightly and gently guided Connie against her. She hoped Reginald was taking above-the-belt shots and no video.

After a couple more love-bumps that had Jade moaning out loud, Connie turned and faced Jade. She draped her arms over Jade's shoulders and looked up at her. Their breaths steamed into the small space between them. Jade's came faster with the intimate contact. She felt like she could drown in Connie's eyes. How had Jade ever doubted she was enough for Connie? The way Connie gazed at her like Jade was her entire world couldn't be faked. Jade gulped with the realization that she held Connie's heart in her hands. Which was fine with Jade, Connie held hers just as surely.

Connie's lips were parted slightly, the softly pink cupid's bow was sweet and inviting. Jade ached to claim her mouth, her entire body burned with the need to taste Connie. She tried to calm her rasping breaths and took Connie around the waist, guiding their bodies to rest snugly against each other. Jade caught her lower lip between her teeth, desire clouding her vision. She didn't care who was watching, she was going to kiss Connie right then and there.

Jade's phone chose to start buzzing just at that moment,

vibrating against her thigh, pressed between their bodies. A jolt ripped through Jade's crotch.

"Jesus," Jade said through gritted teeth. "Fucking Young nearly gave me an orgasm. That man has really shitty timing."

Connie clapped her hand over her mouth.

The mood was broken. Jade sighed heavily, took a step back and yanked out her phone. "Talk to me, Young."

"I guess that's a wrap," Reginald said. He threw his hands into the air at Jade's semi-apologetic look. He got down on one knee and started packing up his camera and various lenses with huffy sighs.

Jade tuned him out and focused on the phone. She locked eyes with Connie and listened intently as Young spoke.

"I dug around a bit more and nothing except the Teresa Kendall case stands out so I tried to get more info on that. The papers weren't really any help, looks like the vic's parents hushed things up. Didn't give any statements or anything."

"Huh, wonder why," Jade said.

"I got a clue from the police records. The vic was with a, ahem, friend. Rachel Evans, now she goes by McNeil."

"Married?"

"Yep. Wife's Laura NcNeil. Folks weren't so open-minded when the incident happened."

Jade sucked in a breath at the same time as Connie. Jade said, "Do you have a current address for this Rachel person? I'm thinking we need to pay her a visit." Jade glanced at her watch, mentally calculating how much daylight they had left.

"I thought you would. I'll send it to you along with the rest of the info I got. It's not much. Your best bet is Miz McNeil." Young paused and Jade heard him drink something, probably a cup of the ubiquitous station coffee. Jade grimaced in sympathy. Young said, "I took the liberty of giving her a call to see if she was around. They're at her wife's folks' place in Winfield today, but they'll be back tomorrow afternoon or evening. How 'bout I send you both addresses?"

"That'd be great, thanks big guy," Jade said.

"Okay then, look out for my text. Later."

"Merry Christmas," Connie added.

"Right back atcha." Jade could hear the smile in Young's voice.

Jade stashed her phone. She took Connie's mittened hand in both of hers and lightly buffed it. "Are you cold?"

"Not at all," Connie replied. She gave Jade a long look through her lashes that had Jade's pulse jumping again. "Actually, I'm pretty hot right now."

Jade glanced around. Reginald and his equipment were long gone, the yard was empty. Jade dropped Connie's hand and cupped her face. Connie closed her eyes and rose up onto her toes to meet Jade in a brief, sweet kiss.

Hand in hand, they meandered back to the resort. Jade's phone buzzed to announce Young's text message. She dug it out one-handed, not wanting to let go of Connie. Winfield was in New Brunswick, a good five hours drive away, but the home address he gave was actually closer to South Aisling than Traynor's Port. They could get there in about an hour. Jade checked her watch. She wondered if a total of ten hours on the road would be worth getting the info a day early. Beside her, Connie held herself still.

"When do you think we should go?" Connie asked.

The wistful tone in her voice tipped the balance. "Tomorrow," Jade said.

Connie gave a little skip. She swung their clasped hands. "Okay," Connie said.

"Why, sweetie?" Jade asked. "What's going on tonight?"

Connie's dimple deepened with her smile. "They're having a hot cocoa making contest. We probably won't win, but I want to at least try. Aunt Addie taught me her secret recipe before we left and Benny gave me some advice about how to tweak it. Your steady hand is going to be the deciding factor."

Jade laughed into the freezing air. She held the front door open for Connie. After they changed into their slippers, they returned the borrowed scarves and hats to Reginald's prop box.

He looked up from the tablet he was tapping away at. "Excellent mood back there. You two were my favorite couple to photograph so far. Fun, lots of sexual tension, plus no bickering."

"Life's too short for bickering," Jade said.

Reginald hooted and said, "You got that right. Anyway, I'll send you the digital copies after I've had a chance to pick the best and pretty them up a bit. Not that two fabulous gals like you need much cleaning up at all. The prints will take a bit longer, but I'll have them to you by early January at the latest."

"Great," Jade said.

# Chapter Twelve

JADE LOADED UP her toothbrush with toothpaste and stuck it in her mouth. Beside her, Connie held out her own brush for a dollop.

Through a mound of bubbles, Jade said, "Fucking hell, who the fuck puts brandy in hot chocolate? Nearly hurled it all back up."

Connie sputtered in laughter. She leaned over to spit and rinse her mouth. "You did a good job of not hurling then. Mel was convinced you liked hers best. Your face when she tried to get you a second cup was priceless."

"It was like drinking gasoline mixed with asswater."

"I thought it was good, actually."

Jade muttered to herself while Connie washed her face and patted on some kind of girly liquid face-stuff. Even though she was still smarting from inadvertently swallowing a cup of nasty, Jade softened. She could never stay pissed off around Connie. She didn't want to. Jade grinned through her mouthful of toothpaste. Connie moved back and Jade took her turn at the sink. She straightened up with a pleased smirk.

"Yeah, well at least Mel had the decency to lose to us," Jade said. She preened and flaunted the first place ribbon pinned to her pajama top.

"Tell me you're not going to wear that to bed," Connie said.

"I dunno," Jade said. She studied her reflection. "I kinda like it. Maybe I'll just wear it for the rest of our stay, you know, to prove once and for all that Mason and Mayflower are an ass-kicking team."

They ended up sitting across from each other on the bed with the contents of the envelope containing the latest mystery question from Mel spread out in front of them. It was more elaborate then the previous ones, consisting of two sets of plastic cards showing red, yellow, and green traffic lights and a printed sheet of instructions.

Jade picked up the instructions and cleared her throat. "Says here we've got to think up as many sexy acts as we can and judge them. Green means you're open to the idea, but it's not necessarily a binding promise that you have to do it. Yellow means okay, but not right now, and red means it isn't something you're comfortable with at present, blah blah, no pressure or judgement, open and honest, uh huh, check in from time to time, nothing set in stone." Jade finished and looked across at Connie with raised eyebrows. "Seems pretty straightforward. How about I start?"

Connie nodded and collected her cards. She was in a silky nightie and Jade had to fight to keep from drooling over the sneaky peeks of cleavage the lacy front gave her from time to time.

Jade pondered her first suggestion for a moment. "I know you're okay with role-play, but how about dial it up a notch with props and costumes and stuff like that?"

Connie perked up with a happy little wiggle. As one, they put down a card each. Jade lifted her hand to reveal a green card, and so did Connie. Jade couldn't help the thrill that raced through her.

"I've always thought you'd make a pretty cool cowgirl, you know with chaps," Connie said. She caught her lower lip between her teeth, then said, "Our afternoon at the motel was really fun, too. I like the idea of going different places and that kind of thing."

"Agreed," Jade said.

"Want to hear my latest role-play fantasy?" Connie asked.

"The latest?" Jade asked with a raise of her brow. "So that means you have more than one?"

"Maybe," Connie said. Her lips quirked up. "In this one, you're a professional sports player of some kind, I haven't really decided which, and I'm the team physiotherapist."

"Good start. Tell me more."

Connie settled into the pile of pillows at her back and clasped her hands on one knee. She looked up at Jade through her lashes. "I got the idea from the massage workshop. I involves you with a strategically placed towel, and me with oil and a naughty wandering hand. And that's all I'm going to say about it."

"Aww," Jade said.

Connie gave Jade a wickedly naughty look. "For now."

Jade grinned. Her mind generated a few scandalous scenarios

inspired by Connie's words. She reached out and poked Connie on the knee. "Your turn to think of something."

Connie threw out the idea of phone sex and sexting, the last was a hard no from Jade and Connie agreed, to Jade's relief. Her introduction to the world of sexting was not a pleasant one. To lighten the mood, Jade suggested they join the budget "mile-high club" which would take place in an elevator and got shot down, similarly to the suggestion of eating sushi off each other, although both of them were okay with the idea of temperature play, which sent Jade's mind off on another little vacation.

At her turn, Connie chewed her lip, then shyly suggested sixty-nine, which earned a green light and a "hell yeah" from Jade and a yellow from Connie, which Jade took in stride.

"I don't really know how it would all line up," Connie admitted.

Jade shrugged. "I don't either, but it's no biggie if we don't." She shuffled her three cards and said, "Okay, kind of a long shot, but how about a threesome?"

"With a guy?" Connie wrinkled her nose and threw out her red card.

"Yeah, that's a no fucking way for me too." Jade paused and asked, "How about with a girl?"

Connie put out a green card, surprising Jade who had her yellow card in her hand.

"Really?" Jade said. She was impressed.

"Yeah," Connie said. She shifted and drew her legs underneath herself, curling up against the pillows. "I've never really been one to get jealous. I don't think I could do it as a permanent thing, but when I'm with you I don't get to see what's going on. I'd really like to watch from time to time."

"Baby girl, there are entire sections of the Internet devoted to exactly that."

"I know, but I can't get into it," Connie said. "I always think about the person stuck filming it and if there's, like a director or someone with cue cards off-camera. I wonder if they had a meeting beforehand and what kind of stuff they'd discuss like the order of panty-removal and who gets on top first."

"Fair enough," Jade said. She swallowed her grin of affectionate amusement.

"Besides," Connie said in a soft but intense tone, "I don't

want to watch people I don't know. I want to see you. I want to see how hot you are when you're making love."

Connie leaned forward as she spoke. Her nightie fell open and gave Jade quite an eyeful. The combination of adorable and sensual nearly undid Jade. Connie looked directly into Jade's eyes, which sent an inadvertent spark of arousal straight to Jade's snatch. Jade swallowed hard and shifted her weight. Unfortunately, the movement pressed the crotch of her pajama pants against her clit, which didn't help matters at all. The idea of Connie watching Jade getting off by another woman, getting hot herself, maybe echoing their movements and trailing her fingers down to tease herself brought a second rush of heat to Jade's body. She felt like she was one second away from needing Connie to use one of her fire extinguishers on her.

Jade pulled at her collar and fanned herself with her green light card. She had to cool down before things got out of hand. Jade glanced at the window and pondered the feasibility of tossing herself into the thick snow banks below. Maybe she could scoop some snow off the window ledge and stuff a few handfuls down her pants.

"You go next," Jade said in a strangled voice.

Connie's face in thought made Jade ache to reach out and cradle her cheeks, pepper little kisses over her throat, and bury her face in the perfect, creamy valley between her breasts. Jade wrenched her dirty mind away from where it wanted to go.

"I don't know, um, how about getting it on in a Jacuzzi or a pool?"

Jade tilted her head in thought, then threw out a green card. "Sure. I think you'd be the sexiest thing alive in a bikini. Until I take it off, that is." Jade waggled her brows with an exaggerated leer.

Connie laughed and threw a pillow at Jade, who caught it and stuffed it into her lap. "Green light for me too. Just not the ocean. Too much fish poop and sand. I don't want to get any sand up my gears."

"Ugh, no." Jade grimaced. She tapped her fingers on the bedcover, thinking carefully about how to bring up her next idea. She decided to just go for it. "How about a strap-on?"

Connie flinched as if Jade had raised a hand to slap her. She shook her head and hugged her knees to her chest.

"No, sweetheart, not like that," Jade hastened to say. "You would use it. On me."

Connie's head came up. Her lips parted in silent wonder.

"What?" Jade said. She spread her hands and shrugged. "We're going for open and honest here, so yeah, the thought has crossed my mind a few times. More than a few, actually. But if it's a red card for you, no problem."

Connie's hand drifted to her array of cards. Slowly, she pushed the yellow one toward Jade, who had to restrain herself from jumping up and pumping her fist. The tension between her legs throbbed harder than before.

"How about we call it a night?" Jade said. She shifted her weight and bit back a groan. "If I get any hotter in the pants, I'm gonna spontaneously cum in my shorts."

Before Jade even finished speaking, Connie rose up to her knees and crawled over to straddle Jade's legs. She grabbed the pillow and tossed it aside. Jade hadn't expected that, or the sudden predatory look on Connie's face, and didn't respond in time to stop Connie from pushing her down and pinning her to the bed.

"Do it," Connie growled in Jade's ear. She grabbed Jade's wrists and held her down. Her grip was painfully strong. A flash of panic jolted Jade into action.

"Connie," Jade said. Her voice shook. "Baby, please stop."

She didn't. Connie lunged and tried to capture Jade's mouth. At the last second, Jade turned away. Her heart seized up. Jade wrenched her hands free. She took Connie by the shoulders and tried to ease her off. Connie fought her, pressing Jade back into the mattress with her entire weight. All thoughts of arousal vanished. Jade's breath quickened in alarm. She got one hand on Connie's chin and pushed her up, but it wasn't enough to get free. The face that looked down at her twisted. For an instant, Jade looked into a stranger's eyes. Jade snapped, "Get off me!"

The spell broke. Connie sat up suddenly and looked around. She scrambled off Jade.

"I'm sorry," she said. Her eyes welled with tears. "I don't know what happened. Oh my God, Jade. I didn't mean to do that. I just couldn't stop myself."

"Hey, it's okay, sweetie," Jade said. She gathered Connie up in her arms. Both of them were trembling. Jade pressed a kiss into

Connie's hair. "Things got a bit overheated, you're okay and I'm okay too."

But she wasn't. Jade lay awake for a long time before the panic faded and she was able to sleep.

SUDDEN COLD AND a sense of loss woke Jade up. She rolled over to find the bed empty. Outside, it was still dark. Jade picked up her phone and saw it was a little past four in the morning. She groaned and burrowed back down into the blankets. After a moment, Jade opened her eyes and sat up. The room was too quiet. Jade threw back the comforter and stood. She didn't bother to find her slippers before she launched herself across the room. A quick peek into the unlit bathroom confirmed it was empty.

Jade's pulse pounded in her ears. Her breaths seemed very loud in the still, dark resort. She padded the length of the hallway, but heard nothing. More uneasy with every passing minute, Jade headed to the lobby. She stopped halfway down the stairs and listened intently. The faintest sound came to her, rough scraping.

"Ass-reaming jizzrockets," Jade breathed. She raced down the remaining stairs and burst into the lobby. A small, dark figure huddled in one corner. It raised a hand and Jade caught the flash of a blade in the moonlight. Jade edged closer until she could make out the word taking form under the blade.

```
unnatural sickness
kill the freak—
```

The figure turned and Jade took a step back in shock. It was Connie.

"Sweetheart, what are—"

Jade didn't get to finish. Connie turned and moved with inhuman speed and strength. Her fingers, white with plaster dust, were curled into claws and aimed for Jade's throat. Automatically, Jade caught her by the wrists and held the scissors Connie had clutched in one hand away from herself. Connie let out a vicious shriek and twisted wildly in Jade's grip. She bared her teeth in a snarl Jade never imagined she would see on Connie's sweet face. The expression sliced into her soul. Whoever was controlling her, it wasn't Connie.

The young woman kicked out and flailed. The scissors came dangerously close to Jade's jugular and her survival instinct took over. She arm-barred her assailant across the throat and slammed her back into the wall. Jade lowered her head to avoid looking at the thing that had taken over Connie. She pounded the hand holding the scissors on the wall until they slipped free and clanged onto the floor. Shrill cries pierced the night, but Jade held on. Bile rose in Jade's throat and tears filled her eyes. She stood strong against the flailing arms and feet.

The lights flicked on and Connie went limp. Jade lunged and managed to catch the unconscious girl in her arms. She staggered back and they both landed on the floor in a pile.

"What's going on here?" Mel asked. She and Doreen hurried across the lobby in their housecoats. Mel had a golf club in one hand. They both stopped and stared at the damaged wall.

Mel dropped the golf club and Doreen pressed both hands to her mouth.

In Jade's arms, Connie stirred. Her body went rigid and she looked around in fear.

"You're all right," Jade said. She smoothed tousled blonde curls away from Connie's face. "It's okay, sweetheart. It's over."

Connie twisted and looked over her shoulder at the wall. She let out a cry and stared at her hands.

"What did I do?" Connie whispered. She folded herself into Jade's arms and buried her head against Jade's chest. Above them came the sound of doors opening.

Doreen backed away. "I'll keep the guests upstairs and take care of the damage," she said. "Lucky we've still got a couple of those cover-up stickers left." Without waiting for an answer, she swept off to the stairway.

Mel dropped down to a crouch and rubbed a hand through her hair. "How about I make us all a nice cup of coffee?"

Connie pulled away from Jade. She was calm, the gentle strength of her resolve floored Jade yet again. Connie met Mel's eyes and gave her a weak grin. "I think I'd like something a bit stronger than that."

Mel laughed. "I can do that, too. Come on, then."

JADE WRAPPED HER hands around her steaming mug of coffee and watched Mel pour two shots of brandy. She put down the bottle and met Connie's wordless toast. Connie downed hers in one go. She put the empty glass down and hung her head with a long sigh that seemed to come from the floorboards.

Mel tilted the bottle toward Connie and she held out her glass for a refill. The second one she sipped slowly and rolled the glass in her hands.

Connie licked her lips. "That's really nice."

"Can't beat a VSOP for flavor and punch," Mel said. She swirled the liquid in her glass and regarded Connie over the rim of it. She opened her mouth to speak, but stopped when Doreen came in and sat down at the table. Mel quickly got up and poured her a mug of coffee.

Doreen speared Jade with a sharp look. "Would either of you care to explain what went down this morning?"

Jade rubbed a hand across her forehead. "Just what it looked like." She enfolded Connie's hand in hers and absently stroked her thumb over the back of her hand. Jade kept her voice as calm as she could. "Something really fucking wants to give us a message. It used Connie. Just like it used Britt."

A long moment passed where Mel and Doreen just looked at each other. Mel was the first to turn away. She lowered her gaze to the glass in her hand.

"So I wasn't wrong," Doreen said with a satisfied smirk.

A rush of rage filled Jade. She rose to her full height, towering over the table. She leaned over to get right in Doreen's face. "Yes, you were." Jade snapped. She jabbed a finger at Doreen. "You're her mother. It's your place to believe your kid, no matter what."

"How can you judge me?" Doreen asked. "You don't know what it's like until you have children of your own. It's different when they're yours."

"No, I'm nobody's parent, but I was somebody's child."

The words were almost there. Jade nearly blurted out how her parents' unwavering belief in her innocence had kept her from hanging herself with her shoelaces the first few years of her incarceration. She kept silent. It wasn't the time or place to lay that truth out.

The need to suppress herself rankled. Jade's head was full of steam. She was ready to bulldoze a path straight out the door when Connie lay a hand on her arm. Jade looked down into her concerned face and instantly regretted her outburst. She fell back into her chair, deflated.

Doreen said, "I guess she told you about how I suspected her."

"I'm not going to say," Jade said. She stared into the black depths of her coffee. "Just, you need to talk to each other. Soon. Let her know you're there for her and that you're going to take her at her word from now on."

Doreen looked ready to launch a counterattack, but Mel spoke before she could.

"I think we've all had enough excitement for today," Mel said in a jolly voice. "And it's still early. Why don't you two go back to bed? Breakfast's not for another few hours and you've got the whole day ahead of you."

"Yeah, that's a good point," Jade said. She pushed her mug away. "Thanks for the coffee."

"And the brandy," Connie said. She swallowed the last mouthful of liquor and put the glass back down with a satisfied nod.

"Anytime," Mel said. Doreen shot her a stern look and swept from the room without another word.

Back in their room, Connie stood next to the bed. She hugged her arms to her chest.

"Are you okay?" Jade asked. "Talk to me."

"I don't want to go to sleep again," she said in a tiny voice.

Jade carefully folded Connie into her arms from behind. She kissed the side of her neck and said, "You don't have to if you don't want to. I'm not sleepy anymore either. We could hang out here, or we could go up to the reading room or something."

"Can we go out?" Connie asked. She held herself very still in Jade's arms.

"Sure, we can get breakfast in town or something," Jade said. She let go of Connie and grabbed a pair of jeans and a new flannel shirt. She turned away and yanked off her pajama top. Behind her, she heard rustling as Connie got dressed as well. Jade concentrated on getting herself together. Connie's voice stopped her.

"It wasn't a male energy," she said.

Jade's grip on her belt buckle tightened. She cinched herself in and turned around. Connie stood still, her face introspective. Jade asked gently, "What makes you say that? Do you remember something?"

"Not anything concrete," Connie said. She pressed her hands to her forehead. "I just felt fear and anger and so much pain. It wasn't trying to hurt me, it was more like, I don't know, screaming out for someone to listen."

Jade froze. "Flaming clown pants," she breathed. "It's Teresa. She's the one haunting here."

Connie lowered her hands. "But why? Why would she do such awful things?"

"Hear me out," Jade said. "I don't know why she'd be in the house, but she's been stuck here since the incident, fighting for her life. She's been living those last moments over and over, trapped in her own mind. She can't let go, she's desperate to stay here."

"But why is she fighting so hard? Why is she still here? There has to be a reason."

"Hopefully, her friend Rachel can help us with that."

Connie's focus went inward. Her normally sparkling aura dimmed. Her brow furrowed in pain. "I can't stand thinking about Teresa, trapped in that hell for so many years."

"She won't be for much longer," Jade said. "Don't worry, we'll take care of her and make sure she finds peace."

Connie looked perilously close to tears. "What if we can't? What if she's doomed to stay in that time loop for all eternity?"

"Don't get lost in the darkness, Connie," Jade said. She couldn't stay still. She moved close to Connie and gently touched their foreheads together. Frustration knotted in Jade's gut and she bit back a sigh. "Fuck, I'd love to live in a world where every problem could be solved by driving really fast."

That caused a smile to break through. Connie stepped back and poked Jade. "It's not like in the movies. I think your driving really fast would cause more problems than it solved."

"I'm a good driver," Jade said. She put her hands on her hips.

"If you say so," Connie said airily over one shoulder.

"I am." Jade strutted downstairs after Connie, who gave her a few exasperated looks over her shoulder.

On their way to the truck, they came across Mel playing with the dogs in the yard. Jade waved. Mel threw the tennis balls she was holding and waded across the snow-covered lawn to them. Behind her, two furry bodies plowed through the snow. Happy barks filled the air.

"I saw you two haven't signed up for any workshops today," Mel said. "Going into town?"

"Yeah, later on we'll go up north a bit. Right now, I just want to get a bit of air after—you know. Any good places to eat that open early?" Jade asked. "Uh, not that the food is anything less than awesome here."

"It's okay. I'm cool with that." Mel bent down and rubbed at Lady's head while Frog pranced around her, tennis ball proudly held in her mouth. "There's a place on Main called Jerry's Grill, right across from the Post Office, that's open twenty-four hours. They've got great pancakes."

"Sounds good," Jade said. Her gaze softened when Connie dropped to her knees and became the recipient of a volley of doggy kisses.

Mel said, "Make sure you're back in time for the dance tonight."

"Uh, yeah, sure," Jade said. Connie twisted around and looked up at Jade with a look of pure happiness and excitement. Uneasy, Jade had to make herself grin back. She'd forgotten about the dance when she made plans to talk to Rachel. With a guilty pang, she recalled how much Connie looked forward to it. Jade promised herself that no matter what happened that day, she'd get Connie back in time to lead her onto the dance floor and be classy and courteous as hell in front of everyone who thought Jade was some kind of psychopath.

After Connie disentangled herself from her two doggy fans, they got in the truck and headed into town. Dawn was still an hour away, and the inside of the truck was dark and quiet, save for the hum of the hybrid engine. Connie kicked off her shoes and curled up in her chair. She gazed out the window, appearing deep in thought.

The silence wasn't uncomfortable. In fact, Jade felt grounded and happy. She found the grill Mel mentioned and parked at a meter in front of it. Connie jumped out, hopping on one foot as she fixed her shoe. Connie put her hands over her belly and laughed.

"Did you hear my stomach growl just now?"

"Nah," Jade said. "I think mine drowned yours out. I hope they've got lots of maple syrup and shit because I'm in the mood for a massive stack of pancakes."

"Me too," Connie said. She scooted over to Jade's side and threaded her arm through Jade's. The pompom on her toque tickled Jades nose, but she wasn't going to complain. She loved having Connie close to her like that.

The inside of the grill was plain and unassuming. Jade was relieved at the absence of overwhelming Christmas decorations and music. A TV in the corner showed the morning news, just loud enough to be heard over the buzz of conversation from the other customers. Even at such an early hour, several tables were occupied and a couple lumberjack-looking people sat at the counter. The air was warm and filled with the smell of hot grease and fresh coffee. Jade sniffed eagerly in anticipation of her breakfast. They found a seat at one of the booths and a waitress approached them. Jade didn't bother with the menu and simply ordered pancakes and coffee. Connie echoed the order from her perch across from Jade, with her chin balanced on her closed fists. Her cheeks were pink and her body language was relaxed.

Jade leaned close to Connie and said in a conspiratorial voice, "It feels like we're cheating on Dixie and her diner with the fucking amazing apple pies."

"Yeah, it does," Connie said. "I won't tell if you don't."

Jade made a zipping motion across her mouth. Their coffee arrived. Jade dumped a bunch of sugar into it before she took a gulp. Two tall stacks of golden pancakes and a generous pitcher of syrup followed and Jade dove in. She finally came up for air after she dragged the last pancake around in the sea of buttery syrup and shoved it into her mouth whole. She downed the rest of her coffee and let out a satisfied sigh.

"That hit the spot," Jade announced.

"I want to try making pancakes in my skillet next," Connie said.

"Fuck, that would probably kill me with deliciousness," Jade said. "But what a way to go." A familiar face passed by and Jade stood abruptly, stopping Percy Havarth in his tracks. He carried a silver Thermos and didn't exactly look happy to see Jade.

Jade stuck her thumbs through her belt to head off him trying to shake her hand.

"Fancy running into you here," Jade said. She scooted over to Connie's side of the booth and slid in. "Don't be a stranger, take a sit and let me buy you a coffee."

Percy looked as if Jade had just invited him to drink drain cleaner. He shook his Thermos. "I was just stopping by to get a fill-up for the road. Christmas Eve or not, the Tourist Information Center is open for business."

"All the better to join us then," Jade said. "Here are two tourists and we're looking for information."

Percy sighed, then resignedly sat down opposite them. The waitress came over.

"The usual, Mr. Havarth?" she asked.

"Yeah," he said in a surly way.

"Put it on my tab," Jade said.

The waitress looked at Jade for a beat longer than necessary, as if trying to gauge Jade's interest. Still frowning, she pocketed her order pad, picked up the Thermos, and swept away.

"So what information can I help you with?" Percy asked.

"Tell me more about Link Porter," Jade said. "Why he was so pissed off he stabbed that girl, for starters. What's his angle?"

Percy let out a long breath. "I deal with the histrorical aspect of this town, not gossip."

"This is history," Jade said. She felt a sheen of sweat gather on her back and shifted in her seat. She increased the wattage of her fake smile, felt foolish, and dropped it. She folded her hands on the table and leaned forward. "Wait, I bet it was mom issues. When did she take off? Was there another guy? Come on, you know what went down back then. It wrecked him."

The Thermos came back with the waitress. Percy grabbed it and stood.

"Can I get you anything else?"

"No, thanks Betty," Percy said. He looked down at Jade and Connie. "There wasn't 'another guy'. Mary-Lynne Porter ran off with a woman."

Jade gaped with the revelation. Beside her, Connie perked up. Without another word, Percy left the diner.

"Huh," Jade said. She met Connie's look with raised eyebrows. "That explains some of it, anyway."

Connie cast her eyes down and idly played with her fork. "I hope she's happy, wherever she is."

Jade's heart swelled. She gently placed her hand over Connie's. "If whoever she's with is half as wonderful, sweet, and amazing as you are, she's happy. Without a doubt."

Connie giggled and poked Jade on the shoulder. "Sweet-talker. Unless there's anyone else here you want to talk to, how about we head back?"

"I'm good," Jade said. She paid the bill and left a generous tip. The drive back was considerably lighter and noisier. Fueled on maple syrup and coffee, Jade pumped the tunes, filling the cab with Christmas cheer. Connie helped by singing along and Jade played the air guitar in support at red lights and stop signs, which made Connie crack up in laughter, interrupting her singing efforts.

BACK AT THE resort, Jade got recruited by Mel to help carry a long stepladder from the house to the event space barn. Jade was rather amused to discover she'd fallen into a role somewhere between hired help, guest, and family. Jade felt very butch indeed when she eagerly hefted her end and didn't miss Connie appreciatively checking her out from the wide window of the lobby.

"That pancake place was great," Jade said. She resisted the urge to swagger.

"Told ya," Mel said. They reached the barn and Mel nudged open the door. "Careful of the edging there."

Together they maneuvered the ladder inside. Jade hesitated for a moment in the tiled hall, wondering if she should take off her boots, but Mel strode right onto the rich carpet so Jade followed suit. They set the ladder up in the arch that separated the entrance hall from the main room. From a large paper bag, Mel produced a handful of leaves spotted with waxy, white berries.

"Mistletoe," she said by way of explanation. "Spot me, Jade."

"Sure thing," Jade said. She held the ladder steady as Mel clambered up, then tied a sprig of mistletoe to a small hook on the arch. She had quite a number of bunches and it took a while to get them all tied up at various places around the room. Once Mel was permanently back on the ground, Jade took a leisurely survey of the room.

It was high-ceilinged with rich, red-draped windows. A small stage was at one end of the room with speakers on it and

Jade hoped karaoke wasn't on the menu for that night. The room was decorated for the season with bouquets of pine boughs sporting red and silver ornaments between the bunches of mistletoe. The main attraction was a gigantic Christmas tree that stood proudly in the corner by the door. It was decked out with glittering plastic icicles and white lights. The trunk was massive. Jade peered closely at the sturdy metal base holding it in place. That tree wasn't going anywhere.

"Nice setup," Jade said. She shoved her hands into her pockets.

Mel looked up from the garland she was messing with and grinned. "I love Christmas. It was my idea to have our grand opening over the holidays." She sobered and stood, echoing Jade's stance. "A lot of LGBT people spend the holidays away from their families because of rejection and abuse. It's a sad fact that many people are vilified and shunned just for being themselves. It should be one of the most loving and wonderful times of the year, but for many it's a stark reminder of how alone they are."

"Yeah, that sucks. At least until they find a new family," Jade said. "One of the heart."

Mel chuckled. "Yeah, agreed. Anyway, we're done here. How about I make you a big mug of my special hot cocoa for your help?"

Jade coughed to cover up the look of dismay on her face. "Very generous, but I'll pass. I fulfilled my chocolate requirements last night."

"Your loss," Mel said. They hoisted the stepladder once more and trekked back to the resort. Jade made her escape and went searching for Connie. She guessed she wouldn't be in their room, so Jade went up to the third floor. She found Connie curled up in a window seat in the reading room with a book resting against her knees. She looked up with a brilliant smile when Jade entered and made a move to put her book aside.

Jade shook her head. "You don't have to stop your reading. I was just checking where you were, that's all. We don't move out until this afternoon anyway."

"Okay," Connie said. She opened her book once more. "I'm at a really good part."

"Enjoy," Jade said. She went to the game closet and found a

jigsaw puzzle that kept her busy for the remainder of the morning.

# Chapter Thirteen

THEY ARRIVED AT Rachel's home at sunset, much later than Jade wanted due to an unexpected closed road on the way in.

The house looked normal from the outside, a typical suburban home with bushes in the front yard. Thick snow covered the seats of a swing set in the backyard, and accordioned on the slide. An SUV sat in the driveway. The front door was flanked by two dilapidated bushes that sported uneven clots of tinsel and a few rough ornaments that looked fashioned by small hands.

For an instant, Jade was transported back to a time when Christmas was magic and dumping out the treasures in your stocking was the best damn thing that could happen to you. She lost herself in that feeling of *home* and wonder and excitement only a child could have.

Jade held her breath. It was so normal, so fucking calm and homey and Jade was going to bulldoze into it, forcing out memories of the most painful moments of a woman's life. Jade let out her breath and turned to Connie.

"Let's do this, babe," she said. Connie met her fist bump and gave her an encouraging smile that filled Jade with confidence. If she was going to wreck someone's day, she wasn't going to half-ass it.

Thundering footsteps met Jade's knock and the door opened a crack. A tow-headed boy held the doorknob and peered up at her. He had something orange and sticky looking all over his mouth.

Jade tried to think of a suitable greeting but ended up just standing there like a dumb fish. She was saved by a stocky woman in a grey sweatshirt and jeans with a buzz cut who opened the door fully. Her cheerful greeting unfroze Jade.

"I'm Detective Young's contact," Jade said. She quickly introduced herself and Connie.

"Come on in," the woman said. "I'm Rachel and this is Caleb. Say hello, Caleb."

"Hey," Jade said. Caleb hid behind Rachel and stared. Then

he took off and Jade heard the high-pitched, shrill scream-talking of what sounded like a zoo full of children and the more low-key voice of another adult who Jade assumed was her wife, Laura. Jade tried to grin through the headache that started to nag at her temples. They hung up their coats and Rachel showed them into the living room.

Rachel said, "I heard you're looking into Teresa's case. The guy from the police didn't tell me the reason. I thought it was all done and sealed. There's nothing really more to investigate."

"Uh yeah," Jade said. She wracked her brain. She didn't think it would go over too well if she mentioned the fact that Teresa was still around and wreaking havoc on any young woman who crossed her path.

Connie jumped in. "That's right, the case is solved, but there are a bunch of things we think were swept under the carpet. The facts don't add up and we're hoping you could help us out with that. We have a vested interest in bringing the truth about Teresa to light." Connie paused and surprised Jade by snuggling up to her side. Automatically, Jade put an arm around her and was rewarded by a flash of understanding from Rachel. She relaxed visibly.

Jade thanked whatever power that was in charge of the universe for sending Connie into her life. Rachel nodded toward the sofa. "Why don't you two have a seat?" Rachel settled into the armchair across from them. Raised voices came from the kitchen.

"Are you okay with talking here?" Jade asked.

Rachel shrugged and opened her mouth to answer, but Caleb and another, smaller, boy came pounding into the room. Caleb threw himself into Rachel's lap.

"Mom! Mom!" Caleb said while his brother clung to Rachel's leg and made incoherent whining noises. "Noah coughed on me! He gots germs!"

"Do not," Noah managed to form the words instead of just making noise.

Jade tried to make herself invisible. Noah wiped his nose on his sleeve and tugged at Rachel's sweatshirt.

"Guys, why don't you go back into the kitchen with Mama? Mom's trying to have a serious talk here," Rachel said. She disengaged Caleb's hands but he kept grabbing at her, all the while keeping up a stream of barely understandable babble. Rachel turned her head and called out, "Laura, hon, can you take the boys in with you?"

Laura appeared with an infant on her hip who was sucking on one of its hands. Her hair was a bewitching shade of red and it was tied up in a messy bun on top of her head. She looked tired and annoyed.

"Okay," Laura said. "Caleb, Noah, stop bothering Mom or you'll lose your screen time for tonight."

"Aww! Mama!"

"What do you want for dinner?" Laura dropped one hand from holding the baby and plucked at Caleb, who twisted away, sulking. "We've got mac and cheese or chicken nuggets."

"Mac!" Caleb's shriek felt like an ice pick being driven through Jade's eardrums.

"Chikkie nuggies," Noah said at the same time.

Laura said, "Well, it is Christmas Eve, so how about both?"

The boys cheered.

"Okay, first one in the kitchen gets to choose the music for dinner."

Pushing and shoving at each other, the two scrambled through the room.

Laura gave Rachel a "you owe me one" look and planted the baby on Rachel's lap. "I've got the boys. You take the baby."

"Sure thing, hon," Rachel said. She jiggled the baby on her knee. It burbled and regarded the newcomers with big eyes. "Sorry about the boys. They're stir-crazy from the drive back and all the sugar grandma kept feeding them."

"Lively bunch," Jade said.

Rachel grinned. She gently bounced the baby. "We were going to stick to two, but Laura had her heart set on a girl, so we tried for a third and ended up with Spencer. I wouldn't trade any of them for a hundred girls, but Lord help us when they're all teenagers."

"At least the world will have three well-behaved guys who respect women," Jade said.

"Hopefully," Rachel said. "It's not like we aren't trying to bring them up right, but you can't force a person to come out the way you choose. My parents wanted a dress-wearing Christian and look what they got."

A crash from the kitchen interrupted them, followed by a trio of shouting. Beside her on the sofa, Jade felt Connie shrinking against her. The discussion was going nowhere fast.

Jade squashed the urge to clap her hands over her ears. She'd lived the majority of her adult life in a no-children environment and the random chaos of small humans put her on edge. Usually, Jade was able to bullshit herself she'd be okay at raising children, but at that moment she severely doubted her own fitness as a potential parent. The realization came with a stab of despair. One more area she would end up coming short for Connie.

"Is there somewhere quiet we can talk?" Jade asked. She barely managed to keep the annoyance from her tone.

Rachel looked embarrassed. "Yeah, sure. Um, how about we go out to the car? It's private and, bonus, the doors lock. I escape out there a couple times a week, just enjoying the silence."

"Lead the way," Jade said. She was on her feet in a second. They got back into their coats and Rachel grabbed a blanket for the baby on her way out. She remotely clicked the locks open and got into the driver's seat. Connie slipped into the back, tacitly giving Jade the lead, so Jade took the passenger seat while cringing. The seats were covered in goldfish cracker crumbs and toy cars littered the floor mat at Jade's feet. Scribbles marred the screen of the navigation. Rachel turned on the heater.

"Sorry about the mess," Rachel said. The baby in her arms squawked and she patted him on the back. "You got any kids?"

"Nope," Jade said. She winced at the abrupt tone and amended, "Not yet, anyway. Kids aren't really my strong point."

"Wait until you get your own. You'll get used to it," Rachel said.

Jade wasn't sure how long their quiet respite would last, so she barreled ahead. "Tell me about Teresa. What was she like?"

Rachel looked surprised by the question. She shifted the baby on her knee. "Funny. Nobody ever asked me that. They were too busy blaming her, vilifying her, making it seem like she deserved it."

"We're asking now," Jade said. She leaned forward in her seat. Jade was all too familiar with being the villain. For the entirety of her trial, all everyone could say about her was how cold, calculating, and *queer* she was. The trial itself was a farce. There was no doubt of anything other than a guilty verdict. Nothing of Jade's life was left unscrutinized, but once those bars closed behind her, Jade was just another number. Another reject who fucked up their life. Another piece of meat for the predators.

Jade shook her head to clear away the clinging fingers of the past. She said, "I know this is difficult for you, but this information lives only in you and it's your chance to set the record right."

Rachel nodded. She took a deep breath and her expression softened, her focus drifted into the past. "Teresa was my first love. She was tiny, but a real spitfire. She got so much flack for being out, but she never let it get her down and she never backed down, not for a moment. She was girly, and that made it hard for her to be seen, I guess. She would shoot her mouth off at the drop of a hat, she did everything at one-hundred percent. That's what drew me to her. She wasn't afraid of anything."

Jade met Rachel's eyes and grinned. For a moment, Jade felt the presence of the vibrant young woman who once lived. Jade said, "It must have taken you a long time to get over what happened to her."

Rachel's hand drifted over her face. Absently she shifted the cooing bundle in her arms. "I was a mess for a while. Meeting Laura actually got me out of it and back to living." She looked down at the baby on her lap and gently stroked a feather-fine hair from his forehead. "My kids and Laura are my life, but sometimes I wonder what if we never stopped at that boathouse."

"Maybe in some alternate universe you didn't," Jade said. "Can you tell me what happened that night?"

"Okay," Rachel said. Her eyes went misty and she gave Jade a half-smile that looked fake. "God, it's been a while since I went back to that place. It's, wow, it's still pretty rough. Give me a minute." The baby squirmed and started fussing. Rachel sniffled and stared into the air with butch bravado.

"Take your time," Jade said even though she surreptitiously checked her watch. It was already past five. The sky was dark. Multicolored Christmas lights twinkled on every house on the street.

"God, I'm sorry," Rachel said. She grabbed for a tissue and awkwardly blew her nose, one-handed. The baby twisted in her arms and nearly slid off her lap. Rachel grabbed him with both hands.

Jade glanced about frantically. She had no idea what she should do. Offer to take the kid or let Rachel handle it herself?

Before Jade could speak, Connie leaned in between the seats.

"If it's okay, I'll hold him for a while," Connie said. Rachel didn't hesitate before handing the squirming bundle over. Jade gaped and felt her face heat up as Connie expertly cradled the baby and settled back into her seat. She spoke soft words for only his ears. Spencer's face lit up and he giggled.

"Wow, Connie. You're a natural," Rachel said.

Jade glowed, just as proud as if the compliment was directed at her. Fuck it, when Connie decided she wanted kids, Jade would be all-in, no matter what it cost her.

Rachel leaned back into her seat. She worried at the tissue in her hands.

Jade waited.

"We were, um." Rachel cleared her throat. She tried again, this time her voice was stronger. "We were driving by the boat-house and Teresa thought it looked really cool. She wanted to take some pictures." Rachel chuckled even as tears welled up in her eyes. "She wanted to be a photographer and always had her camera with her. She loved old maritime buildings. So we got out and she'd gotten some shots, then we, uh, started to, you know, get friendly when all of a sudden *he* showed up."

Rachel stopped and swallowed hard. She clenched her fists. Her hands shook.

"It's okay, you're safe," Jade said.

Rachel's face was set, her eyes distant. Her voice was calm and uninflected as she spoke. "He just appeared behind us, shouting. He was like this crazy person, calling us all sorts of names. Teresa got right in his face and that's when he grabbed her." Rachel drew in a shuddering breath. "I don't know what he was going to do to her. Teresa tried to get away but he was really strong. That's when she pulled her knife on him. I didn't even know she had it, but she always told me she had the means to defend herself." Rachel bowed her head down and pressed her palms to her face. "The knife was like a trigger to him. He just went ape on her, pounding his fists on her. I stood there, frozen, like a dumbass, while she fought for her life. I should have done something, but I couldn't move."

"That's a natural reaction," Jade said. "Anybody in that situation would do the same."

"Yeah, my therapist told me that a few hundred times. Maybe

one of these days I'll actually believe it." Rachel raised her head. Her cheeks were wet with tears. "I don't know what happened. They both went down in a pile and suddenly he just took off. That's when I saw she'd been stabbed. There was so much blood, later they told me she'd pretty much instantly gone into shock. I didn't know what to do, but I saw the lights of the house nearby. I picked Teresa up and ran my ass over there. I'm surprised the old lady who lived there actually opened the door with how crazy I must have sounded."

Jade seized the lead. "What happened after that? Did you go inside?"

"Yeah, she let me take Teresa up to this spare room. I laid her down on the bed. God, I'll never forget how she looked. Barely breathing, but still punching and shoving at me." Rachel swiped her sleeve over her face and sniffled. Her shoulders slumped. "I didn't even get her last words. She was gone before the ambulance even got there. She didn't know I was there. I think in her mind, she was still fighting him until her last moment."

"Tough girl," Jade said. She glanced into the back seat, where Connie was listening intently, her eyes damp with tears.

"She was the toughest," Rachel said. She went to wipe her eyes on the cuff of her sweatshirt, caught herself and grabbed a tissue. Jade studied the dashboard as if it was the most interesting thing ever. Something was missing. The boathouse wasn't their destination. Jade's attention snapped back to Rachel.

"Where were you going?" Jade asked.

"We were going to this LGBT dance in North Aisling," Rachel said. She gave a soft chuckle. Warmth and light returned to her expression. "It was the first time anything like that was being held around here. Teresa was super stoked about it. It was the only thing she could talk about for ages. She'd gotten her dress months before. For her, it was going to be her big moment. Her parents disowned her when she came out, she had to hide at work because her boss was a religious homophobe. She even had to pretend that she had a boyfriend so the busybodies wouldn't set her up with their nephews. It was going to be her one moment of freedom when she told the world, 'Fuck you, I'm queer.'"

Rachel suddenly stopped talking and glanced worriedly into the back seat.

Connie met her with a cute quirk of her lips. "It's okay, he's asleep. And I don't think he'd remember anyway."

"Great," Rachel said. She flopped back. "Laura would kick my ass if his first word was a bad one."

All the while, Jade sat, stunned. A jolt of panic ripped through her. The dance was the key. The LGBT dance, similar to the one that was taking place that evening. Jade jumped up and banged her head on the windshield. She bit her lip to keep from further polluting Spencer's vocabulary.

Connie apparently figured it out too, because she said, "Rachel, thank you so much for sharing this with us. I hate to say it, but we really have to go. Like, now."

"Okay," Rachel said. She looked drained but the raw grief had left her. She took Spencer back into her harms and rubbed a hand over her face. "I hope I helped you out."

"You did," Jade said. "Not only us, but Teresa too. You don't even know how much."

Jade threw herself out of the SUV and clambered into her truck. Connie was right behind her and wordlessly buckled up. Jade threw the truck into reverse and squealed out of the driveway. She slammed on the brakes and twisted the wheel, pulling the truck into a perfect 90 degree turn. She stomped on the gas. The lights on either side of the road streamed by.

The burst of speed sent Jade's adrenaline pumping.

"At least I can get you to the dance on time," Jade said with a wild grin. "Maybe solving problems by driving fast has its merits."

The truck screeched around a corner much faster than it should and Connie grabbed onto the holy shit handle.

"Just don't kill us in the process," Connie said. Jade glanced over, concerned that Connie was scared, but her quick smile put Jade at ease.

"Connie, call the resort," Jade said. She blew through a yellow light and gunned the engine. "Tell them they have to cancel the dance. They can't let anybody into the event space."

"Got it," Connie said. She dug out her phone. Jade held her breath and concentrated on not getting them into a wreck. After a few minutes, Connie said, "No answer, but I'll keep trying. I sent Mel a text too, but it doesn't seem like she's got her phone on her."

"Piss-spewing elephant-fucking crotch bait," Jade said in a

growl. She saw a car pulling out of a driveway in front of them and leaned her entire weight on the horn, stopping the other car in its tracks before they flew by. The driver flipped her the bird through the window. That earned a "dick-chomper" from Jade.

By breaking all the speed limits and taking a few unauthorized short cuts, they arrived back at the resort at seven on the dot. Jade plowed onto the snow-covered lawn and threw herself out of the truck. The event barn's windows blazed with light and a few faint streams of music tinted the air.

"Stay here until it's safe," Jade said to Connie just before she bolted from the truck.

Jade kicked open the door and raced into the ballroom. She stood in the middle of the room, chest heaving, shaking with adrenaline.

"Everybody get the fuck out of here!" she hollered.

"Sweetheart, are you okay?" Garrett asked. He had a champagne flute in one hand and twirled it lazily.

"I'm fucking fine but nobody else will be unless you all get out of here right goddamn *now*."

Silence fell. Jade was very aware of the fact she was standing in the middle of the room with everyone in their fancy clothing frozen in place and staring at her. Once more, Jade was a spittle-flecked freak in the middle of a sea of normalcy. Helen pulled Lisa aside and whispered something to her. The music continued on. A jolt of uncertainty stabbed Jade. Had she guessed wrong?

Mel appeared at her side. "What's this all about?"

"I can fix this," Jade said. "I just need you to clear everyone out and give me some time."

"Got it," Mel said. She spun away and waved an arm over her head. "Let's go folks."

Jade closed her eyes for a moment, trying desperately to sense anything out of the ordinary and came up empty. Jade let out a breath. Maybe they were safe and the only damage was to Jade's already dinged-up pride.

No such luck.

The back of Jade's neck prickled. A cold breath touched her cheek. "Shit!" Jade slapped at the air and twisted around. With a bang, the room was plunged into darkness. The front door opened and in the glow from the moon outside, Jade saw Connie's slim form outlined against the silvery snow.

"Connie, get back," Jade cried out. A babble of startled voices buzzed around her. Something cold and heavy impacted her and Jade fell to her knees. A low, rolling growl started up and grew in intensity until the floor shook. It was affecting more than just Jade. Startled shrieks and shouts filled the air. She caught her breath at the force of the thing. It broke all her preconceptions about spirits and the power they could wield. This one was huge and angry as hell.

"All right people," Mel's voice filtered through the cacophony. "Don't panic, just head for the door. This way, folks." A flickering light from the Zippo she held over her head made Mel a lighthouse in the dark room. The assembled group quieted down and started moving out.

*Nobody leaves.*

Jade didn't hear the words, she felt them vibrate through her. A sick, cracking sound studded with jingles grabbed her attention. "Mangy cock-felcher," Jade breathed.

The huge Christmas tree listed. If it fell, it would block the exit, and crush the group clustered near the doorway. Jade reached forward in impotent agony, her shout temporarily drowned out the popping sound of the trunk splintering one last time. The tree keeled over like a dying giant and Jade braced for the inevitable crash.

When it didn't come, Jade opened her eyes and gasped. Basil was bent over like Atlas with the thick trunk of the tree across his back. He was nearly buried in pine boughs, but he'd stopped the tree.

As if in protest, a vicious wind kicked up in the room. Jade was buffeted on all sides by stinging projectiles. She covered her head and crouched down. She prayed that Connie was out of range.

"Get out of here," Basil said. His voice was strained, but calm. "I can't hold it much longer."

"Basil, no!" Garrett cried out. "What have you done?"

"Garrett, I'm sorry things had to end like this. I'm a fuckup, I know that. I can't do anything right so just let me do this one thing. Let me be a hero. *Your* hero. Just once. Because you're mine and I will love you until the day I die."

A beat of silence followed.

"Basil, you are so dramatic, but so damn sexy when you

butch out like that."

Jade peered through her fingers to see Garrett throw his tuxedo jacket to the floor and run toward where Basil held up the tree. He eased himself under the bough and wrapped his arm around Basil's waist.

"Garrett, get out of here. I've said my bit and I've made my peace. I'm ready to go."

"Nobody is dying today," Garrett said. "If we give this a push, we can land it over there next to the punch table. Easy-peasy, lemon-squeezy. Could we have a bit of help over here?"

The next thing that happened shocked Jade speechless. Mel, followed by Doreen, and the rest of the resort-goers, flocked to the tree. As one, they propped up the leaning trunk. Garrett's piercing voice directed them, even as the wind picked up with a howl that was eerily animalistic. As one they moved, and as one, they set the tree down where it could do no harm. The stinging wind picked up, as if angry its toy had been taken.

As soon as the tree was on the floor, Garrett fought his way over to Jade.

"Coming out, honey?" he asked. "Or are you going to stay for one more dance?"

Jade had to crack a grin. Not even an otherworldly attack and a near-death experience could keep his sass down.

"You go," she said. "I'm a pro at this kind of thing. Get the rest out for me and make sure Connie's safe. I have a job to finish here."

To his credit, Garrett did as she instructed. Soon, Jade was alone against the howling thing. The rage turned into a mental spike of pain and came flying at her. Jade rocked back a few steps with the impact. She clutched her hands to her chest and fought to breathe. It took all the strength she had to make a crystal-clear thought.

"Teresa," Jade whispered. Her mental voice echoed the words. The hungry beast tore at her. Jade felt an abyss open up in front of her.

Unwillingly, she took a step toward it. She couldn't deny the pull.

*Submit.*

It coerced her. Dispair teased her. Jade would never be enough. She would never be whole. How could someone like her expect a happy end? There was nothing left for her. The thing whispered into her ear, dangled all of her failures in front of her eyes, chuckled with a mirthless evil at every single thing Jade had ever fucked up.

Only one thing remained. A golden light beckoned Jade back from the brink. Connie stood before her, outlined in light like an angel. Jade didn't know if she was there in the flesh or just in spirit. Her hair was longer and waved around her face as if she was underwater. She smiled at Jade, and that sent a spear of hope through her. Jade was enough. She was a warrior. Strength returned to her body and mind. The nagging voices quieted.

Jade's voice rang out, strong and confident, "Teresa!"

The slightest pause met her shouted word. The raw rage ebbed for an instant and Jade found purchase for her counterattack.

"It's over," Jade shouted into the maelstrom. She turned in a circle, following the path of the raging wind. "Teresa, Rachel's okay and she's safe. She's happy. She's got three beautiful sons and someone who loves her. She's found peace. The man who did this to you has gone forever. Now it's your turn. Your fight is over. It's been over for a long time. You can rest now."

Jade closed her eyes. She projected peace and security with every last fiber of her being. Everything was going to be okay. The road ahead was not to be feared.

The wind abruptly stopped. All of the items that were caught up in the turbulence dropped in a crashing cascade.

Jade straightened up. Her entire body shook. Pattering footsteps preceeded a warm body landing in her arms. Jade folded Connie into her embrace and buried her face in her cropped curls.

"I was so worried," Connie said into Jade's shoulder.

"Hey, it's me," Jade said with every bit of her old bravado. "Something comes along that wants to kick my ass, I kick it first."

"Just tell me you're okay. Garrett made me go outside with them. I didn't know what was happening here and it was so dark," Connie said. She drew back. Jade ached at the sight of tears on her cheeks.

"Baby girl, don't worry so much, I'm awesome," Jade said. She cupped Connie's face and stroked her thumbs over her silken cheeks, smoothing away the imprint of her fear.

"Is it gone?"

"Not exactly," Jade said. She glanced back over one shoulder. The eerily flickering form of a young woman hovered in the corner. "The bad is gone, but the echo of good remains. I don't exactly know what to do from here."

Connie held Jade by the forearms. Her eyes searched Jade's face. "I have an idea," she said. "Don't say no right away. Hear me out."

"What is it?" Jade couldn't help but be wary. Connie matched Teresa in a lot of ways that Jade could never understand. In sympathy lay weakness. Jade never trusted either.

"Let me give Teresa her night."

"What?"

Connie didn't waver. "Let me give her a night where she can dance in the arms of a proud, out woman in public without judgment or fear. I'll let her take me over and we can give her that moment she fought so hard and so long to have."

"No, I can't allow you to do that," Jade said. Fear ignited a spark of anger. She squashed it down and deliberately kept her stance neutral and non-threatening. "You saw what it did to Britt—and I saw what it did to you. I can't let that happen again."

"This time is different," Connie said. "The anger is gone, and this time, she'll have my permission. She can have me for as long as she wants. More than anything, you'll be there."

Jade bowed her head down. The weight of Connie's gift humbled her. "I can't decide for you, but I will promise to keep you safe."

"Good," Connie said. Her lips quirked up in the mischievous grin Jade loved. She said, "I already made a playlist of oldies—um, hits from twelve years ago. All you have to do is get yourself into your tux."

# Chapter Fourteen

"THIS IS INSANE," Jade breathed out as she carried the two garment bags from their room. Snow was falling thickly, almost obscuring the view of the main house the farther she got from it.

When she returned to the event space, the emergency lights were on. They filled the room with an otherworldly green glow. Connie took over the larger bathroom while Jade slipped into the smaller, single one. She quickly changed into her starched tuxedo shirt, stepped into the slim trousers and buttoned the white form-fitting vest. The long tails of the pristine white jacket swept down to her knees. She kept the collar of her shirt rakishly unbuttoned. Jade swept back her long hair and twisted it up, securing it with a clip. Her bangs hung into her eyes and she impatiently brushed them aside. She gazed at herself in the mirror. Fuck, she felt good and looked like a million bucks. She couldn't wait to see the dress Jordan and Benny fixed Connie up with.

Jade's boots sank into the rich carpet for the few steps needed to take her to the middle of the dance floor. The scene felt surreal; the refreshment table was tipped over, bits of sandwiches littered the floor along with torn decorations. The wall sported a dripping red stain from the punch. The huge tree lay on its side, spilling needles and icicles all over. Ripped up mistletoe was scattered all over. The disco ball still spun, casting subdued diamonds of light all over the room. Jade felt like the last survivor of a zombie apocalypse.

The door opened and Jade's world narrowed to one point. Her breath wouldn't come. Connie was radiant in a dress of the palest violet. Sheer material covered her bared shoulders over a delicately sculpted bodice that showed off her slender curves. The skirt was layers of filmy chiffon that stopped above her knees in the front and trailed to her ankles in the back. Her feet were delicately strapped into purple high heels. She wore no jewelery other than a sparkly star-shaped pin in her hair. In her hands was a folded rectangle of silky material. She met Jade's eyes, held her for an instant, then *changed*.

Jade knew the instant when Connie was no longer there. Her muscles sat differently over her bones, her eyes deepened and her entire aura shifted. Jade's vision blurred. She blinked. She wasn't looking at Connie anymore, but a vibrant young woman with unruly russet hair and a mischievous look on her face. The young woman looked around in wonder. The first strains of the sweet, simple melody started up from Connie's phone, propped on the stage.

"Hi," Jade said softly. "Teresa, it's me, Jade. I've been waiting for you."

Teresa took a step toward Jade. Her expression was wondrous, as if she could barely believe she was there. Jade felt much the same way, but she was determined to act the part. As if noticing for the first time, Teresa looked at the material in her hands. She shook it out and revealed the scarf, dyed to match her dress.

"I guess this is for you," she said. Her voice was clear, light as a summer breeze and filled with laughter.

Jade held herself still as Teresa stepped closer to her and very gently draped the scarf around her neck. She tucked it under Jade's collar and smoothed her hands down the silken lengths of it, flirtatiously close to Jade's breasts.

"May I have this dance?" Jade asked. She bowed and held out a hand.

Teresa drew in a breath before she stepped into the circle of Jade's arms. Instead of taking the proffered hand, she draped her arms lightly over Jade's shoulders. "You certainly may have this dance, and anything else you desire," she said with a decidedly naughty note in her voice.

Jade couldn't help but chuckle at that. Damn, but she was a sucker for a cute, flirty femme. Nobody would take Connie's place in her heart, but Jade didn't stop herself from enjoying the moment. It was important that moment was real, for both of them.

Against all logic, the music swelled and enveloped them. The ruined room faded away and was replaced with walls full of rainbow streamers, balloons filled the corners and the scent of a hundred blossoms enveloped them. Jade put her hands on Teresa's waist and guided her into a slow, spiraling dance. Voices filled her ears, and Jade became aware of the crowd surrounding them. Some were in dapper suits, others in dresses, some with lush feather boas and sequins, all of them focused on the pair in the middle of the dance floor.

Jade couldn't help but spin Teresa out and whirl her back. Teresa landed nestled in Jade's embrace. Hoots and cheers bolstered her. Jade felt proud and free. Teresa gazed up at her as if Jade was her entire world.

"Do you know how fucking hot you are?" she asked.

Jade just replied with a raised eyebrow. She agreed, but that night wasn't about her, or them. Jade took one of Teresa's hands in hers and gently guided her to turn around and stand with her back pressed to Jade's front. Jade wrapped her arms around Teresa's waist.

She bent her head and spoke softly, so only Teresa could hear, "Look at them. They're here for you. They're proud of you. You did it. You broke the mold and beat the system. You dared to walk the road you wanted and fuck everyone else. Take pride in that."

"You're right, and thank you."

"No. This is your moment. You fought for it, you never gave up and here you are."

"How long has it been?" Teresa asked.

The question shocked Jade. She felt the ballroom scene slipping away. The voices grew faded and echoey. The glittering lights dimmed.

"Twelve years," Jade said.

"I'm glad Rachel's okay. That she's happy."

"She is. She's the reason we figured out how to help you."

Teresa's expression grew soft and introspective.

"It's Christmas, right?"

"That's right." Jade paused. "You've been here all this time, but now you're free. Are you ready to go?"

"Almost," Teresa said. She disengaged herself from Jade's loose hold and took a step away. She turned back to face Jade. "I'm sorry for...everything. I want you to thank Connie for giving me the best night of my life. You're lucky to have her."

"Yeah, I know," Jade said.

Teresa took one more look around, then closed her eyes. Just like that, she was gone.

Connie opened her eyes.

"What happened? Did it work?"

"Yes, it did," Jade said. She shoved her hands into her pockets and leaned back with a grin. "Teresa says thank you. You did it, Connie."

"We did it," Connie said. She pressed a hand to her lips and smiled. She took a slow survey of Jade, who held herself still and proud in her tux. Connie's gaze on her was like a tangible thing. While dancing with Teresa was flattering, Jade never felt the hot, aching need Connie's sultry look called up.

"I owe you a dance," Jade said.

Connie practically flew into Jade's open arms. She pressed herself against Jade and sighed, relaxing completely into the embrace. Jade pressed a kiss into Connie's hair. She was complete. Her world was right again. The music from Connie's phone was tinny and faint, broken glass crunched under their feet and shredded decorations lay in drifts around them, but Jade was in heaven. She wouldn't feel as rich with any other woman in the entire world in her arms, not even in the most opulent ballroom that ever existed.

Jade was content to dance with Connie, wearing her second-hand tux in that refurbished barn in small town Nova Scotia, where she'd probably racked up a hundred speeding tickets, and Mel was going to kick her ass for parking her truck smack-dab in the middle of the front lawn.

"Does mistletoe count if you're standing on it?" Connie asked in an innocent voice.

"Hell yeah," Jade answered immediately. She cupped Connie's face and they met in a full, deep kiss that outlasted the song. When they finally parted, Jade calmed her heaving breaths. "How about heading back?"

Connie nodded. She looked down at her shoes and wrinkled her nose. "Let me get changed. I'll freeze my feet off if I try to walk back through the snow in these."

"Not a problem," Jade said. She bent down and swept Connie up in a princess carry. Jade couldn't help herself. Seeing Connie in a fancy dress always brought out the Prince Charming in her.

Connie laughed and nestled against Jade. "Don't drop me."

"Never," Jade said. She took them over to the stage to let Connie grab her phone, then headed out. The lights of the Wellness Room blazed over their heads. Jade guessed their ingenious hosts were holding some kind of secondary event there, to make up for the disruption of the formal dance. The blinds were drawn and shadows swirled across them in a merry rhythm. The snow was tapering off, but they were still dotted with snowflakes by the time Jade cleared the front door.

Jade's biceps were on fire by the time they got back to their room, but she didn't allow herself to show any weakness. Her purpose was to carry Connie and she did it with stubborn pride. She eased the door closed with her heel and they ended up in a frothy pile of purple chiffon on the bed.

"Wanna pretend it's prom night and we're horny teenagers?" Jade asked. She nuzzled against Connie's neck and slowly smoothed her hand up the front of the boned bodice.

Under her touch, Connie arched and purred. Her hands trailed up Jade's back and tangled in her hair.

"I think that would be—"

A ping from Connie's phone interrupted the moment. They both froze. Jade forcefully swallowed the curse words.

"If that's not Mel," Jade said, "I'm personally killing whoever sent that. And not quickly either."

Connie rolled over and grabbed her phone. "It's a text from Mel. She wants to know if we're okay. What should I say?"

Jade held out her hand. "Let me talk to her."

She dialed and put the phone on speaker.

"Hey," Mel answered immediately. Her voice was almost drowned out by happy Christmas music.

"Can you talk?"

"Yeah, just a minute." The music faded. The sound of a closing door followed. "What happened?"

Jade briefly summed up the crime against Teresa and the aftermath.

"My God," Mel said. "That poor girl. How awful. She's not still around, is she?"

"No. She's at peace now, and she'll never bother anyone again," Jade said.

"That's good to know. By the way, I'm telling everyone it's a gas leak, just so you know."

"Okay, I'm an expert at gas," Jade cracked.

Mel's laugh echoed over the phone. "Thank you so much, Doreen and I really appreciate all you two did for us. You are officially invited to stay for the holidays next year too, no charge of course."

"No shit? That's really generous of you," Jade said. Her grin fell off her face when she looked over at Connie. She didn't look happy. Far from it. Her head was down and she had her hands pressed to her belly as if she had a stomachache. Jade abruptly grabbed up the phone, "Look, I gotta go. Have a good night."

She ended the call.

Connie rose and agitatedly swished up and down the length of the room.

"What is it, sweetheart?" Jade asked. "You don't want to come back here?"

"It's not that." Connie absently picked at one delicate cuff. She swayed on her feet for a moment longer while Jade died a thousand times. She didn't dare breathe. Connie sat on the bed, just far enough away that Jade would have to move to touch her.

"I wanted to have this discussion later," Connie said. Her hands twisted around each other in her lap. "But maybe now would be better, before we make plans we might not be able to keep."

Jade couldn't speak. She felt like a truck hit her in the chest.

Connie was silent for a heartbeat, then blurted out, "I don't want children. I mean, I like them and I'm good with them, but I never want to be anyone's mother." Even though her eyes swam with tears and her voice trembled, Connie held her head up with pride. "If it's your plan to start a family with someone, I want you to find her before we get too entangled in each other's lives. I would hate myself if you missed out on any life experiences because of me."

Connie's shoulders fell with the last word of her confession. Jade, on the other hand, felt like a huge weight just came off hers.

"That's a fucking relief," Jade blurted out. She was rewarded by Connie leaning forward. Her eyes were wide and her cheeks flushed. Jade raked a hand through her hair. She wanted to laugh with the sudden release of tension. She said in a rush, "Here I was all this time feeling like I had to fake being on track with the life script so I wouldn't mess up *your* dreams. I really proved what happens when you assume shit. I can't believe what a massive idiot I was. Am."

Connie's perfect lips parted. "Really?" she asked. "You're not just saying that because I did?"

"Sweetheart, I'd be a shitty parent," Jade said. "I'd mess up any kid unlucky enough to have me as its mom. I also know I would do anything to make you happy. I got it into my head that meant having a kid or two, maybe not now but someday. I swore I'd do as good a job I could, even if it cost me my sanity." Jade shifted one butt length closer to Connie and gently took her hands. "Not having kids isn't a deal breaker for me. Even if I did kind of want them, I would be the dumbest person on Earth to give you up for some random sack of DNA who doesn't even exist yet and has a million times more chance of becoming a drug dealer than curing cancer."

"You'd give up having a family for me?"

"No way," Jade said. "*You* are my family. I don't need anything more than what I have now. Do you understand, Connie? I choose you."

With a squeak, Connie leapt into Jade's arms. Jade held her and stroked a hand through her hair and down her back. Connie shivered. Jade wasn't sure if it was from the release of tension or residual nerves.

"What do you say, baby girl?" Jade murmured into Connie's soft hair. "Do you choose me back?"

Connie rubbed a hand across her eyes, but she was beaming. "Let me think about it—*yes!*" She threw herself backwards onto the bed and gave a lithe stretch Jade thoroughly enjoyed watching. Connie let out a long sigh and looked up at Jade with nothing more than joy on her face.

Jade slung herself down beside Connie and playfully dropped kisses to her cheeks and hairline. Jade paused in her kiss attack to say, "Good, because I'm pretty sure there's nobody else on this planet who'll put up with my bullshit."

"That's not true," Connie said. She squirmed and giggled. "But nobody cuter than me."

"You got that right. And you forgot smarter and better at talking to people and braver and more intuitive. I don't know how the hell I ever got shit done before you came into my life. I could never have solved this case without you."

A pink-cheeked Connie said, "We did it as a team."

"The best team ever," Jade said. Connie snuggled closer.

"Now that we cleared the air," she said, "I'm totally okay with making plans to come here next year. If you are."

"Sweet," Jade said. "I'll talk to Mel about it tomorrow."

Connie started to say something, but interrupted herself with a yawn. She covered her mouth and looked apologetic. "Sorry. It's been a long day." Connie said, "Since we have the room to ourselves once more, I was planning on keeping you up all night, but I don't think I can stay awake. I don't mean to be boring but I just want you to hold me, kiss me, and whisper sweet dreams into my ear."

"You know what, I'm going to be boring too, because that sounds like my idea of a good time" Jade said. She surreptitiously rubbed her lower back. She loved her tux, but wearing it for a long time made her tense in weird places.

When they were in their comfy pajamas, Jade perched on the side of the bed where Connie was snuggled under the quilts, looking cozy and adorably sleepy.

Jade cupped her hands around a small velvet box. "This isn't a Christmas present," she said. Her palms sweated. Jade fidgeted. Connie sat up.

"What is it?"

"Just open it," Jade said. She awkwardly thrust the box at Connie, who eased it open.

Her head came up at once, her eyes wide. "It's beautiful," Connie breathed. She drew the platinum chain from the box and reverently cupped the pendant, a star sapphire in a delicate setting. She shook her head. "Jade, I can't accept this. It's too —"

"Yes, you can," Jade said. Beads of sweat prickled at her forehead. "I got it because it reminded me of you and it makes me happy to give you stuff. How about this? Consider it insurance, like if you ever run out of money or something you can pawn it. Or, I dunno, bribe someone with it."

"Romantic," Connie said, but she was smiling and seemed at ease once more. She turned around. "Could you put it on me?"

Jade couldn't resist kissing the bare nape in front of her before she gently draped the chain around Connie's neck. Connie turned back around. Her eyes sparkled, eclipsing the sapphire a thousand times.

"Thank you, Jade."

"It looks good on you," Jade replied. She paused and cocked a brow. "Don't tell me you're going to sleep with it on?"

"Yes, I am," Connie said. "You get your hot cocoa ribbon and

I get this."

"Fair enough," Jade said. She proudly flapped her ribbon before being tackled by Connie and dragged into the warm nest of quilts.

"And to think, I only got you fuzzy socks," Connie's voice was muffled by the fluffy blankets.

"That's awesome! I happen to love fuzzy socks," Jade said. "And I already told you it wasn't your Christmas present. For that, I got you socks too, actually."

Connie's tinkling laugh filled the darkened room before they both fell into sleepy silence. Just before sleep took her, Jade thought she saw a fluffy black cat watching over them from the windowsill.


THE NEXT MORNING, Jade stood in the lobby and checked her watch for the seventh time. She leaned against the wall and tried to be invisible. The other guests around her exchanged last-minute greetings, some passed business cards and typed into each others' phones. The floor was littered with suitcases and shopping bags full of souvenirs.

After putting in her year-in-advance reservation, Jade thought it might be fun to hang out in the lobby, but she was wrong. The cheerful crowd kicked in her old survival instincts. Jade mentally urged Connie to hurry up with her morning prep upstairs so they could get on the road.

"It's a good thing you found out about the gas leak," Garrett's voice cut through the babble of voices. Jade shouldered her bag and studied him cautiously. Garrett didn't sound sarcastic, which meant he bought Mel's story. Beside him, Basil shifted his weight from one foot to the other and looked nervous.

Jade shrugged and said, "I was tipped off. It's a good thing nobody was hurt. Basil, you were something else. You saved the day."

"About that, thanks," Basil said. He reached out and took Garrett's hand. The look they shared was sweeter than any Jade saw pass between them until that moment. "We, uh, talked a lot last night. Cleared up a bunch of issues. I think we're gonna be okay."

"Yes," Garrett said. "Who would have thought that Basil

nearly getting himself killed would be so damn hot?"

"You weren't bad yourself," Basil said.

"Glad to hear it," Jade said. She tried to smile, but it came out rather anemic. Connie pattered over and Jade gratefully turned from Garrett and Basil making goo-goo eyes at each other. Connie ducked under Jade's arm and hugged her unselfconsciously. The sapphire pendant glowed against her white turtleneck.

Garrett nudged Basil and gave him a significant look that both intrigued Jade and set off a few warning bells. Basil cleared his throat and said, "I was wondering if you and Connie would like to keep in touch. We're based in Shannon's Falls just outside Portsmouth, and it would be great if we could hang out together, maybe have regular get-togethers so our kids could grow up knowing each other."

Jade gaped. "What?"

With a proud toss of his head, Garrett jumped in. "We are looking for a surrogate and are willing to offer you a deal. You know, one for you, one for us kind of thing until we have two and you have as many as you want. You can choose who you'd rather be the father. If possible, we'd prefer our two to have at least one parent in common."

Connie drew back and shared a long look with Jade. They both knew the answer.

Jade said, "I appreciate the offer, but I'm afraid we'll have to turn you down." She looked Garrett straight in the eyes and intoned, "It's unethical to breed a rescue."


THE BACK OF the folding chair was cool through the thin cotton of the white collared shirt Jade wore in combination with the jeans that made her butt look great. Jade knew the outfit was Connie's favorite. Jade's feet were warm and snug in their navy and white striped fuzzy socks. She looked around, hoping for a reason for the text from Connie that asked her to go into the living room and sit on that chair. The TV was off, the curtains were drawn, and only one small lamp was lit. A frisson of unease stirred in Jade's mind, but the particular wardrobe decision Connie insisted on changed the unease into a vague feeling of anticipation.

In addition to that, Jade was more than intrigued by the

thought she would finally find out what Connie was planning.

Since they got back from the retreat, three days ago, Connie acted secretive. She often checked her phone and, at least a couple times a day, Jade noticed her listening to music on her earphones and making little moves as if practicing a dance routine. The day before, she abruptly left Jade's place for hers, citing a delivery. Since they had the family talk, Jade was reasonably sure Connie wasn't about to suggest they break up or anything like that.

Jade heard someone coming up the stairs. Was that bells along with the light footsteps? Jade still had the puzzled expression on her face when the door eased open.

"Are you sitting down?" Connie asked from the other side of the door.

"Yup, just like you asked," Jade said. She cracked a grin and added, "Commando, also like you asked."

"Good. Now close your eyes and no peeking." Connie's tone dropped to the sultry level Jade loved to hear. "I promise I'll make it worth your wait."

Jade immediately buried her face in her arms. "Done," she called back out in a muffled voice. Jade heard the door ease closed and more jingles accompanied soft footfalls. Jade's proximity alert tingled.

"Okay, you can look now."

Jade raised her head and her jaw dropped. Connie stood before her in a red miniskirt, trimmed in white fur and a little matching cape that didn't even start to cover the red satin bra. Her sapphire pendant hung between her breasts, nestled into the creamy curves. She was barefoot, but had a length of holly studded with tinkling silver bells around each ankle. A jaunty Santa hat was on her head with blonde curls framing her face.

"My God," Jade breathed in absolute awe. Her sex woke up in a tingling rush. Jade squeezed her thighs together. "Fucking beautiful."

Connie gave her a wicked little smirk and put her cell phone into the holder. A dance remix of *Last Christmas* filled the room. She turned around and gave a little shake of her hips that sent her skirt whirling out, high enough for Jade to get a momentary glimpse of two perfectly curved, bare cheeks. Jade's entire body hummed with anticipation.

"Consider this a late Christmas present," Connie said. She rolled her shoulders and turned around. She caught the clasp of the cape and whirled it off. She dropped it to the floor and leaned over. She put her hands on Jade's knees for an instant, before she straightened up and flicked her skirt a few times. Jade tried to stop drooling and fought the urge to bend down like the total perv she was to see exactly what Connie was hiding under that skirt.

Jade's brain managed to remember how to form words. She licked dry lips and asked, "Is this what your private lesson was?"

Connie nodded and sexily bit her lower lip. At that moment, she looked like the naughtiest Christmas elf ever. "I'm going to give you a lap dance you'll never forget. If that's okay?"

"Oh hell yeah," Jade said. She hitched herself a bit higher in her chair and purposely adjusted the crotch of her jeans with one hand. With the other, she made a beckoning motion. "Come over here and lay it on me."

"Not so fast, cowgirl," Connie said with a saucy wink.

Jade replied with a groan.

In time to the music, Connie took a few steps back and knelt on the floor. She spread her legs and gathered her skirt into her lap. Jade gulped. Not seeing everything was sexier than if Connie was simply standing there undressed. Then Connie got on all fours and wiggled her sweet little ass in the air and Jade lost her train of thought.

Connie bent over so the skirt's hem flipped up and slithered along her back, revealing a tiny red g-string with a sassy bow tucked into the cleft of her cheeks. The breathtaking vista lasted only a moment before Connie stood once more.

Jade breathed out a reverent, "Oh fuck me," when Connie delicately stepped up to her and settled down on Jade's lap, legs spread. The soft weight of Connie's backside on her thighs nearly sent Jade rocketing into the stratosphere. She was glad she wasn't wearing any underwear because it would be ruined already by how much her pussy was gushing with lust. Jade felt like she was going to leave a puddle on the seat. She made a move to take Connie around the hips but was stilled by a stern look.

"Hands to yourself," Connie said.

Guiltily, Jade held both hands up. "Sorry baby girl. Please continue."

Connie replied with a nod. She lowered her head and looked up at Jade through her lashes. "May I?" Connie asked.

"Uh huh," Jade replied.

She had no idea what she'd just agreed to, but she wasn't going to deny Connie anything. Jade had to hold in her moan of longing when Connie reached out and started unbuttoning her shirt. Jade helped a bit at the end by yanking her shirt out of her waistband. Connie delved inside the shirt and effortlessly stripped it from Jade's shoulders. Jade didn't even register it hitting the floor before Connie bowed down and licked her nipple. She glanced up once more, then kissed the other one. Jade was already rock hard. The light, teasing caress sent ripples of pleasure through her. Jade couldn't help but rock her hips up, lightly bucking Connie.

The music caught Jade's attention for a split second. The vocals were female. Trust Connie to think of even the smallest detail. Jade caught her breath and forgot everything else when Connie reached behind herself and unhooked her bra. She kept her eyes glued to Jade's face. Her hands cupped her breasts, holding the bra in place while the straps hung down uselessly. Jade's breath quickened.

She was more in love with Connie at that moment than ever. She loved the sassy, sweet, confident woman who sat on her lap, who teased her and knew exactly how to get her going. First times, what the fuck ever, Jade was never going to get enough of Connie. A lifetime was not going to be anywhere long enough for her.

The bra slipped off. Connie held Jade by the hips and pumped against her crotch, like she was ready to fuck her. Her breasts bounced with the motion. Jade's eyes rolled back in her head. She came back to earth abruptly when Connie half-stood and pressed their bodies together. Connie's lips played with the sensitive skin of Jade's neck. Hard nipples brushed Jade's own. Connie's exquisite softness thrilled Jade. Her pulse pounded between her legs. She clenched her fists to keep from grabbing Connie. The naughty teasing was driving her crazy, but Jade wasn't going to move without permission.

"Jesus Christ, baby girl," Jade moaned. "I want you so bad. Let me touch you, please."

Connie's words were hot and wet against Jade's skin. "Yes,"

she whispered.

The skirt dropped to the floor, Jade wasn't sure how, but she assumed it was by divine intervention. That left Connie on her lap in only a tiny red thong. If Jade wasn't already about to explode into an estrogen neutron bomb, Connie definitely didn't help by pulling aside the crotch of her panties to reveal a fully-bare pussy. Connie looked Jade right in the eyes as she ran her fingers up and down her pouty lips before she braced herself by placing her hands on Jade's knees and leaned back, legs spread in invitation.

Jade wasn't going to waste time now that she'd been given permission to act on all of the horny urges crowding out her reason. She unclenched one hand and delved between Connie's thighs. When she parted the slick inner lips, Connie welcomed her with a shimmy of her hips and a soft moan of pleasure that zinged straight to Jade's clit. Jade reverently pushed two fingers deep into Connie's willing entrance. The heat that encircled her was intense. Jade couldn't help but rock her own hips as she pumped into Connie.

"Yes, yes," Connie squeaked out with each deep thrust. She met each one with a jerk of her hips. Jade's world narrowed to that tiny cleft, those sweet, wet lips that parted for her and held her tight. Jade's pussy clenched. Connie had barely touched her and Jade was rocketing fast on her way to an orgasm. The trigger came when Connie looked Jade straight in the eyes, licked her fingers, and started stroking her own clit. Jade loved watching Connie touch herself.

The first wave hit Connie and bucked her against Jade, who grabbed onto Connie's ass with her free hand. Jade buried her face against Connie's shoulder, breaths coming even faster, breaking off into ragged gasps as a wave of tension unfurled between her legs.

"Fuck, oh *fuck,* I'm coming babe," Jade gritted. Her hips juddered with her release. The crotch of her jeans was soaked. Jade was firing on all thrusters, desperately trying to keep up with Connie as she rode out her climax on Jade's lap.

Connie finished first. She collapsed onto Jade's chest just as the final frissons of orgasm faded away. Jade gathered her up and held her, gently rubbing one hand up and down her back.

"Wow," Connie said. She pulled away and shifted her panties to cover herself again. Jade pouted in disappointment, but the veiled look Connie gave her assured Jade the coverage was only temporary.

"Yeah, wow," Jade agreed. She let her gaze wander slowly over Connie's body, enjoying the slight flush of the creamy skin of her chest, the hard nipples Jade planned to have in her mouth, and that miniscule red triangle of satin that held the softest, most beautiful blossom in Jade's world, which Jade also planned to have in her mouth. Soon. Very soon.

Connie didn't flinch under the scrutiny. She stood and trailed one hand down the platinum chain, while the other rested suggestively at the waistband of her panties.

"Want to relocate to the bedroom?" Connie asked. She turned and addressed Jade over her shoulder. "Of course, I'll lead the way."

"In that case, hell yeah," Jade said. She levered herself upright and followed Connie, unable to take her attention from her perfectly round, blushing cheeks.

They melted into each other's arms, and the rest of the world fell away. Jade was complete. She was loved and the center of Connie's world. They were complete in each other. For one moment, all of creation was perfect. Jade didn't know what the next day would bring, but she was ready to meet it. First, though, she had to get those panties off Connie. Everything else would come after that.


THE END... FOR NOW

# About the Author

Mildred Gail Digby has a BSc in geology, however Takarazuka, pachinko, and no laws against drinking beer outside lured her to teach in Japan. Her favorite thing to do is add lesbians to any situation and make a novel about it. She dreams one day of working as a professional beer taster and devotes a good deal of her time honing her skills in that area which, to an uninformed outsider, appears to be simply drinking a lot of beer.

She shares her non-angst-filled life with her wife of nearly ten years where the most excitement they have is deciding where to eat and forgetting where they parked their bicycles. Mildred is a sucker for oddball characters, opposites attract, and women getting what (and who) they want. She will squeeze a happy ending out of anything and still blushes when she writes love scenes.

# Other Mildred Gail Digby titles to look for:

## *Stay*

Jade Mayflower sees ghosts, can curse with enough vitriol to strip paint, and drives like she's in an action movie. In short, she's not a typical Private Investigator. Which is just as well because Connie Mason isn't a typical client. She's a disembodied spirit who appears in Jade's office one night with a job: Find out what happened to her and who did it.

Jade takes the case, not only because Connie has one of the cutest butts Jade has ever seen and a cute personality to match, but also because of Jade's righteous sense of justice — the tusche is a nice bonus, though. With Connie as her vaporous partner, Jade investigates Connie's life and the truth begins to take shape. In spite of herself, Jade is drawn to the sweet, and sometimes spicy, young woman who has a habit of blushing adorably when Jade flirts with her — and who flirts right back.

Even as their friendship deepens into something much more than that, Connie is being called over to the other side and she can't resist forever. Time is running out as Jade races against the clock to solve a crime where she is falling in love with the victim.

ISBN 978-1-61929-422-9-6
eISBN 978-1-61929-423-3

## Uncovered

Lindsay Ryan spends her days hidden in the basement of a medical university's archives and her nights online as a pro mah-jong player. She is invisible, anonymous and most of all, safe. Lindsay lives only through the novels she devours every spare moment of her time.

Dr. Gwen Mukherjee invades Lindsay's sanctuary with coffee dates and conspiracy theories—both of which wreak havoc on Lindsay's solitary existence. Inexorably attracted to the odd but charismatic doctor, Lindsay can't keep her distance from Gwen. Neither does she want to. For the first time, Lindsay experiences romance outside the pages of a book.

When Gwen discovers a horrible truth about the town they live in, the unscrupulous company responsible will do anything to keep their secrets safe. And that includes setting Lindsay up as a wanted fugitive to use her as bait to trap Gwen.

Lindsay is thrown into the spotlight. Now, to have a future with Gwen, all she has to do is make it out alive.

ISBN 978-1-61929-430-1
eISBN 978-1-61929-431-8

# *Bloodring*

Lark Greenpool became a Guardian at just the wrong time. A forbidden artifact known as a Bloodring has been awoken. It released a malevolent energy that threatens to destroy the barrier that protects Lark's world from the Outside and it's the Guardians' job to put it right.

Help arrives in the form of an ambassador from the Ringsworn, the people who made the Bloodring. Violet Ironwrought is prickly, most likely very dangerous, dislikes everyone, and is completely fascinating to Lark. After a rocky start, friendship blossoms between the two women, and slowly grows into something much more than that.

When circumstances threaten to separate them, Lark has to decide where her loyalties lie, and what she is willing to risk to protect not only herself, but the woman who has become the most important part of her life.

ISBN 978-1-61929-444-8
eISBN 978-1-61929-445-5

## Perfect Match: Book One

After a tragedy derailed her life, Dr. Megan Maier crawls back to the land of her birth to take a job in a private Jewish hospital. There, she meets Syler Terada, a pediatric surgeon with a brash attitude and a lack of respect for authority who incidentally rocks a tuxedo. She captivates Megan with one glance. Conservative culture and rules against fraternization can't stop Megan. However the secrets she's running from can. The weight of her guilt prevents Megan from making the promise of forever, even though that's the only thing Syler wants from her.

ISBN 978-1-61929-414-1
eISBN 978-1-61929-415-8

## Perfect Match: Book Two

Dr. Megan Maier is on her way to happiness and professional success when a hurdle to both appears in the form of Charles Brockman, the son of the hospital's president who has decided that Megan is the perfect partner for him and proposes to her. Megan turns him down cold, certain nothing could make her even consider his offer. Nothing except for Megan's secrets. Incriminating documents go missing and Megan has to face the truth that the cost of protecting herself, and the victims of her shattered past, is betrayal of the woman she loves.

ISBN 978-1-61929-416-5
eISBN 978-1-61929-417-2

# Phoenix

What would it take to make you ditch your career, your pride, and run from everything you believe in? In private investigator Ashe Devon's case, it's the fact that her client ended up dead while under her protection. Out of the P.I. business, Ashe is just trying to survive the daily grind of her boring, vanilla life when her former boss calls her out of retirement for one last job: protect a local DJ from a violent stalker. Ashe is fully prepared to turn down the case until she meets the client.

Mystral Galbraith, aka Phoenix, is unashamedly gay, just a tad awkward and musically brilliant. Ashe is instantly captivated by her and can't ignore the fierce young woman's plea for help. Neither can Ashe ignore the stirrings of long-forgotten emotions that set both her heart and her boxer briefs on fire. While Ashe struggles to keep her relationship with Mystral professional, the tension between them simmers just beneath the surface.

More than Ashe's pride is involved — failure could cost Mystral her life. But is Ashe the right person for the job? If she doesn't get her hormones under control, the undeniable pull between them could compromise her judgment and open the door for history to repeat its tragic lesson.

ISBN 978-1-61929-394-6
eISBN 978-1-61929-395-3

# MORE REGAL CREST PUBLICATIONS

| | | |
|---|---|---|
| Brenda Adcock | Soiled Dove | 978-1-935053-35-4 |
| Brenda Adcock | The Sea Hawk | 978-1-935053-10-1 |
| Brenda Adcock | The Other Mrs. Champion | 978-1-935053-46-0 |
| Brenda Adcock | Picking Up the Pieces | 978-1-61929-120-1 |
| Brenda Adcock | The Game of Denial | 978-1-61929-130-0 |
| Brenda Adcock | In the Midnight Hour | 978-1-61929-188-1 |
| Brenda Adcock | Untouchable | 978-1-61929-210-9 |
| Brenda Adcock | The Heart of the Mountain | 978-1-61929-330-4 |
| Brenda Adcock | Gift of the Redeemer | 978-1-61929-360-1 |
| Brenda Adcock | Unresolved Conflicts | 978-1-61929-374-8 |
| Brenda Adcock | One Step At A Time | 978-1-61929-408-0 |
| K. Aten | The Fletcher | 978-1-61929-356-4 |
| K. Aten | Rules of the Road | 978-1-61919-366-3 |
| K. Aten | The Archer | 978-1-61929-370-0 |
| K. Aten | Waking the Dreamer | 978-1-61929-382-3 |
| K. Aten | The Sagittarius | 978-1-61929-386-1 |
| K. Aten | Running From Forever: Book One in the Blood Resonance Series | 978-1-61929-398-4 |
| K. Aten | The Sovereign of Psiere: Book One In the Mystery of the Makers series | 978-1-61929-412-7 |
| K. Aten | The Lost Temple of Psiere: Book Two In the Mystery of the Makers series | 978-1-61929-448-6 |
| K. Aten | Burn It Down | 978-1-61929-418-9 |
| K. Aten | Embracing Forever: Book Two in the Blood Resonance Series | 978-1-61929-424-0 |
| K Aten | Children of the Stars | 978-1-61929-432-5 |
| Georgia Beers | Thy Neighbor's Wife | 1-932300-15-5 |
| Georgia Beers | Turning the Page | 978-1-932300-71-0 |
| Lynnette Beers | Just Beyond the Shining River | 978-1-61929-352-6 |
| Lynnette Beers | Saving Sam | 978-1-61929-410-3 |
| Hartley Blaze | The Place I Call Home | 978-1-61929-450-9 |
| Sky Croft | Amazonia | 978-1-61929-067-9 |
| Sky Croft | Amazonia: An Impossible Choice | 978-1-61929-179-9 |
| Sky Croft | Mountain Rescue: The Ascent | 978-1-61929-099-0 |
| Sky Croft | Mountain Rescue: On the Edge | 978-1-61929-205-5 |
| Mildred Gail Digby | Phoenix | 978-1-61929-394-6 |
| Mildred Gail Digby | Perfect Match: Book One | 978-1-61929-414-4 |
| Mildred Gail Digby | Perfect Match: Book Two | 978-1-61929-416-5 |
| Mildred Gail Digby | Stay | 978-1-61929-422-6 |
| Mildred Gail Digby | Stay for the Holidays | 978-1-61929-452-3 |
| Mildred Gail Digby | Uncovered | 978-1-61929-430-1 |
| Cronin and Foster | Blue Collar Lesbian Erotica | 978-1-935053-01-9 |
| Cronin and Foster | Women in Uniform | 978-1-935053-31-6 |
| Cronin and Foster | Women in Sports | 978-1-61929-278-9 |
| Emily L Quint Freeman | Failure To Appear: Resistance, Identity and Loss | 978-1-61929-426-4 |

| | | |
|---|---|---|
| Melissa Good | Eye of the Storm | 1-932300-13-9 |
| Melissa Good | Hurricane Watch | 978-1-935053-00-2 |
| Melissa Good | Moving Target | 978-1-61929-150-8 |
| Melissa Good | Red Sky At Morning | 978-1-932300-80-2 |
| Melissa Good | Storm Surge: Book One | 978-1-935053-28-6 |
| Melissa Good | Storm Surge: Book Two | 978-1-935053-39-2 |
| Melissa Good | Stormy Waters | 978-1-61929-082-2 |
| Melissa Good | Thicker Than Water | 1-932300-24-4 |
| Melissa Good | Terrors of the High Seas | 1-932300-45-7 |
| Melissa Good | Tropical Storm | 978-1-932300-60-4 |
| Melissa Good | Tropical Convergence | 978-1-935053-18-7 |
| Melissa Good | Winds of Change Book One | 978-1-61929-194-2 |
| Melissa Good | Winds of Change Book Two | 978-1-61929-232-1 |
| Melissa Good | Southern Stars | 978-1-61929-348-9 |
| K. E. Lane | And, Playing the Role of Herself | 978-1-932300-72-7 |
| Helen Macpherson | Revolving Doors | 978-1-61929-440-0 |
| Kate McLachlan | Christmas Crush | 978-1-61929-195-9 |
| Kate McLachlan | Hearts, Dead and Alive | 978-1-61929-017-4 |
| Kate McLachlan | Murder and the Hurdy Gurdy Girl | 978-1-61929-125-6 |
| Kate McLachlan | Rescue At Inspiration Point | 978-1-61929-005-1 |
| Kate McLachlan | Return Of An Impetuous Pilot | 978-1-61929-152-2 |
| Kate McLachlan | Rip Van Dyke | 978-1-935053-29-3 |
| Kate McLachlan | Ten Little Lesbians | 978-1-61929-236-9 |
| Kate McLachlan | Alias Mrs. Jones | 978-1-61929-282-6 |
| Hope Milam | Welcome Home, Bailey | 978-1-61929-438-7 |
| Lynne Norris | One Promise | 978-1-932300-92-5 |
| Lynne Norris | Sanctuary | 978-1-61929-248-2 |
| Lynne Norris | The Light of Day | 978-1-61929-338-0 |
| Schramm and Dunne | Love Is In the Air | 978-1-61929-362-8 |
| Rae Theodore | Leaving Normal: Adventures in Gender | |
| | | 978-1-61929-320-5 |
| Rae Theodore | My Mother Says Drums Are for Boys: True | |
| | Stories for Gender Rebels | 978-1-61929-378-6 |
| Barbara Valletto | Pulse Points | 978-1-61929-254-3 |
| Barbara Valletto | Everlong | 978-1-61929-266-6 |
| Barbara Valletto | Limbo | 978-1-61929-358-8 |
| Barbara Valletto | Diver Blues | 978-1-61929-384-7 |
| Lisa Young | Out and Proud | 978-1-61929-392-2 |

Be sure to check out our other imprints,
Blue Beacon Books, Mystic Books,
Silver Dragon Books, Yellow Rose Books, Troubadour Books,
and Young Adult Books.

CPSIA information can be obtained
at www.ICGtesting.com
Printed in the USA
LVHW101306211120
672268LV00021B/991